wayward SON

wayyard
SON

JAY CROWNOVER

To family.
Be it the one you were born into,
The one you created,
The one you found,
Or the one that found you.
(I am aware this dedication sounds
like Dominic Toretto wrote it.
That makes it ten times cooler than it already was!)

author's NOTE

I know I typically drone on in these little pregame messages. I think I can keep this one short and sweet since *Wayward Son* is a pretty cut-and-dry type of story. Obviously, I recommend reading the previous Forever Marked books for maximum enjoyment, but even if you just pick up Aston and Zowen's book by itself, it will be a good read. There isn't the complicated backstory and connections in the book like there was in *Son of a Gun.*

As always, I preface these second-generation novels by saying that, while the content is set in the future, I did not write a sci-fi novel. I spend my time and energy on the characters and connection, not futuristic phones and cars and clothing. If this feels like a modern setting, it is.

I am also aware that jail and prison are two very different things and are not used interchangeably in the real legal system. However, there are only so many times you can refer to one thing, in one way, without it getting monotonous and repetitive. I think normal folks probably interchange the two regularly. So, please excuse my use of either or throughout this story. It's like trying to find a new way to describe any and all the things that happen during the sex scenes. There's only so many ways to say the same thing.

Going along with that, you'll notice as you read, I don't designate a specific brand name for Zowen's motorcycle. I know from real-life experience exactly how important what type of bike a rider chooses is to their identity. Are they an Italian bike person, a Japanese bike lover, or any other variety that might be preferred these days? I also know the name brands for their riding gear play a huge part in their vibe. Since this is the future, I didn't want to have to be tied down to a Ducati or a Gixxer or a Ninja. If you're a motorcycle person, feel free to fill in your favorite as you read.

I do keep the names of things that would be considered vintage, be it now or when the story is set, only because those things would exist as they are in this time period.

I know by the time you are done with this novel, there will be more than a handful of you reaching out to ask about the other kids and more books in the series. For now, this is the end of the Forever Marked series, but I never say never to anything. I never thought I would write a second-generation series in the first place. Maybe this book will be an exception to the rule and sell remarkably well. If that's the case, I can always be persuaded to keep going … I'm going to tell anyone who wants to negotiate for more books that I must know down to my bones that it's worth the time, creative energy, and mostly money before I can commit to adding more to a series.

Even if this is the end of Forever Marked, there will be more books on the way.

I already have what I'm going to work on next fighting for time and space in my mind.

I hope you've enjoyed the kiddos as much as you loved their parents. It's been a delight to come full circle with so many readers who have been on this ten-year journey with me. I hope you can all tell I'm a much better writer now than I was at the beginning, LOL.

Happy reading!
XOXO!

Love & Ink,
Jay

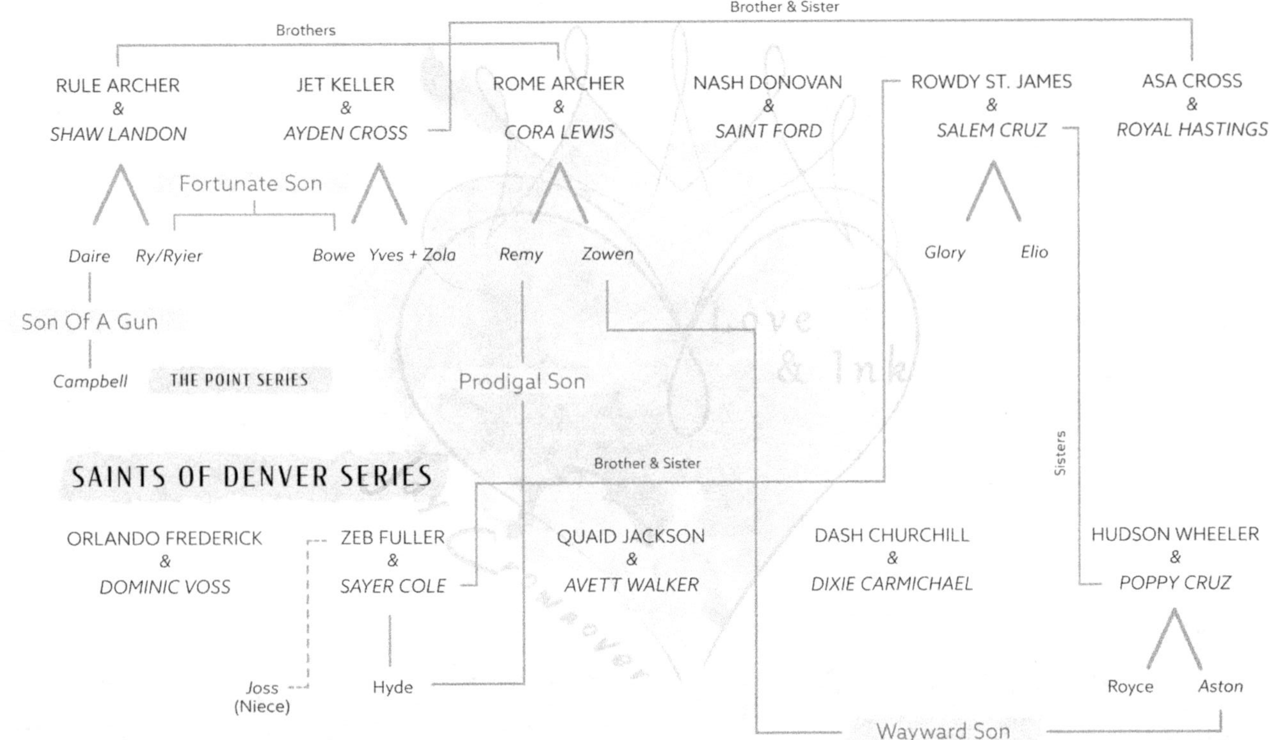

MARKED MEN SERIES
Brother & Sister
Brothers
RULE ARCHER
&
SHAW LANDON
JET KELLER
&
AYDEN CROSS
ROME ARCHER
&
CORA LEWIS
NASH DONOVAN
&
SAINT FORD
ROWDY ST. JAMES
&
SALEM CRUZ
ASA CROSS
&
ROYAL HASTINGS
Fortunate Son
Daire
Ry/Ryier
Bowe
Yves + Zola
Remy
Zowen
Glory
Elio
Son Of A Gun
Prodigal Son
Campbell
THE POINT SERIES
Sisters
SAINTS OF DENVER SERIES
Brother & Sister
ORLANDO FREDERICK
&
DOMINIC VOSS
ZEB FULLER
&
SAYER COLE
QUAID JACKSON
&
AVETT WALKER
DASH CHURCHILL
&
DIXIE CARMICHAEL
HUDSON WHEELER
&
POPPY CRUZ
Joss
(Niece)
Hyde
Royce
Aston
Wayward Son
Love & Ink

PROLOGUE

Zowen

"We, the jury, unanimously find the defendant guilty ..."

Everything after the word *guilty* was a blur. I barely registered the charges of which I had been found guilty. Anything the judge added after that went in one ear and out the other. It was important that I listen to how long the man with a stern expression, wearing the serious-looking black robe, was sending me to prison for. But I could not bring myself to care.

I *was* guilty.

Whatever punishment was handed down to me was a consequence I deserved.

Being sentenced to any amount of jail time didn't feel like it would be enough to alleviate the weight of the remorse crushing everything inside of me. Culpability pressed down so heavily inside of my chest that there was barely any room for my heart to beat properly. Regret hung from every inch of my soul; I couldn't remember the last time I had taken a step where I didn't feel like

I was wearing concrete shoes. Every thought and feeling that had lived within me for the last year was filtered through a haze of guilt.

I looked over my shoulder without turning around when the bailiff moved to snap handcuffs around my wrists in front of me. I didn't want my mom to see me being chained up and hauled away like a criminal ... even though the guilty verdict officially made me one.

She was crying. My dad was holding her tightly as her entire body shook. She'd been crying for me for over a year. Ever since the night I had gotten arrested. The entire year I had been out on bail, waiting for the trial, and now, as soon as the verdict came in. It was too much for her; she cried enough that I worried I might drown within the depths of her sorrow before they managed to lock me up.

My dad just looked disappointed. He had handled everything from my initial arrest to the trial preparation and everything else that piled up much better than the rest of my family. He was always the rock the rest of us anchored ourselves to when the seas got particularly stormy. I could see that my situation had started to chip away at his stony surface. My dad's disappointment was harder to handle than my mother's devastation.

I tried to force a smile to let my family know I would be okay. I'd never been the type to shirk my responsibility or run away from the consequences of my actions. I'd inherited my bone-deep responsibility from my old man. I knew he understood why I wasn't putting up much of a fuss at being found guilty and sentenced.

My gaze shifted to my older sister. She was staring at me like she could see directly inside my head. The expression on her face landed somewhere between resignation and rage. Throughout the entire legal process, she'd surprisingly been the one to offer me the most consistent shoulder to lean on. She was also the one with the most reasonable advice.

My mom believed the outrageously expensive lawyer she and my dad had hired was going to convince a jury I was innocent. After all, I was a good kid. I'd never been in any kind of major trouble before. I kept my nose clean, and compared to Remy, my older sister, I was practically a saint.

My dad was more realistic. No matter how skilled or experienced my lawyer was, there was solid, irrefutable evidence that I had been involved in the crime I was charged with. He'd hoped I would get house arrest, probation, or a lighter sentence since I was a first-time offender. That hope had died when I refused to testify in my own defense and the stern judge handed down a five-year sentence.

From the start, Remy had known I wasn't doing much to help my case. I thought she could tell from the jump that I was resigned to taking whatever punishment the state saw fit to give me. She understood I was searching for atonement by staying silent and letting the legal system do its worst. She didn't agree, but realized there was nothing she could do to convince me otherwise.

Before the bailiff took me away, my lawyer muttered something to me that I purposely ignored. My mom reached across the railing separating us and hugged my neck so tightly that I couldn't tell whether she was saying goodbye or trying to choke me. I couldn't hug her back because my hands were cuffed in front of me.

I could only whisper to her, "It's okay. Mom, I'll be fine."

My words made her cry even harder. My dad eventually had to pull her away. He gave me a long look and then sighed so heavily, the sound was clearly filled with every emotion a parent could have toward their child in such a dire situation.

"Take care of yourself, Zowen. We'll come see you as often as possible."

I winced at the reminder that not only was I going to prison, but I was also going to prison in a state a thousand miles from home. It'd been exhausting, traveling between Colorado and California after I was arrested. My folks were well off, all things considered, but for the last year, they'd done nothing but spend a fortune trying to help me and traveling to be by my side while my life imploded. Every way in which they had helped added another layer to the guilt I was currently buried under.

I nodded to my father and straightened my shoulders. The least I could do was make sure they didn't have to worry about me taking care of myself while I was locked up and separated from everyone who loved me.

Remy leaned closer to me as the bailiff started to get impatient. Her eyes were intense, and the grip she had on my shoulder was tight enough to hurt.

Her voice was low enough that I could only hear her when she whispered, "Once we know where you're going to serve your time, Uncle Benny is going to make sure there is someone on the inside to watch your back. If you get into trouble, be sure to call Daire. She's the closest family member, and that boyfriend of hers has connections that frankly terrify me. I need you to remember that you are not alone while you're in there, and you won't be alone when you come out. Archers stick together, no matter what."

Uncle Benny was a friend of the family. Whenever any Archer got into a bind they couldn't get out of, he was the first person called in to try and make the best out of a bad situation.

I sighed slightly and bent forward so I could touch my forehead to hers. We had a complicated relationship. Even though Remy was several years older than me, I'd always been the one to take care of her. I kept her out of trouble and saved her impulsive ass every single time she got in over her head. I didn't blink twice at being her savior in whatever form that happened to take. It was an unsettling experience, having the tables turned and Remy being the one looking out for me.

"I'll call Daire if I get in trouble. Promise."

Daire was my cousin and currently the only Archer who was living in the same state where I'd been sentenced. She'd recently moved to San Francisco to attend art school and work as a tattoo apprentice. San Francisco wasn't exactly close to Los Angeles, but it was a whole lot closer than Denver. She was sitting in the back of the courtroom.

I couldn't look in her direction throughout the entire trial because she hadn't been alone. It wasn't her intimidating boyfriend, Campbell, who kept my gaze off her. It was the pretty young woman with soft brown eyes and dark hair with a red cast that looked like hidden fire sitting next to her that I couldn't risk making eye contact with.

I hadn't wanted Aston Wheeler involved in any of what was happening to me.

I hadn't wanted to see the look in her eyes when my guilt was announced to the world. I didn't want her to cry over me or be disappointed in me. I wanted her to forget I existed and to move on with her life like we'd never known one another.

I pulled away from Remy and gave my family one last shaky grin before being led away. There was pressure in the back of my throat and wet heat pushing at my eyes. I was resigned to my fate, but that didn't mean I wasn't terrified of whatever awaited me once I was taken away and locked up. I wanted to be brave and accept the punishment stoically and somberly. It was hard because my entire life had been turned upside down. I'd willingly surrendered my freedom, and all the shattered pieces of the man I'd thought I was were now falling in every direction. There was no way to catch them with my hands restrained in handcuffs.

I knew in time, the guilt wouldn't feel as heavy and some of the sting might fade. I was young, and even after being sentenced and serving my time, I still had a lot of life and opportunity in front of me. I understood I was an Archer, and nothing—I mean, *nothing*—would ever cause my family to turn their backs on me.

They would love me even though I was guilty.

And they would love me even though I was a murderer.

Murder was something that would never fade. Murderer was a title and stigma I was going to have to bear regardless of what happened to me.

No matter how inadvertent or accidental my actions had been that night, I'd killed someone.

I was a murderer.

· · ·

The Previous Year

I knew I shouldn't have let the kid goad me into a reaction.

Kid being the operative word.

He couldn't be more than sixteen or seventeen years old. I mean, he still had acne and a baby face. The bike he was so proud of had noticeably been bought with his parents' money, and it was obviously too powerful and too much of a machine for him.

I had known all of that, and yet I'd still let him get under my skin.

I'd hauled my bike all the way to the desert outside of LA for an exclusive race that only a handful of riders had been invited to. I'd been toying with the idea of taking some time away from college and seeing if I had what it took to race professionally. The invitation to the desert race was the first step in pushing my limits and challenging myself. I didn't tell anyone I was going. The race was only known by a handful of people in the street race circuit, and any leaks would not be tolerated.

Besides, my parents didn't love that my favorite hobby was flying across the asphalt as fast as possible on a two-wheeled death trap. My mom begged me more than once to quit messing around with motorcycles and focus more on school. But racing was more challenging than school.

I was smart. Very smart. And I had a particular affinity for anything electronic. Computers were like a kid's toy in my hands. In another life, I could've made a name for myself as a hacker. Instead, I became a gamer who loved anything that went fast and made a lot of noise. I also liked sports cars as much as I liked street bikes. My dad had always ridden a Harley, and some of my fondest memories were riding on the back behind him when I was growing up. Which was how I ended up with a passion for motorcycles.

I was all raced out in Denver. There was nothing new or anyone worth getting excited about racing against anymore. I'd spent so long in the local scene that it got boring. So, when the invite for LA came through, I jumped at the chance to experience something different and see where my skill level ranked.

There was also a slight chance that the temptation of being in the same state as Aston Wheeler and getting to see her without all our family and history hanging over us had played a big part in my desire to haul my bike halfway across the country.

I couldn't have imagined that it was a decision that was going to end anything before it even got a chance to start.

The races in the desert had gone off without a hitch. I won more than I lost and learned there were some modifications I hadn't considered to make my ride even faster. I talked to a couple of professional racers and chatted with a couple of scouts who were at the event on a low-key basis. It was a good time, and I planned to walk away with a better idea of what I wanted to do with my future when the kid I'd beaten in the final race of the event tracked me down and threw a massive fit.

It had been obvious from the start that the kid had more money than skill. It was also clear he wasn't used to losing.

When he accused me of cheating and demanded the event organizers go over my bike from fender to fender to make sure I didn't have any prohibited enhancements, I laughed. I thought it was funny and that I could just brush him off and go about my business—until my bike was really pulled for inspection.

I was pissed.

I'd never had my integrity or honesty called into question in such a blatant way. Plus, I was used to being a big fish in a small pond back in Colorado. I had no idea the scene in LA was swimming with sharks. Or that the right amount of money could make the version of events coming from the person paying become the accepted truth..

I was appalled when my bike was disqualified and every win and record I'd obtained during the event was voided. My entire trip became a waste of time and effort. I was so angry that I couldn't see straight.

I should've punched him and let that be the end of it. But I didn't. I challenged him to a race. A street race. One that would absolutely be illegal and where I would be at a complete disadvantage because I was in an unfamiliar city. One twice the size of Denver with triple the traffic and police presence.

Of course, the kid couldn't turn me down. Not in front of a bunch of other racers who were looking down on him for buying his win at the event. There was no way for him to decline and save his childish ego, so we had set up a race on one of LA's notoriously busy roads.

When the time came, I didn't think the kid would show. He was over an hour late, and when he and his crew finally appeared, I could tell he was frazzled and nervous. He seemed even younger than he had when he was screwing me over in the desert.

A flash of reason infiltrated my anger, and I offered to call the entire thing off. It was stupid and pointless. I didn't have anything to prove to some teenager with more money than sense. And even if my wins at the race had been voided, I still had someone I wanted to see, and she meant more to me than bragging rights.

The teenager insisted we go through with the high-risk race. He was as prideful as he was nervous.

I shrugged and agreed to go through with it, figuring I could take it easy and still more than likely win. The kid had a nice bike and zero idea how to coax the most out of it. I let him set the terms and quietly climbed onto my own ride to consider all the hazards and obstacles that came with racing along a busy street. It wasn't only the rider's life at risk, but also all the innocent commuters who had no idea they were in the middle of a racecourse and were in danger. As much as I lived for the adrenaline rush and thrill, I always worried I was going to be the reason someone else got hurt.

Things started out as normally as any illegal race could. Both of our bikes zipped in and out of traffic at high speed. Lights flashed by, and startled drivers honked their horns. I was so focused on making sure I wasn't causing an accident that I didn't notice when the kid went flying past me on a turn when the road opened up and the traffic thinned out. In a normal race, I would applaud the move, but on a city street, it was insane. You should never hit the gas when you didn't know what was waiting for you around the corner. I didn't even care if I lost at that point. I just wanted to make it to the end of the race in one piece with my bike intact. With every fiber of my being, I regretted letting the kid get to me. It was the middle of the night, so things could be much worse. However, the timing meant we weren't the only reckless drivers on the road that night.

When we came out of the curve, there was a dark SUV driving without any lights on. The only reason I caught sight of it was because the teenager's headlights reflected off the black paint. I saw the kid brake too hard and knew that powerful bike of his was going to react faster than his reflexes could keep up with. I tried to catch up to him to slow him down, but it all happened so fast that there was zero time to react.

The kid flew over the front of the bike and tumbled head over feet toward the back of the SUV. His bike kicked out sideways and clipped my front tire. I went down almost as hard as he had, but I hadn't been going as fast and didn't have a big vehicle in front of me.

I managed to limp to my feet and tried to make my way toward the kid who was lying prone on the street. He didn't look like he was in good shape, and I needed to get him out of the middle of the road.

The driver of the SUV pulled over and was screaming and yelling at the top of his lungs. A couple of other cars stopped amid the chaos, and I could hear sirens in the distance. Just as I was about to limp my way to where the kid had landed, the world seemed to narrow down to the bloody asphalt and the darkness surrounding me.

• • •

I didn't remember the semitruck that had come barreling down the road.

I didn't remember the impact when it had run over the fragile body and sent both crashed motorcycles flying into oncoming traffic like expensive shrapnel. I couldn't recall the other drivers screaming and crying or the driver of the SUV getting sick and passing out since he was as close to the carnage as I was. I didn't remember getting put in an ambulance and being raced to the hospital because I had been hit by a piece of my own bike. I was rattled and battered against the asphalt, but all my riding gear had done its job, and the worst injuries I'd ended up with was a dislocated shoulder and a severely sprained ankle. And I definitely didn't remember the first night I'd spent in an LA jail cell.

Everything that had happened after the bikes crashed was a blur. The only reason I had any idea what had happened after the crash was due to all the different dashcam footage from the surrounding traffic that the LAPD used as evidence against me on the charges of reckless endangerment and vehicular manslaughter. Little did I know, the kid had been streaming the race, so he had effectively recorded his own death and firmly placed me at the scene.

My family had a devastating history with motor vehicle accidents. It was heart-wrenching to know I had been the cause of another family having to face the loss and grief mine had also suffered through.

All throughout the trial, which happened months after the accident, I had to watch the crash and the horrifying outcome—repeatedly. As did my parents and sister. It was burned into my brain. The images from the accident were the only things I could see when I closed my eyes. They were all I dreamed about.

All I wanted was to go back in time and walk away from the stupid challenge that had not only ruined my life, but also robbed a family of their son.

It had been so preventable that it made me sick whenever I looked back on that night.

There was no end to the guilt I suffered.

There was no penance I wasn't willing to pay.

At the top of the list of things I was willing to give up was the girl I had loved since I had been seven years old.

Even if the stars finally aligned and there was a slim chance we could figure out how to be together with all the history and complications between us, she deserved someone better than a guy who was a murderer.

chapter ONE

Zowen
Five Years Later

I closed my eyes and tilted my head back so the sun could hit my face. I took a deep breath and let the fact that I was finally a free man sink into my bones.

When I had been a dumb kid, spending five years behind bars as punishment for my wayward actions hadn't seemed like much of a big deal. I knew I deserved to pay some kind of penance, and some would say five years wasn't even close to being long enough. Now that I'd done the time and spent the first half of my twenties locked up, I knew with every fiber of my being that I'd underestimated how hard serving a five-year prison sentence would be.

I wasn't the same Zowen Archer as I had been back then. And it had nothing to do with me hovering closer to thirty than twenty. I felt like being locked up for any significant amount of time altered a person down to their very base level. My perception of the world was different from the one I'd had when I went in. As was my perception of myself and the kind of man I ended up being.

Time hadn't stood still for the five years I was stashed away. I felt like a visitor in a new land, trying to learn new customs and familiarize myself with the people and their traditions.

"Are you ready to go?"

A soft voice shook me from my introspection. I lowered my head and met Daire's bright green eyes. Even from the distance separating us, I could see she was holding back tears, and her hands were tightly clenched together to keep them from shaking.

"You can't possibly be reluctant to leave this place behind?"

I let out a low chuckle and opened my arms. The next second, my cousin was wrapped in a hug that was tight enough to crack ribs. I felt my eyes tear up as well. It had been way too long since I'd been able to hold a family member this close.

"Thanks for coming to get me, Daire."

Originally, my parents were going to make the trip to the outskirts of LA for my release day. However, my dad had been caught off guard by a sudden cardiac event the weekend before and was still recovering in the hospital. He was going through a multitude of testing, and my mom was too worried to leave his side.

My sister also couldn't make the trip because she was heavily pregnant. She was already a mom to an adorable little six-year-old, who had come as a package deal with Remy's long-term boyfriend. I didn't think anyone was as shocked as she was when she decided she was ready to add to her family. She'd proven to be a fantastic mother over the years; at least, that was the report I had gotten whenever she managed to visit me.

All my immediate family was still in Colorado for valid reasons, so it had fallen on Daire to be my chauffeur. She was the Archer I'd had the most contact with during my incarceration. She and Campbell came to see me every available visitation day. Her regular presence made me feel less alone. Plus, there was something about Campbell showing up with her that made the other inmates give me a wide berth when word got around that I was acquainted with him. I'd always meant to ask Daire why her fiancé garnered such a strong reaction from an institution full of felons, but there was something in her eyes that warned me not to pry.

Daire squeezed me back and reached out to grab my hand so she could take me away from the pickup area toward an old, very cool-looking Bronco. It was the type without the top and had to be from the '70s; it was very retro and looked like it was suited for cruising along the beach, not the steep hills of San Francisco.

She glanced at me over her shoulder and said, "Ry wanted to come with me, but he got called in for a last-minute shift for his residency. He said something about getting to observe a specialty surgery. I know he feels awful that he couldn't make it."

I shook my head and waved a hand to dismiss any concern. "It's fine. I'll let him know it isn't a big deal next time I talk to him."

Ry was Daire's older brother and my closest friend. We had been inseparable, growing up, but he'd moved away after hooking up with his one true love. While I had been incarcerated, he had ended up marrying his girl-friend, Bowe, in a last-minute Vegas wedding while she was playing a weekend festival in the city. It was wild to think that he was a husband now. I would never admit how badly it stung when I realized that not only had I missed the wedding, but I'd also missed standing next to him as his best man. The honor was an unspoken certainty that always existed between us. We were supposed to be by each other's side for all the big milestones. Neither of us had planned that I'd fuck up as badly as I had.

"It's not like I'm graduating or getting married. Getting out of jail isn't exactly an event that needs to be celebrated." I tried to keep my words light and easy, which wasn't how I was feeling on the inside.

I was secretly relieved the entire Archer clan wasn't waiting for me outside the prison walls. I had no idea what I'd have said to them. Or if I would have had the wherewithal to act appropriately around the family I'd been separated from for so long. I needed a minute to find my footing and figure out how to approach everyone now that I was older and fundamentally altered from living the past five years in a constant state of do-or-die.

"You're wrong." Daire gave me a serious look, which conflicted with her overall angelic appearance. "We're getting you back. That is one hundred percent something worth celebrating. We're moving forward. Not just you, Zowen, but everyone who has been waiting for this day too."

I grunted in response because I wasn't sure what to say. I couldn't comprehend how my family could miss a murderer and couldn't fathom that they still viewed me as the same Zowen I had been before the accident.

I changed the subject to save my sanity and to stop the impending spiral of self-degradation I knew was building. "How are your parents? I haven't spoken to Uncle Rule in a long time. Are you still planning to take over the tattoo shop when he's ready to retire?"

Daire shrugged as we reached the big four-wheel-drive vehicle. "I'm not sure I want to go back to Denver. I like San Francisco, and so does Campbell. I want to open a branch of Marked Men here in California and see if I can be successful with my own shop before I contemplate taking over the flagship stores. Dad's been very understanding. He's got a good crew working for him these days, which leaves time for him to take my mom on vacation. Right now, they're in Portugal. Dad wanted to come home when he heard about your dad's medical issues, but your mom told him she had everything under control. They've been doing a lot of traveling since my mom shifted gears and opened a private practice. She's not working as much as she was, and she seems to have chilled out. They're both still furious that Ry got married without telling them. He and Bowe had to promise they would let both sets of parents throw a real wedding for them once Ry's done with his residency."

I let out a low whistle and hopped into the passenger seat. For the past five years, my days had been blindingly boring and similar, but everyone in my family seemed to have moved ahead at warp speed.

"Remy is pregnant. Ry got married. You and Campbell are engaged." I looked down at the unique black diamond that sat on her ring finger. "Everyone has shifted into sixth gear." And I was stuck in neutral.

Daire gave me a look out of the corner of her eye as she started to drive toward downtown LA.

Initially, my plan for after I was released had been to head back to Denver immediately. I was worried about my dad's health, and I wanted to be there for the birth of my newest niece. Frankly, if I never saw California again, I wouldn't be sad about it. Unfortunately, none of my plans wanted to work out.

As soon as the family of the teenager who had died in the accident knew I was getting released from prison, they had filed a civil lawsuit for wrongful death against me. I was looking at another year or so of litigation and getting caught up in the legal system. It didn't make any sense to go back to Colorado until everything was said and done.

I was going to visit home once I got settled in my temporary place in LA. Daire and Campbell had wanted me to come and live with them in San Francisco, but the thought of traveling on the interstate between the two cities every time I had a meeting with my lawyer or needed to appear in court made me sick to my stomach.

Luckily, Daire had a good friend who had recently relocated to Los Angeles, and they'd agreed to let me crash in their pool house until the civil suit was settled. My cousin had been vague when I asked for details about the friend. They were probably one of the shady connections everyone alluded to Campbell having, so I let it slide. Beggars couldn't be choosers, and I was fortunate anyone was willing to take a newly released convict into their home.

"You've asked about everyone *but* Aston. Aren't you curious how she's doing? She told me you refused to see her every single time she came to visit you." Daire kept the question playful even though the subject was anything but.

Aston was Daire's best friend. She was also Ry's ex-girlfriend. I loved her from the moment I first saw her when we were little kids. Sadly, at least for me, it was obvious we were never meant to be.

"I spent the last five years doing my best to let Aston go. I forced myself not to think about her. There was no way I could see her or let her see me while I was in that place. I hope she's doing well. I hope she's happy. I want her to live the life she's always wanted. I know there is no place for me next to her. There never has been." I kept my tone firm and tried to hide the quiver in my hands while talking about the one person I'd never been able to let go.

The wind whipping through the open vehicle made conversation hard once we hit the highway. The desert outside LA quickly turned into a big city, and I tried not to throw up as Daire navigated through heavy traffic. I honestly had no idea if I would ever be able to get behind the wheel again. The idea of driving or riding a motorcycle put my entire body into a cold sweat and made bile rise in the back of my throat. Daire wasn't a reckless driver by any means, but I still wanted to yell at her to pull over and demand she let me out of the car. At one point, she answered a call from Campbell and replied that we were about half an hour away from our destination. It took every drop of self-control I had not to rip the phone out of her hand and throw it out of the vehicle.

I could tell that the accident from that night had left deeper scars and done more damage than prison had.

Admittedly, that was probably because, just like Remy mentioned on the day I was taken away, Uncle Benny had pulled some strings behind the scenes. I was placed in a cell with a lifetime convict named Bruno. I couldn't take a step without the behemoth of a man watching my every move. The other inmates already steered clear of me because of him. So, combined with whatever threat knowing Campbell added to the equation, I didn't have much to worry about behind bars. On my last day of lockup, Bruno had pulled me to the side and quietly told me to remind Uncle Benny they were now even. His debt was paid, and he hoped he never had to see or speak to the well-dressed man again.

Daire sensed my unease and quickly ended the call. She concentrated on the road and let me stew in my own anxiety and thoughts while driving through a well-established neighborhood on the outskirts of the city. The house was located back up in the hills and surrounded by more nature than I thought one would find in such a large and heavily populated city. She stopped in front of a brightly painted bungalow that didn't look very big but had to have cost a fortune, considering the location.

I hopped out of the old four-wheel drive and slung the duffel bag of personal belongings Daire had brought for me over my shoulder. When I glanced at my cousin, I caught a look of trepidation on her pretty face. She was quick to hide it, and within seconds, she went back to looking like an angel without a halo. The hair on the back of my neck stood on end. I frowned as she walked over to me and grabbed my elbow to tug me toward the front of the house.

"It's a cute place, isn't it? This is a terrific location. You can go out and exercise and enjoy nature. I'm sure that'll be a nice change from your previous environment. The guesthouse in the back isn't big, but it's perfect for one person. I think you'll like it here. The owner is awesome. The two of you will get along great." She was talking so fast; it was obvious she was trying to hide something.

I frowned as I let her tow me along. "How do you know this person again? You never explained why a total stranger was willing to take someone into their home for a year, much less a convicted felon. It seems like an extreme act of goodwill."

Daire hummed in agreement and practically skipped up the steps leading to the front door of the cheerful home. "There are good people in the world, Zowen. There are people who recognize you are not the sum of your bad choices." She turned her head and gave me a pointed stare. "You know I learned that particular lesson the hard way. When I say that the person who is letting you stay with them is a friend, I don't mean they're only my friend. They're your friend as well. Even if you tried to push them away and sever ties since your arrest."

The duffel bag fell off my shoulder and landed at my feet with a *thud* as my whole body went numb.

"Daire …"

I couldn't think of what to say as a million chaotic possibilities flooded my mind. There was no way in hell she would do this to me ... *right?* There was no way she was dropping me on the doorstep of the last person I was ready to face, was there? She couldn't be that cruel. She couldn't be that calculating.

As soon as the front door opened, I realized my cousin could indeed be as diabolical and deceptive as people seemed to think her fiancé was. Apparently, she had picked up some of his sinister habits while I was away.

"Welcome home, Zowen. It's so good to see you." Aston's voice was eerily calm, and the pleasant expression on her beautiful face didn't move an inch as all the blood drained from mine.

My eyes roved over every inch of her like a blind man seeing light for the first time. Aston was as stunning as I remembered but appeared far less timid. She was always a petite person who came off as fragile and delicate—in part because she'd been so ill as a child. When we were growing up, I always thought if I moved wrong or said the wrong thing, she would shatter into thousands of pieces. That was one of the reasons I'd kept my feelings for her to myself for so long. I never wanted to be the one to break her. I never wanted to cause her harm.

I shifted my gaze between Aston and Daire and felt my heart lodge in my throat.

"You've got to be kidding me." The words felt like sandpaper on my tongue.

Daire nudged me hard with her shoulder, and Aston's dark eyes flickered with a hint of uncertainty.

"This is the best place for you to be right now, Zowen." Daire snorted and defiantly crossed her arms over her chest. "It's not like you have a lot of options at the moment. You either stay here with Aston or come back to the Bay Area and stay with me and Campbell."

Aston blinked and cocked her head to one side. Her wavy, dark hair slithered across her shoulders, and I felt my breath catch. Other than violent and bloody nightmares, Aston Wheeler was the only thing I had dreamed about the entire time I was incarcerated.

"The guesthouse has a separate entrance and its own kitchen. We don't have to interact at all if you don't want to. I'm happy to have you here, Zowen. I missed you."

Unsaid was that she was hurt I had refused to see her for the past five years. I could see thinly veiled pain in her eyes.

I turned to glare at my cousin. I wanted to swear at her. I wanted to call her names. I wanted to turn my back and walk away. I felt like Daire had tricked me, and Aston had been in on the setup. It was the best friends versus me, and I was the clear loser. I had nowhere to go. Just like Daire had said, my options were sadly lacking.

I reached up and shoved a hand through my shaggy, dark hair in frustration. All I could do was look Aston in the eye and quietly tell her, "Thank you."

When we had been younger, I'd always fantasized that I would be the hero who got to save her from every scary thing the world was going to throw at her.

Never in a million years had I imagined the opposite would be true and she would have to save me.

chapter TWO

Aston

Reluctance was oozing from every pore of Zowen's large body.

His expression was blank, but I could see that he wanted to be anywhere but standing in front of me. He'd made it clear he didn't want to see me for the last five years. Any correspondence I'd sent appeared to die in his hands without a reply. I was certain he was doing everything within his power to kick me out of his life, and I wanted to be mad at him. His actions hurt my feelings and made the chunk of my heart that always had his name engraved on it throb painfully. However, I was guilty of trying to shut him out first.

When I'd surprised my entire family and all my friends by dumping my long-term boyfriend and packing up and moving to the West Coast for college, I'd specifically made sure Zowen was the last to know. And for my entire first year, I buried my head in the sand and barely spoke to anyone back home. Zowen included.

I thought a clean break would help me figure out the conflicting feelings I had toward the Archer boys. I was hopeful a new city and new people would erase the lingering love I had for both Ry and Zowen. Those new people and experiences made me realize just how good the boy I had left back home was. The realization came too late. When I had been ready to sit down and have a true heart-to-heart talk with Zowen about the decades of missed opportunities between us, he had been arrested and slowly started to turn into a man I no longer recognized.

Even now, everything about him screamed somber and distant. Zowen was never the Archer who was goofy and outgoing. He wasn't the one who strove for perfection. Or the one who liked to rile everyone up and cause a scene. Zowen was the reliable one. The smart one. The steady Archer whom all the others turned to when they needed sound advice and a shoulder to lean on. He was steadfast and always there when someone else in the family needed him, especially his older sister. He was the problem solver and the mastermind. Growing up, I'd felt like there was never a situation he couldn't fix.

When I saw him today, he came across like someone who would fit in more with Daire's scary fiancé than the Archer family. I wasn't foolish enough to believe him spending five years locked away with the worst society had to offer wouldn't change him, but I'd held out a lot of secret hope that Zowen would retain all the traits that made him so special. He was the best Archer in my opinion, and I couldn't see much changing my mind.

I cleared my throat to break the awkward silence and stepped aside so Daire could lead him into the house. I was so lost in my own thoughts that I didn't realize the cousins were arguing over the keys to the Bronco.

"I drove it up here for you to have while you're in the city. You can't walk anywhere in this town. Once you get your license back, you'll need a way to get around. I'm riding back to the Bay with Campbell." She motioned to a discreet black sports car that was parked along the incline of the hill.

It was a low-key car for being as expensive as it was. It unironically matched the unusual diamond on Daire's ring finger. She shoved the keys into Zowen's hand. I watched his complexion pale. His fingers curled around the metal, and his mismatched eyes twitched nervously. He looked like he wanted to chuck the keys into the bushes and forget about them. Daire had told me he had his license suspended for reckless driving. It had only been revoked for a year, so all he needed to do was get a new one now that he was out of prison. However, the idea appeared to make him very uncomfortable.

Fortunately, the impending argument was broken up by Campbell's arrival. He dipped his chin in greeting and motioned for Zowen to follow him through the house.

I blinked in surprise.

It was my house. I should be the one giving Zowen the grand tour. He seemed stuck at the doorway while facing me but managed to move his feet when his gaze locked on Campbell. The two large, tattooed men maneuvered their way through the relatively small house toward the back, where the French doors leading to the guesthouse were located. I watched the twin broad backs with a frown as Daire grabbed my elbow and pulled me to follow.

"Don't worry about his reaction. He's surprised to see you after all this time. I know he's grateful to have a place to stay and that he's happy to see you. He's emotionally tapped out for the day. He's got to catch up on five years' worth of things he missed. Zowen's a genius, but he's still human."

She patted my arm and lowered her voice so the men in front of us couldn't catch the conversation. "Plus, Campbell has a lead on a job for him while he's here. Zowen asked Remy to sell every single possession that he owned to help his parents pay for all his legal fees, and if he has to pay restitution to the family after the civil trial is done ..." She trailed off and shook her head. "His finances are nonexistent. He can't afford to go anywhere else. There's no way in hell he'll stay here for free even though you offered, so he needs to work. He needs to feel useful and have a purpose again."

I watched as Zowen nodded his dark head at something Campbell had said and saw his shoulders slightly relax.

Before his arrest, Zowen and Campbell had seemed to be on opposite sides of the personality spectrum. One was quiet, mysterious, and exhaled danger and secrets with every breath. The other had been bright and brilliant. He had been achingly honest and gone out of his way to take care of the people he loved. Now, they both hovered closer to the middle of that gradient and seemed like they were tinted similar shades of gray. Campbell loved Daire in a way that was beyond reason, which meant he could—and would—do *anything,* no matter how questionable, to keep her happy and safe. Prison seemed to have dulled down most of Zowen's shine. Those unusual-colored eyes of his that I used to be able to read like a book now hid thoughts and feelings I couldn't name. His presence wasn't as suffocating and oppressive as Campbell's, but it was no longer warm and comforting. I used to feel reassured just by knowing he was close by. That feeling had now turned to unease. Everything about Zowen felt cold. Like his heart and soul had been encased in ice.

Which was fine. I had nothing but time while I waited for his vital parts to thaw.

"This is a nice place. I'm a little surprised you moved to LA. I thought you liked the Bay Area."

It took me a second to realize Zowen was speaking to me. I cleared my throat and nervously fiddled with a strand of hair that curled around my face.

"I do like that area, and I like that I have friends there."

Not only Daire, but also another girl named Nobel—whom I had gone to college with and become close to—was in San Francisco. Both Daire and I had lived with her for different periods of time while finishing school and figuring out our next steps. Daire had moved out when Campbell permanently moved to the area. These days, the two of them lived much closer to a suburb I wouldn't be caught dead anywhere near at any time of day.

"I got a job promotion six months ago that required me to move here. This house belongs to my boss. She's letting me rent it for cheap because she's overseas, working to establish a European branch of the business. She comes back once every four or five months to check on things." I offered a slight smile. "I could never afford to buy something in this kind of location on my current salary."

Zowen blinked at me like I had suddenly started speaking Spanish, then asked in a quiet voice, "What do you do for work?"

The question was like an arrow through my heart. He and I used to know everything about one another. He knew me better than anyone else, including his best friend, whom I had dated for the entirety of my teenage years. But now, even the very basics were foreign. His question hammered home the fact that I was about to share my house, the place that was my safe zone, with a stranger for at least a year.

I shifted my weight nervously and told myself to get it together. No matter what, the man in front of me was still Zowen Archer. Regardless of how much he had changed or how different he was, I refused to believe the boy who had always treated me like I was some sort of precious treasure was lost. So what if we were strangers? What we needed to do was start over from the beginning and get to know each other again. If we were strangers, we didn't have to deal with all the baggage that had forever been stacked up a mile high between the two of us.

"I work in public relations and marketing. My company handles actors, authors, influencers, and various other types of entertainment professionals. I spend a lot of time researching trends and figuring out how to leverage social media for our clients." I gave him a crooked grin. "And occasionally, I have to run errands and play personal assistant for our really, really famous clients."

Having to interact with legitimate celebrities had gotten me over my shyness really quick. If I was meek and weak-willed, I'd get run over in a heartbeat in this industry.

Zowen made a noise in his throat, and his blue eye glittered with suppressed humor. The eye that was dark brown was always better at hiding what he was thinking. "That sounds very LA."

I laughed. "It is. It's not where I expected to end up career-wise, but I'm good at my job. It's interesting and always changing. I enjoy the challenge of it."

That was one thing he and I always had in common. We were constantly searching for things in life that would test our limits and force us to be our best selves.

One of the main reasons I had broken up with Ry was because our relationship was too easy. He and I were similar. He cared for me too much and never allowed me to be in a situation where I might struggle or suffer. It was like I was living my life in a plastic bubble. After a while, I forgot there were things in the world that could hurt me. My emotions had been numb, and I'd realized the longer Ry and I stayed together, the more of myself I was going to lose.

"As long as you like it, I'm sure it's a good fit for you. I always knew you would find your place in the world when you had the opportunity to spread your wings." He cleared his throat, as if he felt like he'd said too much, and inclined his head toward the tiny guesthouse. "Let's take a look so I can throw this down." The duffel bag on his shoulder was bulging with stuff.

I knew Daire and his sister had spent a lot of time making sure he would have anything he might want or need on hand as soon as he was released. There was even a high-tech computer set up in one corner of the small living area of the guesthouse that Campbell had hurriedly put together when Daire left to pick up Zowen.

I stepped around everyone so I could unlock the door and hand Zowen the key. "It's small, but it has everything you need. And my boss had it remodeled recently because she was going to use it as an office before she decided to move overseas. There's a gate on the side of the yard, so, like I said, you have your own entrance without having to come through the bungalow. It's quiet and private back here, and there are a lot of mature hiking trails you can take up into the Hills. This neighborhood is home to several famous people, so it's pretty secure."

The corner of Zowen's mouth turned down, and his mix-and-match gaze landed on me like a ton of bricks. His voice was more of a growl than anything else when he asked, "Does your boss know you're letting a felon move into her guesthouse?" His dark eyebrows lifted, and a sardonic look crossed his handsome face. "I doubt she wants someone like me hanging out in a neighborhood like this."

I frowned when he called himself a felon. Even if it was true, he was so much more than that. At least to me, he was.

"No. I told her I was going to let an old friend stay with me because that's the only truth that matters. That's what I will always see you as, Zowen. You're my friend. Everything else is incidental."

He sighed heavily and let the duffel bag drop to his feet. He raked a hand through his dark hair, and his eyes were far more serious than I ever remembered them being. "After all these years, you still see me as a *friend*? I don't know if that's a good or bad thing, Aston."

He used to want me to see him as more, but now, it felt like he wanted me to see him as less.

Unsure of what to say, I waved at the single-bedroom dwelling and told him to make himself comfortable. Like Daire had said, he was more than likely maxed out emotionally. Having to deal with the surprise of seeing me after all this time when he obviously didn't want to must have been enough to push him past his breaking point. I didn't want his first day of freedom spent rehashing old feelings and asking questions that were impossible to answer. He'd been surrounded by people and had his every move watched for the last five years; he had to be ready to enjoy his own space and to do things according to his own wants and needs. I planned to stay out of his way until he gave me the green light to get close to him.

Daire wrapped her arm around my shoulders and leaned her head against mine. "Let's get something to eat. I'm sure Zowen will appreciate a home-cooked meal. He needs a minute to get his bearings. Don't take anything he says to heart."

I huffed a frustrated breath and let her guide me to the main house. Campbell stayed behind.

I heard the door to the guesthouse click shut and asked Daire, "You don't find it weird that the two of them are so close these days?"

It was tricky to talk to Daire about Campbell. He was someone so different from the kind of people we had grown up with. There was no question he was good for her and good to her, but none of that canceled out his questionable past or the distinct changes Daire had undergone since getting involved with him.

My bestie had always been reckless and a bit wild. She treated everything as a game with little thought to the consequences. After a tragic accident had nearly killed her brother, she had shut down and appeared to reevaluate how her impetuousness might adversely affect others. I was always worried about her. And I was always envious of her.

I wanted to live life to the fullest and experience what it felt like to be reckless and carefree. I was too cautious for that. I'd always been too sheltered, and I couldn't bring myself to make my parents worry about me the way Daire's did. My mom never let me forget how close they had come to losing me right after I was born.

Now that Campbell was in the picture, Daire seemed to have embraced her chaotic nature fully. She was messy and often a lot to handle, but Campbell was always there to balance out whatever hectic situation she was in the center of. If Daire was a scream that could make a person's ears bleed, then Campbell was the type of eerie silence that gave a person chills. Instead of them carving out a place for one another in their very different worlds, they created their own. If you wanted to step into it, you did so while accepting exactly who Daire was and being aware that there was more to Campbell than would ever meet the eye. He made my best friend threateningly confident, and she made him quietly domestic. Well, as domestic as a predator could be.

Daire sighed and knocked our heads together hard enough to hurt. "It would be weird if it were the old Zowen you're asking about. The guy who played video games and wanted to hack into satellites for fun didn't have anything in common with Campbell. When he was the smartest guy in the room and wouldn't hurt a fly, it wouldn't have made any sense for the two of them to be close. But that's not who he is anymore." She sniffed as if she was holding back tears. "Zowen will always be a genius, but now, he's also dangerous. He had to be to survive in that place for so long. Even with someone watching out for him, he still had to be on guard. When you spend all day, every day, watching your back and staying vigilant against an attack, it's bound to alter who you are and how you live your life. Campbell knows exactly what it feels like to wake up and wonder if today is going to be his last. Zowen needs someone who won't judge him for who he's become. He needs someone who understands him without having to ask questions and poke at open wounds. Campbell is that someone."

I wrapped my arms around myself in a loose hug. "Is it a bad thing if I admit I want the old Zowen back?"

Daire might enjoy life living with a deadly and unpredictable man. I wanted the opposite. At least, that was what my mom had drilled into my head and heart for as long as I could remember. Stable and secure. Exactly how Zowen had been before his arrest. However, I conveniently ignored that those were the exact reasons being with Ry for so long had ended up being duller than dirt.

Daire hummed a soft sound of acknowledgment and bumped our temples together again. "Hope for the best, plan for the worst. Who he was or who he is now is all a matter of perception. Any part of him that seems unrecognizable now was always there. He never needed to rely on them before, so we never saw that side of him in the past. Plus, he's no longer a kid. We're all older now. All of us who grew up together should know more and have all kinds of different experiences that have shaped us. His experiences just happen to be a bit more extreme, and we weren't allowed to witness any of it. He's still Zowen, and that won't ever change. I think that's what you should focus on while trying to mend fences."

I nodded, but wasn't so certain on the inside.

I knew what to do with the Zowen who had wanted to get close to me and protect me.

I had no idea how to handle the one who pushed me away and looked right through me.

I doubted we could even figure out how to be friends again—let alone any of the other things I'd started to imagine when I finally figured my own feelings out.

THREE

Zowen

"Your sister wanted to make sure I gave you this."

I grunted as Campbell shoved a destroyed motorcycle helmet into my hands. The visor was cracked into a spectacular spiderweb. There was a place on the side where all the paint and decals were worn away because it had been dragged across the asphalt, which, in turn, acted like a cheese grater. There was also a split where the safety device had taken the brunt of the blow when I was hit with flying pieces of shrapnel. Anyone with eyes could see that the owner of the destroyed helmet was beyond lucky to be alive.

"Remy isn't very subtle, is she?" I set the helmet down and wandered around the small space that would serve as home base for the foreseeable future.

It was about the size of the dorm room I used to call home while in college, though infinitely nicer. I could tell Aston had gone out of her way to make the space cozy and welcoming.

"I want to get back to Denver before she has the baby. And I need to see for myself that my dad is doing okay." I glanced at the redheaded man.

Campbell was hard to read on a good day, but I felt like I had a better understanding of him after spending so long locked up with men who had given off similar vibes. When a dangerous man was quiet, they were less of a threat. When they had something to say, you'd better listen because whatever it was could mean the difference between life and death.

"I know you think the stress you put your parents under is part of the reason your father suffered a cardiac arrest. Once you've taken the blame for one mistake, it becomes much easier to start taking responsibility for everything that goes wrong around you. I've been there. I've carried that weight unnecessarily." Campbell shook his head and crossed his heavily tattooed arms over his chest. "Your father has always had pieces of a fragmented bullet stuck in his chest. Remy gave me the rundown of how he was injured while your mom was pregnant. Those leftover pieces have always been a threat to your old man. She told me every Archer knew those fragments put your dad at a higher risk of having something go wrong with his heart. Making yourself feel awful for something that you had no control over doesn't do anything to make those who love you feel better."

I snorted, a little surprised he could pinpoint the exact idea swirling around my mind. "Even if he didn't end up in the hospital because of me, I'm still at fault for not being able to be home when my family needed me. The responsibility for that falls solely on my shoulders."

I pointed at the helmet and told him, "I'll let Remy know you passed her gift along the next time I talk to her. I meant to ask Daire how my sister is handling her pregnancy, but I couldn't even hear myself think over the wind blowing through the Bronco."

Campbell shrugged, and a slight grin tugged at the corner of his mouth. He had a big scar that made the gesture look far more menacing than the average smile. "I think Remy's doing good. She seems excited. She's mentioned more than once that she hopes the baby takes more after Hyde than her. Hyde keeps telling her that he hopes the baby is exactly like her. Your sister has done a fantastic job in raising Hollyn all these years. I don't think she has anything to worry about."

He motioned to the keys Daire had forced on me while at the front door. "Daire bought the Bronco especially for you. It's old and built like a tank. It doesn't go over sixty-five miles an hour. Because it has an open top, it's the closest thing you're going to get to feeling like you're back on your bike. Your cousin thought long and hard about what kind of welcome-home gift to give you. Don't let your pride or fear diminish how desperate your loved ones have been to have you back." He waited a beat until our eyes met. The expression in his stony gaze was enough to send a shiver down my spine. "Even if you do it unintentionally, I'm not willing to let you hurt Daire ... or Aston."

"Yeah, about that. Thing is, I have nightmares about being on the road. I nearly hyperventilated when Daire was driving me here from the prison. The thought of reinstating my driver's license makes me want to throw up.

I don't want to diminish or hurt anyone. I just might be unable to accept certain acts of kindness right now." I blew out my frustrated breath and dragged a hand down my face. I was suddenly exhausted and felt like I could fall asleep right where I was standing. "Agreeing to stay in this house, even though it's so close to Aston, is the biggest concession I can make right now. Everything within me is screaming that this is going to be a disaster and I would be better off sleeping on the streets or in that Bronco. But I'm going to bite the bullet and accept her generosity." Even though it felt like a spectacular mistake in the making.

Some of the tension surrounding Campbell eased, which made the atmosphere in the small house feel less oppressive. I was glad that somewhere along the way, he'd decided I was a friend and not an enemy. He wasn't someone I ever wanted to cross or get on the wrong side of.

His voice was low and serious when he told me, "Aston isn't the same girl you remember from high school. She graduated from Stanford with honors. She works her ass off. She's nowhere near as shy and timid as she was when Daire first introduced me to her. She isn't hung up on the wrong Archer anymore." He gave me a pointed look.

"She dated on and off while you were away, but nothing was ever serious. It seems to me like she's been patiently waiting for you to get your shit together and get free. Daire insists though that she just hasn't met the right guy yet." Campbell snorted, and a slight furrow wrinkled his forehead.

"She's got a new client. An Italian guy named Cassio Vinci. He's making the move from amateur sport bike racing to the MotoGP league this season. Cassio seems interested in having more than a business relationship with Aston. She told Daire that he likes the fact that she's familiar with motorcycles and the sport. He wanted to fly her to Tokyo for qualifying this month, but she refused because she was getting this guesthouse ready for you. I had him vetted once he started seriously hanging around and couldn't find any red flags."

I frowned back at him and asked, "Why are you telling me this? I don't have any say or opinion when it comes to who Aston decides to spend time with." I'd lost that privilege way before these last five years.

"I'm telling you because you need to know what you're up against. You need to see that there are people who aren't scared of the things that terrify you. Your fear will make others more powerful than you. And I'm sure you've figured out that power is everything once you've had none."

"If she has someone who makes her happy and treats her right, I'm happy for her," I lied through my teeth.

Campbell scoffed. "Ry made her happy and treated her well. Were you happy for her when she was dating him?"

That was a low blow, and I hated how easily this man could see through my secrets.

"You really are a ruthless son of a bitch, aren't you?" I still couldn't believe that I was going to share a last name with someone like him.

The redheaded man shrugged. "Never claimed to be anything else. I'll let you rest. You look like you're ready to fall over."

He moved to the door; however, I stopped him before he opened it.

"Are you sure the guy I'm going to work for is legit? I can't afford to get messed up in anything that might be adjacent to illegal with the civil trial pending."

Before I had been released, Campbell had informed me he could get me a job working with computers. Uncle Benny had put him in touch with a husband-and-wife team that ran a nonprofit, searching for missing and exploited kids. Their methods were extreme but highly successful. Campbell had endorsed the operation and the couple behind it because they were responsible for helping him get his younger siblings away from his abusive father.

"I'm sure that whatever role they plan to have you take is above board. I can't promise that your new boss isn't on a government watchlist somewhere, but I can assure you that he is much better at walking the line between black and white than my boss is. He won't have you working on anything that might land you back in jail."

I nodded and silently took his word for it. Because even if Campbell was generally indifferent to anything and everything that wasn't related to my cousin, I knew, for Daire's sake, there was no way he would put me at risk.

Once I was alone in the small space, I allowed myself to collapse on the comfy-looking gray couch. My gaze strayed to the battered helmet and my sister's unspoken reminder to be thankful that I was alive. Regardless of how things had played out' or of all that had been lost, and the changes that had occurred, I was lucky to still be around to wade through the muck and mire. It was a blessing to be around even if it was to simply wallow in remorse.

I wanted to close my eyes and rest, but I couldn't stop myself from digging through the duffel bag Daire had packed and looking for the new phone she'd told me was in one of the pockets. I didn't start the phone so I could call my parents or text my sister. I didn't send a message to Ry or check in with my lawyer.

No, the first thing I did was search the internet for the Italian racer who had his sights set on Aston.

I should've waited until I got some sleep.

I should've listened to my initial instinct and ignored anything having to do with Aston Wheeler.

It was like I was looking at a picture of what my life might've been had I not screwed everything up.

The guy was younger than me, and yet he had achieved everything I had hoped to. He was also handsome and appeared to be rich as hell. His family owned several famous vineyards in Tuscany. He had a legion of fans and seemed to be a pretty big deal across social media. All his posts were related to racing and were full of pictures of his bike and his crew. There were a few sponsored posts sprinkled throughout. I wasn't shocked that I recognized a lot of the brands that paid to advertise with him. It was impressive, considering he hadn't gone pro yet.

My hand clenched the phone tighter when I saw that the only post he had up that seemed to be personal and not related to racing was a candid picture of Aston with the caption, *Tesoro mio*. She had her head tossed back and was laughing at something. Her dark eyes sparkled in the image, and the hidden hints of red in her hair glowed like fire. She was stunning. And she looked so happy.

Happier than I could ever remember seeing her.

Even when she had been dating Ry and they were the king and queen of our teenage social circle, she'd never looked that carefree and joyful.

I threw the phone on the coffee table next to the helmet and slumped down on the couch. I closed my eyes and tossed my arm across my face. I wanted to shut the world out. I wanted to numb all the feelings flooding through my heart. I could feel my soul shake against everything I had worked so hard to repress for the last five years and try to break free. Campbell was correct when he'd said power was important when you had none. Right now, I didn't even have enough strength to make my mind and body follow my commands. My fingers twitched, and my eyes burned with emotion. I'd lost count of how many times I wanted to cry myself to sleep over the last five years, but I never allowed it. It was a weakness that might've gotten me killed if I let it escape.

But now that I was in this meticulously decorated home, cared for by family and friends who had genuinely missed me, I no longer had the willpower to keep those agonized tears at bay. They stung fiercely as they squeezed past my closed eyelids and rolled down my face.

I cried for the loss of that teenage boy.

I cried for the loss of my future and all my plans.

I cried for the lost love I'd always had for Aston even if it was unrequited.

I cried for the kid I used to be who was never going to get a chance to be anything other than a murderer.

I cried for all that I'd put my family through and for every struggle we were bound to face now that we were about to be reunited.

Being released from prison was supposed to be a happy event, a new lease on life and a chance to start over. For me, it felt like an impending doom. I knew who I was and how I was supposed to act while I was locked up behind bars and caged in cement.

I had no clue what I was supposed to do or how I was supposed to interact with my family and friends now that I was free.

I lost track of how long I sat there and let the tears fall. I must've fallen asleep at some point because when I opened my eyes, my neck was stiff, and it was dark outside. My face felt dirty and sticky from my earlier breakdown, so I dumped the duffel bag and took some of the brand-new clothes into the bathroom so I could change after I took a shower.

It had been so long since I could enjoy as much hot water as I wanted and didn't have to be extra vigilant when I was most vulnerable. I stayed until the water ran cold. When I looked at myself in the foggy mirror, I noticed that my hair was too long. I needed to get it cut. I also took note that I no longer looked like a young man who was just entering his twenties. There was no more youthfulness to my features. My face was sharp and starkly defined. My eyes were always notable because they were two distinct colors, just like my mom's. One was a light shade of brown, and the other was the familiar bright blue all the Archer men had been blessed with. They used to be lively and full of curiosity. Now, both colors appeared dull and hollow. I thought I'd gotten taller while locked up. I'd gained some muscle mass. There wasn't much to do other than workout and read. And Bruno had aggressively reminded me at least once a week that it was better to look like a guy who wouldn't lose a fight than to look like a pushover.

I didn't just feel like a stranger in my own life; I looked like one.

I swiped my hand across the fog and blurred the image out. I rubbed a towel over my wet hair and walked back into the living area just in time to catch a knock on the door. Figuring it was Daire coming to check on me before she and Campbell left to drive back up the coast, I opened it and surprised Aston mid-knock. She had a small tower of plastic storage containers in one hand and a shocked expression on her pretty face.

"Daire and I made dinner. She tried to call you a couple of times to eat with us, but you never answered. Campbell came and knocked on the door before they left. I figured you were asleep when there was no response. I just wanted to make sure you had something to eat. I was going to leave it on the doorstep if you didn't come to the door. I didn't want to bother you." She spoke so fast that some of her words rushed together.

I looked over at the phone I'd tossed away earlier and noticed there were notifications glowing from the screen like crazy.

"Daire and Campbell left?"

She nodded and shoved the stack of food containers into my hands. "Daire has to work in the morning, and Campbell had some sort of meeting he needed to get to later on tonight." She cocked her head to the side and blinked her dark eyes innocently. "I've learned it's best not to ask him too many questions about what he does and who he does it for."

"That *is* for the best." I looked at the meal, and my stomach growled as the scent hit my nose. "Thanks for this. I can't tell you the last time I ate something that was identifiable."

She shifted nervously and reached up to push her hair behind her ears. "It was mostly Daire. She's a decent cook these days. But she's always mastered anything she sets her mind to. I get takeout and order delivery most nights when I'm home."

I lifted an eyebrow and rested my shoulder on the doorjamb. I didn't want to give her the impression I was going to invite her in to hang out and have a chat. Even though she had taken me in like a wounded stray, I still thought it would be best if our lives intersected as little as possible.

"Do you eat out with clients when you're not home?"

I bet the Italian guy knew all the best places in LA to take her. I bet he could get into the kind of places where you needed a reservation years in advance.

Aston shrugged, as if her response was no big deal. "Sometimes. LA is expensive. If it's business-related and the client is paying, I don't mind getting a free meal every now and then."

She must've sensed my unwillingness to invite her inside because she took a step back and waved in the direction of the house. "I'm headed to bed soon. Let me know if you need to be anywhere over the next few days. I'm working from home this week, and I know you won't be able to reinstate your driver's license overnight. Daire mentioned you more than likely needed to meet up with your lawyer. I'm happy to take you to and from."

"It's already enough that you offered me a place to stay, Aston. You don't have to be my driver or my personal chef. Don't worry about me. I can take care of myself." It sounded harsher than I'd meant it to, but I didn't want her to feel like she needed to adjust her life now that I was back in it. I refused to be a burden on anyone while I reintegrated into the world I'd left behind.

Aston paused and gave me a look I couldn't fully decipher. Campbell was correct when he'd told me she wasn't the Aston who had lived in all my most cherished memories. There was an edge to her now, a toughness she hadn't had before. There was no indication she might crumble just because I was being outright mean to her.

"I know I don't *have* to do anything for you, Zowen. I *want* to do those things for you. I want to help you. I want you to know that you aren't alone anymore." She flipped her hair over her shoulder and tilted her chin so that her head was held high. "Enjoy your meal and have a good night."

I watched her walk away, too stunned to speak.

I wasn't sure I was equipped to handle a confrontational Aston Wheeler. I hadn't known she had that kind of sass buried within her.

I shut the door and looked at the food, feeling a bit bewildered. I was well aware of how drastically I'd changed while I was away. I hadn't been prepared at all for how the people from my past differed from the enshrined recollection I'd had. Apparently, I wasn't the only one who was a different person than I'd been five years ago.

I had a sinking feeling that staying so close to this woman, who was so unlike the girl who had always owned my heart, was going to be far more difficult than serving time.

chapter
FOUR

Aston

"How are things going with your new houseguest?" My brother's deep voice held a hint of humor, and I could tell he was walking outside because the background of the call was full of city sounds.

Royce lived on the opposite side of the country in New York. When he had decided to move to the city full-time after I graduated from high school, it was one of the big factors to me finally being brave enough to break away from the protective bubble I had grown up in. Royce and I had different biological mothers. Which meant each of us grew up with a bonus mom who treated us like their own. Royce spent the school year in Denver with me and our parents, but every summer, he left for the East Coast. As we got older, I could tell it wasn't just his mom he missed when he came back to Colorado.

My older brother was an artist. He specialized in modern art and creating unbelievable sculptures out of reclaimed materials and massive pieces of recycled metal. And while Denver was delightful and open to all avenues of entertainment, the art scene was not the same there as it was in a big city. Royce needed to be somewhere he could thrive. Since moving, he'd seen more of the world than I could imagine. He spent a year abroad, traveling through Italy and France. He spent half a year in Barcelona after falling in love with a ballet dancer. He had backpacked through the Netherlands and spent his final year of college in Berlin.

I was jealous of all his experiences, and I was happy he was finally back and settled in Brooklyn. We tried to visit each other at least every six months and go home for at least one major holiday a year. Even if we didn't see each other as much as I would like, Royce never failed to check in through video chat or a phone call at least once a week.

I looked at the French doors that led to the guesthouse in the backyard and shrugged in response. "I haven't seen very much of him for the last two weeks. After Daire dropped him off, he shut himself away for the first few days, and he had a bunch of meetings with his lawyer. This week, he disappears in the morning before I get up. Yesterday, I watched him get dropped off in a serious-looking black sedan. The guy driving looked like a Secret Service agent from a TV show. So, maybe he's working for the government ... or the mob."

Royce snorted. "Those two things are pretty much the same. And I highly doubt Zowen is stupid enough to get tangled up with either."

"Whatever he's doing, he's going out of his way to avoid me." I couldn't hide the hurt in my voice.

I'd anticipated a chilly reception after Daire tricked him into staying at my place, but I was in no way prepared for the total freeze-out. Ever since the moment we had met, Zowen Archer had looked at me with his heart in his eyes. I spent a lifetime looking past it so we could maintain a friendship and so there was never a rift between him and Ry. I ignored his infatuation deliberately and, admittedly, cruelly. So, I couldn't say that I didn't deserve the indifference and frost that gazed back at me now. It took every acting skill I'd honed over the years of pretending to be fine—when I was far from it—to keep up an unbothered facade.

Royce hummed a sound of sympathy and swore as something honked loudly in the background. His life was so full of sound and energy. It often felt the opposite of my quiet and staid existence.

"He's probably just busy. His whole life was on hold for five years. Longer if you include everything leading up to the trial and sentencing. All of that happened when he was just a kid. He was barely old enough to drink legally at the time. Not only does he have to figure out how to navigate everything he missed while he was away, but he also has to learn how to be the adult everyone expects him to be even though he never had the opportunity to grow into that version of himself. I bet he's under more pressure than any of us can imagine, and as kind as your offer to let him stay was, it's another weight on his shoulders. When Zowen was a kid, he loved you without question. Now that he's had to grow up so fast and in such a rough way, that love has more than likely turned into something else. He needs to sort his feelings out."

I sighed and tossed my head back in frustration to stare at the wood beams on the ceiling. "What if I don't want his love to turn into something else?"

What if I'd finally realized that it was the thing missing from my life all along? No matter how independent I learned to be, no matter how much I challenged myself, no matter what steps I took to become the woman I always wanted to be, I felt like there was a hole inside myself that would never be filled. I could shovel achievements and accomplishments into it all day long, but the void remained. It felt like it got deeper and darker the more time went on ... and the longer Zowen was out of reach.

Royce swore again, but this time, it was directed at me. "You ignored Zowen's feelings for you for years. You dated his best friend even though anyone with eyes could tell Ry was in love with someone else the entire time you were together. You moved to California and didn't tell Zowen. It's not fair that you expect him to pine over you forever, Aston. That's just cruel, and I know you are not that type of person."

I scowled, but my ire was directed at myself. My brother wasn't wrong in his assessment. I had been unkind to Zowen a lot of the time when we were younger. Not because I wanted to be. Because, while I couldn't tell at the time, I was living the life my mother wanted for me, not the one I envisioned for myself. I hadn't known the difference until it was too late and Zowen was forcibly taken away.

"I want to make amends. I tried the entire time he was in prison, and he refused to see me. He wouldn't talk to me. I was never able to explain why I was the way I was back then. I never got the chance to apologize. I hoped when he came to stay here, he would see my sincerity and we could start over and at least figure out how to be friends again, but he doesn't want anything to do with me."

And I hated it. It gave me a whole new appreciation for how he must've felt when I shut him out and left for California without much warning.

Royce sighed and softened his tone. "Everything you just said is about you, Aston."

I blinked at his words, and with a jolt, I sat up straight in the chair I had been sprawled across.

"*You* want to apologize. *You* want to be forgiven. *You* want to make amends and have your sincerity acknowledged. What about what Zowen wants and needs? Have you taken a second to consider him in all of that?"

I closed my eyes and threw my forearm across my face. "When did I become such a selfish person?"

I really hadn't given much thought to what was best for Zowen beyond giving him a roof over his head. A roof he'd never even asked for.

My brother chuckled, and I heard him stop and make baby talk to a dog before he turned his attention back to our conversation. "I want to make a joke about you learning how to be selfish because you spend so much time around Daire, but the truth is, she's very good at knowing when to make something all about her and when it needs to be about someone else. She puts herself first, but now that she's engaged to Campbell, she makes sure to keep him right at the top, next to her. Loving someone else doesn't always mean they have to come first; you just have to love them as much as you love yourself. And if you can't figure out how to love yourself, you're never going to figure out how to love someone else the way they deserve to be loved."

I felt my eyes well up with tears. Royce was always more eloquent and in tune with his emotions than I was. It had to do with our different mothers. His was a bit more of a free spirit and much more daring than mine. Both women had had some significant trauma in their pasts. However, instead of being overprotective and hovering like my mom, Royce's encouraged him to push boundaries and jump into anything scary headfirst. She believed the only way to learn was to make mistakes, whereas my mother wanted me to live a life that was low risk and filled with success. I very rarely failed at anything while growing up. In fact, breaking up with Ry Archer right before moving on to the next *big* step in our perfectly planned future together could be considered my first real, purposeful decision I'd made for myself. It was the first loss I'd suffered and, to this day, still one of the hardest and scariest choices I'd ever faced.

"I feel like you're not the guy who should be handing out relationship advice so freely. You've had, like, three different girlfriends and two boyfriends since the start of the year. You go through relationships like other people go through those disposable coffee pods."

It was a long running joke between us that Royce had a lot of love to give, and that was one of the reasons he needed to move to a bigger city and travel abroad. He had already dated everyone there was to date in Denver.

"Because I haven't met anyone I like as much as I like myself. We both know how great I am."

I couldn't help but laugh at his brazenness. No one would ever accuse my brother of lacking self-confidence.

"You are great. I miss you. When are you going home next?"

As I asked the question, I noticed movement outside the French doors. While I was on the phone, Zowen had returned from whatever mysterious place he disappeared to during the day. His attention was on his phone. However, before he entered the guesthouse, he turned his head to look at my house. I felt like our eyes met through the glass door, but he went inside before I could figure out if I was imagining things.

"I won't be free to visit until Christmas. I have a new commission that's going to take the rest of the year to complete, and my mom hasn't been feeling well. She's been doing a bunch of medical testing to pinpoint the problem. I won't feel comfortable leaving her until we know exactly what she's dealing with. Mom also got a new puppy I offered to help her take care of. She hasn't felt up to walking him. He's a handful." He sounded concerned, and I felt bad for monopolizing the conversation.

"Well, if she's still not feeling well when my next vacation-time allotment rolls around, maybe I can come and visit you. If you need me there, you have to let me know."

Royce was someone I would drop literally anything for.

"I'll keep you updated. Hey, I bet Zowen plans to head home for the birth of his sister's baby. You can always tag along on that trip with the excuse you were planning to see Mom and Dad anyway. It would be a good chance for the two of you to catch up. Plus, you'd have the nostalgia of being back in Denver working for you."

He stopped talking to me, and I heard him muttering to someone else. When he came back to the call, he told me he had to go because he reached his studio, ending his walking commute to work. Royce asked me to keep him updated about my guest and waited to hang up until I agreed.

I hung up the phone and stared out the back door. I was turning over Royce's suggestion about inviting myself along on Zowen's trip home. As tempting as the idea was, I didn't want to force myself on him any more than I already had. Right now, he was avoiding me, but he was still close enough to see and touch. Not that I was brave enough to reach out and grab him. Taking him dinner his first night here had been about the limit of my fearlessness. Even though I'd quietly rejected him for the duration of our friendship, I wasn't equipped to deal with him doing the same to me. I felt like my heart was going to shatter each time he looked right through me.

While I was silently stalking my backyard, Zowen stepped out of his door. He was still looking at something on his phone, but he had changed into a more casual outfit. This was the first chance I had to look at him and take note of everything that was different about his physical appearance over the last five years.

Zowen was always good-looking. All the Archers were. Attractiveness ran as deep in that gene pool as the very, very blue eyes did. He was tall like his father but built a bit slighter. Probably due to his mom's petite frame. He had brown hair. It used to be sandy with hints of caramel since he spent so much time outside in the sun, but now, it was all dark. It was longer than he'd ever worn it when he was younger. But the darkness went beyond his hair color. Everything about him seemed to be shades deeper and harder to see through than before. His face, while still pretty and eye-catching, had no softness to it. No hint of carefree youth. He didn't look like a young man growing into a typical Archer. He looked like an Archer, period.

He had his father's hard-earned wisdom stamped on his face.

He had his uncle's wariness and rebelliousness etched within the colors of his unusual eyes.

He carried himself like both men did even though he was decades younger.

It made me wonder just how hard life had been for him during the past five years.

When I realized he was walking around the guest-house and headed somewhere, I impulsively grabbed my keys and darted after him. The sedan wasn't parked in front, and he walked right past the Bronco like it wasn't even there. I had no clue where he was going, but there was nothing within walking distance.

I jogged to catch up to him. When I was close enough to grab his arm, I reached out, but immediately withdrew my hand. Royce asking me to consider Zowen's wants and needs was still lingering in the back of my mind. It was a given he didn't want to be surprised or touched without permission. I cleared my throat loudly until he turned around and acknowledged I was behind him.

"Where are you going? Would you like me to give you a ride?" I kept my tone light and stayed a step behind him so he didn't feel pressured or attacked.

"I'm going to a bar." He looked over his shoulder at me and indicated the GPS program on his phone. "It says it's only a thirty-five-minute walk."

"A bar?" I racked my brain, trying to think of where he might be going. I drew a blank. "There's nothing like that in this neighborhood."

He showed me his destination marker on the phone screen, and I laughed.

"That's a wine bar. It has a dress code. You won't get past the front door." I waved my hand toward the distance where the Hollywood sign was clearly visible. "Remember, this neighborhood is considered upscale even if it's older."

Zowen sighed and tucked his phone away. He stopped walking and looked at the ground for a minute before asking, "Can you tell me a place that is busy and low-key? Somewhere I won't have to pay sixteen dollars for a beer."

"I can take you somewhere."

Though everywhere in LA was expensive. I did know of one or two dive bars closer to the beach where the prices were okay. They were a bit of a drive from where we were located, but they would suit Zowen's current vibe better. Royce was the one who had found them when he came to see me. I was reluctant to let Zowen out of my sight. I wasn't sure if it was his first time letting loose since getting out of prison, but if it was, I thought it might be better for him to have someone watch over him. He didn't need to be in any type of situation that might affect the impending civil trial.

Zowen swore and finally lifted his head to look at me. As always, his eyes were cold, but there was something in the brown one that felt familiar. It wasn't warm or friendly. It was hot. Like an inferno.

"I want to go alone. I'm not going to drink."

I cocked my head to the side and considered him seriously. "Not going to drink? Then, what do you want to go to a bar for? You can't tell me you want to make new friends. I won't believe it."

He was the type who preferred his own company or the people he played games with to big social circles. He always said it was hard to make friends when you were smarter than everyone else.

He grunted and took a step away from me. "I do want to make a new friend. But only for a couple of hours." He gave me a pointed look, and a sarcastic smile curled the edges of his mouth. It was an expression I'd never seen him wear before. "I was locked away from *everything* for a long time, Aston. I missed some things more than others."

I blinked and felt my heart trip over itself.

I wasn't naïve. I'd known Zowen for most of my life. And regardless of what Royce had implicated, it wasn't like Zowen had lived a chaste and celibate life while waiting for me to come around. There was a period right around the time I decided to break up with Ry where it seemed like he and my brother were competing to see who could have the higher body count. While he'd never had a serious girlfriend as long as I'd known him, he was rarely without willing company. It should've occurred to me he had other needs he needed to attend to aside from the bare-bones basics.

"Ohhhhh … okay. I can still take you someplace. I can be your wingwoman." I tucked a piece of hair behind my ear and forced a smile. The last thing I wanted to do was help him hook up with some stranger, but if it opened the door to him being willing to have a conversation with me, I could grin and bear it. "I won't get in the way. I just think it's better you don't go out on your own the first time out. I mean, this is technically still a new city for you to be in."

Zowen narrowed his eyes at me and let out a long, frustrated breath. "Forget it. You're probably right. I'm just going to end up looking for trouble. I'll get something to drink delivered through an app and save myself the money and headache." The reluctance was obvious in his tone.

I didn't care that he was unwilling. I latched on to the opportunity presented with both hands.

"Great. You get something to drink, and I'll get dinner delivered. We can have a mini welcome-home celebration. You can tell me about the guy in the suit who picks you up in the morning, and I can catch you up on anything you want to know that's been going on outside of the Archers while you've been gone. It'll be fun." I could see the instant refusal on his face, so I finally mustered up my courage to grab his arm. I held on tight and gave him a look that was nothing more than me begging. "Please, Zowen."

Indecision crossed his strong features, but eventually, he relented. I lost count of how many times he sighed as I practically dragged him back up the hill toward the bungalow.

I purposefully ignored his hesitation.

I also willfully ignored the taunting voice in the back of my mind that kept telling me if Zowen needed someone to spend a few oblivious, delirious, fantasy-fueled hours with, I would be more than happy to volunteer myself as tribute.

I mean, if he refused to be my friend, maybe there was a chance I could get him to come around to being my lover instead.

chapter FIVE

Zowen

I was drunk.

I was also angry.

The first seemed to amplify the second. It wasn't like I had been much of a drinker before getting locked up. I never got the chance to develop any type of tolerance. It only took two beers and a shot of something that tasted like a piece of cinnamon candy from hell to make my surroundings spin and put Aston's pretty face into a slight blur.

I was mad at myself for being so easy when it came to Aston.

I'd caved as soon as she said "please" and flashed her big doe eyes in my direction. I was constantly telling myself I was immune to her after so long, but I folded the seconds she started to act cute. I felt as if I'd learned nothing and that all the distance I'd fought to put between us shrank down to mere centimeters. Aston was back to living under my skin and in my mind, rent-free.

I hated it.

However, nothing ever made me hate her. My default programming always booted back up to Aston being the only person outside of my family I'd ever loved. It seemed like I was *always* going to love her regardless of being worthy of those feelings or not.

"The guy you currently work for is friends with Uncle Benny?" Aston seemed like the liquor was having a negligible effect on her. She was drinking that candy-flavored liquor and chasing it with soda. She seemed unfazed by the burn and proceeded to ask me a million questions now that the booze had loosened my tongue and made me too dizzy to run away from her.

I dipped my chin in a slight nod. "I don't know that Benny has friends per se. My boss is someone he trusts and someone he knows from back in the days before he married Echo and moved to Denver. The nonprofit is based out of San Francisco, but they recently opened an office here in LA and one in New York. Campbell is more familiar with the couple in charge than Benny is. He's worked with them in the past."

It wasn't my place to lay out Campbell's complicated family history. I figured she had to know more than others because she was so close to Daire. I left my explanation at that.

I spent a lot of time doing the same thing she did, scoping out social media and digging into public information. The difference being, I was looking for predators and clues that might help law enforcement track down missing and endangered kids. And since I was an avid gamer, my boss added combing through online game chats to the list of highly probable places for predators to hunt. The job was on the up-and-up. However, it didn't slip my notice that the company had several secure offices that very scary-looking men walked into every day. They clearly were not doing the same kind of work I was doing for the company. They often looked even scarier when they were finished with whatever their task was for the day. In another life, I'd be interested in knowing what went on behind those closed doors. I had a plethora of computer skills that weren't being adequately utilized. What I was doing now was too easy and had minimal risk.

There was a part of me that was always going to crave a bigger, badder challenge. Even if I got burned by the outcome.

"Do you enjoy it?" Aston's curiosity was genuine, and I could tell how happy she was that we were finally having a conversation and I wasn't freezing her out.

"It's fine. It's the kind of work I can do in my sleep. It's very disturbing to see how many kids are at risk, and their parents don't even know because they aren't paying close enough attention to what's happening online. It's also disturbing how many kids go missing and no one seems to notice or care."

It was heartbreaking.

No matter how badly I fucked up or how deeply troubled Remy became because of her mental health, our parents never gave up on us. They might be disappointed and frustrated with us, but they never once made us doubt how deeply we were loved. It wasn't just my parents. It was the entire Archer clan. There was always someone there to reach out a hand when you stumbled and always someone there to pick you up when you fell on your face.

"It sounds like you are helping a lot of people." She sounded impressed, but it was unfounded.

"I took the job to get a paycheck. Not for any idealist reasons you might be spinning in your pretty little head. I'm in debt up to my eyeballs. I'll never be able to pay my parents back, and who knows what's going to happen with the next trial? Plus"—I took another shot of the sweet and spicy liquor and felt my head spin, and I breathed fire— "it's not like I can say no to someone willing to hire me, knowing exactly where I spent the last five years. I'm never passing a background check for an average job ever again."

Aston hummed lightly and lifted her auburn eyebrows in my direction. "It might be a means to an end, but that doesn't take away from the fact that it's a difficult job with a measurable impact on a group of people who are incapable of protecting themselves. I think it is an honorable way to make a living."

I snorted and tilted my head back so I could look up at the stars in the sky. It was peaceful. It made some of the anger simmering in my system cool down. "I'm not honorable. You need to stop projecting all the things you remember about me from when we were younger on to who I am now. We don't know each other anymore, Aston." I squinted at her through the drunken haze. "I'm not like that Italian guy you work with. I'm not shiny and clean and perfectly packaged for the camera. I'm not a guy on the verge of making it big with endless opportunities in front of me."

I scowled more because I couldn't control my face when I thought of her picture on his social media. It never occurred to me that she had no idea I'd secretly peeked into her life and the sloppy words would give me away. I was also frustrated because she never wavered in her endless optimism where I was concerned.

"I am definitely not the kid who was foolishly in love with you. I don't even remember why I was so hung up on you back then."

I was being mean. She didn't deserve to be the sole target of my ire. I felt like I couldn't help but lash out at her.

I heard her gasp at the harsh words. Part of me wanted to take them back. A bigger part hoped she would finally get it through her head that we were basically strangers and didn't owe each other anything. It would be best if we acted like landlord and tenant and nothing more.

Aston looked like a puppy dog who had been scolded, and her voice was quiet when she muttered, "You were never mean before. That's something that's clearly changed."

I met her sad gaze unblinkingly. "Can you tell me one thing that being nice got me in the past?"

She narrowed her eyes at me as we faced off under the stars. It was the first time we'd ever had a real confrontation or disagreement. When we had been younger, I'd acquiesced to everything because Ry was my best friend, and I didn't want to make Aston responsible for my feelings. After the accident, I'd flat-out refused to see her, so there wasn't an opportunity for us to clash. It was interesting to see her demeanor change as if she were preparing for battle.

"Name one thing that being mean has gotten you, Zowen." She looked at me like she had all the time in the world for me to come up with a suitable response.

I swore under my breath because she had a razor-sharp point. Being mean and stubborn was what had landed my stupid ass in jail. Not willing to let her know she'd very succinctly put me in my place, I tried to change the subject but somehow ended up back on the Italian motorcycle racer.

"Why didn't you go to qualifying in Tokyo? That seems like a dream trip. I bet your dad wanted you to go."

Aston's dad co-owned a bunch of custom automotive stores with my dad. One of the big reasons I'd first gotten into street bikes was because her dad helped me fix up an old beater of a bike when I was a kid. It was fun to get my hands dirty. I liked taking things apart and putting them back together. And I liked to go fast. Something her dad understood more than mine did. I couldn't imagine how delighted he must be now that Aston was standing so close to a professional racing team. It had to be a car guy's dream come true.

Aston's expression changed to one of confusion as she sipped from the glass in her hand. "Wow. You are shockingly informed about what's going on in my life for a guy who refused to have anything to do with me for the last five years. That doesn't seem very fair."

It didn't seem appropriate to rat Campbell out for having a big mouth and telling me about her client. She might not believe me if I told her he was the one spilling her secrets. It wasn't like the guy was known for being overly chatty.

I kept staring at her, the alcohol at war with my common sense. "Why didn't you go?"

After a long pause, she shrugged her shoulders and told me, "I wasn't interested. Honestly, everything having to do with motorcycles is kind of triggering for me. I can't stand the way they sound. It makes me queasy when I see them racing up and down the freeway. Whenever I see someone riding without a helmet, I want to chase them down and yell at them. Everything that has to do with any kind of bike seems too dangerous to me after your accident. I haven't stepped foot inside my dad's shop in over five years. Cassio's future might be tied to a sport bike, but yours was taken away because of one. Logically, I know the machine isn't to blame, but it's easier than cursing the person in control. Especially when that person is important to you." She sniffed as if she was getting emotional. "Besides, it wasn't necessary for me to go. He's got a social media manager who does a better job of handling his public image than I ever could. I'm willing to go above and beyond for my clients, but there is a limit. My friends and family will always come first."

The liquor loosened my tongue, and I realized I wasn't as in control of myself or the situation as I wanted to be.

"I never asked anyone to wait for me." Not when she had left for California as a teenager. And not while I had been locked up. "I didn't expect the world to stop while I was on the inside. I'm a murderer. I know that changes how people—even family and friends—see me. I have very realistic expectations for my loved ones regarding how I'll be viewed and treated by people moving forward."

At least, I thought I had. Now that I was slightly drunk and caught up in a melancholy mood, I could admit to myself that it'd hurt, walking out of prison and not having my mom and dad or my sister there, waiting for me. I knew the circumstances were working against a family reunion at such an inopportune time, but that didn't take away the churning undercurrent of disappointment.

Aston put her glass down and leaned forward so she could put her hand on my knee. It was a light touch, like a butterfly brushing against me, but I felt it like a thunderbolt.

"That's the thing, Zowen." She pressed closer, her gaze locked on mine in an unwavering way. "You didn't have to ask those of us who really, truly know you to wait. We were going to do it regardless because we never thought you were as guilty as you thought you were. We don't think you're solely responsible for what happened that night." She squeezed my knee harder, and it made my heart clench and my blood pump so loudly between my ears that I barely heard her say, "Out of the two of us sitting here, the only person who thinks you deserve to be called a murderer is you."

I didn't know how badly I'd needed to hear someone tell me that.

I didn't know how desperately I'd needed someone who had known me most of my life to tell me they still saw things within me that had been there before I became someone who stole another person's life.

I'd convinced myself I was okay with the people I loved looking at me like they never saw me before, but it was one lie on top of the other. The tower I'd tried to force myself to believe was impenetrable was bound to topple sooner or later.

All the defenses and walls I'd put in place to protect myself crumbled into sand under Aston's touch and words. Maybe I could rebuild all the barriers I'd erected to protect myself when I sobered up in the morning. For now, she was the victor who laid claim to the fallen castle.

I surrendered.

To the alcohol.

To her.

To the memories.

To the comfort that practically radiated off her.

To the night.

My hand reached out and wrapped around the back of her head so I could pull her closer. She practically fell off the edge of her chair when my lips landed on hers. The liquor bottle that smelled like candy and fire spilled all over the patio pavers and tickled my nose.

I'd wanted to kiss Aston Wheeler for as long as I could remember. It was something I dreamed about. It was something I beat myself up over the entire time she was with Ry. It was something I had been sure was never going to happen in my lifetime.

Even as my lips moved over hers and my hands held her in place, I waited for her to pull back and stop the madness. She didn't. She leaned toward me and grabbed the front of my T-shirt to tug me closer.

My ears were ringing, and my heart was pounding. The parts of my body I was long used to ignoring were more active and excited than they had been allowed to be for the last five years. I was dizzy all over again, but it didn't feel like it had anything to do with drinking too much.

Aston went to my head faster than the liquor did—and she was more potent.

Maybe I lost my mind because I'd always wanted her or because I'd been alone and lonely for so long. I knew if I were thinking straight, I wouldn't be so willing to make this mistake I prided myself on how cautious I'd learned to be after the accident. I wasn't someone willing to walk into a situation bound to be filled with regret ever again. Or so I'd thought. All of that went straight down the toilet the moment Aston kissed me back.

Lips, teeth, and tongue tangled and clashed in a kiss that was far more violent than romantic. She tasted sweet and spicy like her drink, but her mouth was soft, and the way she kissed me was almost as desperate and hungry as I felt. Her hands clutched me tighter than where I was holding her, and her lips were more restless than mine. When she breathed my name, I shivered.

It'd been a long time since I'd experienced anything that made me passionate enough to feel parts of my body shake. Whatever smidgen of control that might have lingered way, way down in the very bottom of my being was lost when Aston launched out of her seat and settled onto my lap. Her arms wrapped around my neck, and all the warmest, softest parts of her pressed against the hardest, loneliest parts of me.

The kiss quickly burned out of control. Teeth nipped, and tongues tangled. Things were wet and messy. I forgot how to breathe. I forgot where and who I was. Kissing her, holding her, touching her were akin to every fantasy I'd had coming true.

Aston and I weren't supposed to be possible. Not in the past. And not in the future. There was no part of me that had been prepared for this drunken turn of events. It was overwhelming in all the best ways.

Aston's tongue twisted around mine, and her fingers tugged at the shaggiest part of my hair. The edge of her teeth sank into my lower lip. It was more than a playful nip. She felt hungry. Ravenous even. Almost as if she'd been waiting for this flashpoint between the two of us as long as I had.

When I heard her make a small whimper, I pulled back because I wasn't sure if the sound had come from a place of pleasure or pain. We had gotten in over our heads so quickly, and I needed to make sure neither one of us was going to drown.

I moved my hands to her waist and gave my foggy head a shake. It was on the tip of my tongue to apologize to her for acting rashly and putting my hands on her without explicit permission. Something like that might not have been as important in the past, but these hands of mine were no longer clean. Which meant they didn't have the right to take hold of things just because I was greedy and wanted them to be mine.

I didn't get the chance to say a word, let alone apologize for my drunken behavior before Aston climbed off my lap and grabbed both my hands in hers. She pulled me to my feet and started to drag me toward her house before I could put a coherent thought together. Outside, under the night sky, somehow felt safe. There was no way things could go too far or get too heated under the stars.

Once we were inside, this became something that wasn't a simple mistake fueled by too much to drink and the right type of mood. It became deliberate. It became a choice that was being made.

"Aston"—I should be embarrassed that my voice cracked on her name— "what are we doing right now?"

I really needed her to be the voice of reason. She had to be the one to stop this impending disaster before it started because I wasn't capable of it. It was a pitiful move to make her responsible for whatever was happening between us—I knew that—but I wasn't strong enough to turn the tide.

"What we're doing—no, what I'm doing is, I'm going to welcome you home, Zowen." She looked over her shoulder at me, and her dark eyes were defiant and slightly dangerous. "And when I'm done, you'll know exactly how much I missed you while you were gone."

I couldn't tell whether her words were a promise or a threat. Either way, I was inexplicably excited to find out.

chapter
SIX

Aston

It happened so fast.

I was worried if I gave Zowen too long to think about the implications of what we were doing, he would change his mind. I relied on a lifetime of unrequited love and years of repressed passion to steamroll over Zowen's hesitations and reluctance. The plentiful alcohol and his low tolerance were also lending a hand to my mission to get as close to him as possible. He had worked hard to make sure there was a noticeable division between us since coming back into my life. I was about to toss all that effort and resolve into the garbage. Hopefully, I'd never have to see it ever again.

I was nowhere near as drunk as he was, just floating on a slightly inebriated cloud. If I were totally sober, there wasn't a chance in hell I would be bold enough or daring enough to think the best way to build a bridge between the past relationship I'd shared with Zowen and the future one I desired was to have sex with him. I was also coherent enough to judge whether he could consent to things going too far. Lust and desire were powerful motivators. They made a person greedy and hungry, but I wasn't so far gone that I was willing to be another person who compromised Zowen's autonomy.

Only recently had he been allowed to take his power and control back.

Under no circumstances was I going to be someone in his life who tried to take those things away from him. I had done plenty of that when we were younger. I refused to accept what he offered me back then, but couldn't force myself to let him go. I selfishly couldn't bear the thought of him having feelings for someone else, even when I had known there was no way for us to be together at the time.

We didn't make it to my bedroom.

We didn't even make it to the very comfortable couch a few steps away in the living room.

It was as if Zowen had seen the first flat surface to cross his narrowed gaze and deemed the spot good enough. Before I could catch my breath, he hoisted me up onto the edge of my dining table. Good thing it was an antique and made of sturdy wood because he wasn't exactly gentle when he touched me. I was on the small side, so being roughly handled when things became heated wasn't new. However, there was an underlying restraint in all Zowen's movements, which belied the fact that he was someone who had cared deeply about me for an exceptionally long time—or at least, he had.

I felt like I was his favorite piece of candy. One he'd long been denied. But for whatever reason, he was now allowing himself to have a taste. He was ready to savor the sweetness and let the flavor melt on his tongue. He was hasty when he ripped the wrapper off, and I found myself very naked and laid out in front of him between one breath and the next. Zowen was still fully clothed, but I didn't get a chance to complain because he stepped between my legs and bent over my body. He braced his weight above my head with a bent arm and lowered his head until our lips touched.

This kiss was softer and more restrained than the one outside. Zowen took his time flicking his tongue against mine, and I felt him leave a damp trail across my parted lips. He kissed his way down to my neck, pausing to nip at my earlobe on the way. Every inch of my exposed skin erupted in tiny bumps of excitement, and my hands curled into fists where they rested on the table. I wanted to grab him and pull him closer. I wanted to wrap my legs around his waist so he couldn't pull away. But again, I didn't want him to feel trapped. I wanted Zowen to know he could step away at any time and I wouldn't put up a fight. There were enough regrets between us as it was, and I didn't want to be the cause of any more.

Hopefully, he was as caught up in the moment as I was. In a perfect world, this moment felt as inevitable to him as it did to me.

When Zowen dragged the tip of his tongue down the side of my neck and across the crest of my breasts, my nipples instantly puckered, and the spot he was pressing against between my splayed legs quivered uncontrollably. I couldn't resist reaching for his dark hair, my fingers curling possessively in the soft strands. It was a heady feeling to be completely covered by someone who was so much bigger in stature than I was while feeling like I was the one calling the shots. Regardless of how much or little Zowen had changed while he was away, I knew he would never physically harm me. He might be the biggest threat my heart had ever had to face, but the rest of me was perfectly safe and achingly cherished in his big, rough hands.

He dropped biting kisses that were sure to leave marks down my stomach and across the dip in the valley between my hip bones. My hands slipped from his hair to the sides of his face, and I used the edge of my thumb to trace the curve of his harshly arched eyebrow. This face was still handsome enough to make my heart skip several beats. But it was admittedly different from the face that used to torment my teenage dreams. I knew everyone had thought it was easy for me to pick Ry and ignore Zowen's blatant infatuation back in the day. But it wasn't. Trying to be happy and forcing myself to fake being in love with someone I wasn't ate away at my insides for years. I knew Ry deserved better. I knew Zowen deserved more. And most of all, I knew I was wrong.

I was the problem.

My cowardice and my inability to make choices for my own happiness versus what my parents wanted turned me into the kind of villain who deserved whatever heartbreak was waiting for them in retribution. I was sure I could face the consequences of my actions and own up to being insensitive and immature. Only Zowen had been ripped out of my life before I got the chance to make amends and explain to him it was a different Aston who had treated his youthful infatuation so terribly. The Aston I was now had the skills and knowledge to be much kinder and gentler with those complicated emotions.

I gasped when he moved his head, and I felt his teeth bite into the fleshy part of my inner thigh. His face was dangerously close to the most intimate part of me. It was a big jump to go from being purposely ignored to ending up like a buffet in front of a man who had been denied food for a long time.

I closed my eyes and shivered when he dropped to his knees in front of me and pulled me closer to the edge of the table. He hooked one of my legs over his broad shoulder, and I felt the heat of his breath against what I was sure was an obviously damp center.

"I missed you, Zowen." I sighed while moving my hands to stroke along the front of my body. My voice was thin, and my breath hitched when his mouth ghosted over the softest and most secret part of my body.

I bit my lip and threw my head back as he used his tongue to lick through my wet folds. My entire body felt electrified, and the only parts of me left touching the table were the back of my head and my shoulders. I arched my back and dug my heel into his back to urge him to move closer. I sighed and tried to absorb the ludicrous amount of pleasure coursing through my body as he licked into me. Things that were warm turned blazing hot. And things that were damp ended up soaked and quivering uncontrollably. Knowing I was the first person he'd touched and tasted in so long only added to the intensity of my emotions and the sensations spiraling through my limbs.

"I miss when you used to like me, Zowen. I know that isn't fair, and those days were awful for you. But they meant everything to me. I want you to give me a chance to show you that I like you the same way you *always* liked me. I've had a lot of time to figure out who it is I want and how I can make that person as happy as they make me."

The words drifted off when he switched his attack from only using his tongue to probe against the soft opening to licking against my clit and using his fingers to explore all the wet folds in front of him. I was panting heavily and curled my legs around his head in a very wanton manner. My hands found my breasts, and while in a typical situation where I was so exposed and vulnerable, I would silently worry about how unsubstantial all of me was ... there was none of that insecurity with Zowen. This man had been present when I was at my worst, when I had no concept of who I was and no idea of who I needed to be in order to be happy, and he'd still loved me.

Zowen moved back, but his fingers never stopped touching and teasing. I writhed shamelessly under his manipulation, my body feeling like it was out of my control.

"I had a lot of time to figure things out too." His deep voice was rough and quiet. "Kind of like being nice, liking you didn't get me very much, Aston. And the fact that I'd liked *only* you felt kind of pathetic when I had nothing else to think about. I'd always thought I was too smart to get hung up on something or someone unattainable. If I wasn't back then, I most certainly am now.

Which means you should put an end to this before it goes any further."

He spread his fingers apart, and his dark eyebrows lifted in a taunting manner. His mouth was wet from the way he had devoured my body. He didn't look like a man who regretted his most recent decisions.

"No."

I wiggled around so that I was bent over the table on my stomach. I was short, so I had to stretch out and reach with the very tips of my fingers to snag the strap of my purse, which had been dropped haphazardly on the other side. I dumped the entire thing out. My wallet, phone charger, lipstick, random receipts, breath mints, a pack of travel tissue, and hand sanitizer scattered into a mess across the surface. Fortunately, my makeup bag was within reach, and I had no trouble digging out the emergency condom that lived inside. I had no clue how old the thing was, but it was all I had available. I didn't want to ask Zowen if he had any type of protection on him. It would make him trolling for a hookup earlier all too real, and I refused to believe he would rather be with a stranger right now than with me. I handed him the little packet over my shoulder and caught a glint of surprise in his two-toned eyes.

"I'm not going to stop this, and I'm not going to let you keep pushing me away. You loved me for a long time. And I waited for you for a long time. Shouldn't we finally get to have what we've always wanted?"

He visibly wavered for a moment, but eventually lowered his inhibitions, and decades of unrequited love and desire won over common sense. He opened the condom and suited up with fluid movements, then leaned over so he could kiss the back of my neck in the spot where my hair parted to the side. I felt his warmth all along my back and felt his fingers dig into my hips. I didn't love that I couldn't see his face. I figured if he wasn't walking away, I could endure whatever he was about to do.

He kissed his way down my spine, and one of his big hands moved to palm my ass. Since I was petite, there was often a size discrepancy between myself and whomever I was with at the time. It wasn't something that ever stood out as a turn-on or a particular rush—until the other person was Zowen Archer. There was something about being completely covered by his strong body that made my toes curl and had my fingertips tingling.

I made a sound that was something between a whisper and moan when his hand landed next to my face to brace himself on the table. His lips touched the shell of my ear, and his breath was ragged and uneven when he used his foot to push my legs even farther apart. I squeezed my eyes shut when his hardness rubbed against my ass in an unmistakably provocative manner. And when he finally pressed into me, the tip of his cock gliding seamlessly through my wetness, I forgot how to breathe. I forgot how to think. I forgot there was a lifetime of hurt and harm between the two of us.

Zowen didn't. Just as I started to move against him, searching for more contact, looking for more connection, one of his hands landed on the back of my neck and kept me pinned to the table in front of him. All I could do was whimper and wiggle ineffectively as he fucked me.

He set a relentless pace that felt both desperate and angry. His breath was choppy above me, and I swore at one point, I felt something wet slide across my naked shoulder.

Was he crying? I couldn't tell because he wouldn't let me move so I could see his face.

His teeth tugged at my ear, and the sounds our bodies made when they collided had me blushing to the roots of my hair. In a million and one years, I never would've imagined that being with Zowen would be so brutal, almost bordering on the edge of violence. In the back of my bewildered mind, I knew he wanted me to be frightened. It was obvious he wanted me to regret letting things get this far between us, but I wouldn't.

For so many years, Zowen had silently been exactly who I needed him to be even if he suffered for it. I knew it was my turn to be who he needed me to be. I had to prove I was strong enough to withstand whatever emotional storm had been brewing within him for the past five years. I knew Zowen well enough and had cared about him for long enough to know any and all storms were bound to pass.

Even as rough as his handling was and how disconnected the sex seemed to be, it still felt really good. He kept hitting the exact spot that was guaranteed to make me come. And when he skimmed his hand down between the table and the front of my body and added his fingers to the mix, I didn't stand a chance. As soon as his touch circled my clit and slicked through my wetness, my vision went white, and I moaned his name loud enough to make my ears ring. If I didn't have alcohol swirling around in my system and if I wasn't being fucked to the point of forgetting how to think, I would've been embarrassed by my brazen response.

However, Zowen must've liked my overt reaction because he soon followed me over the peak of pleasure. He swore softly and dropped his forehead to rest on the back of my neck. Again, I felt something warm and wet trickle against my skin.

He sighed and whispered, "The difference in us getting what we want is that you knew I was waiting for you, Aston. It didn't matter. Not then and not now."

I sighed heavily and told him everything I'd been holding inside since he had been torn out of my life. "When I say I missed you, Zowen, what I missed was the way you always looked at me like I was special. I missed the way you always seemed to know what I was going to say even if I couldn't find the words. I missed the way you laughed, even when I wasn't funny. You have my favorite smile, probably because you're so stingy with it. I missed being able to ask you anything and you knowing the answer because of that giant brain of yours. I missed you coming by my dad's shop, looking for an excuse to sit and talk with me for hours." I gave him an unwavering look. "You *always* mattered."

He pushed himself up and took a step away from me, allowing me to finally lift a little bit.

He didn't comment on the litany of ways my life had been lesser without him in it because at the same time I realized I was wet and messier than I should be from the excellent orgasm he had given me, he stilled and asked, "How long have you had that condom in your purse?"

I frowned and reached for my discarded shirt. "I don't know. Longer than a year? More than likely longer than two or three."

Zowen muttered something under his breath and gave me a look that belied how much he'd had to drink earlier. "We have more than one problem on our hands. That condom was not the strongest soldier. It broke." He sighed and dragged a heavy hand down his face. "I shouldn't have been so rough with you. I'm sorry. I couldn't control myself ... for more reasons than I want to dredge up."

I tossed my hair behind me and tried to marshal a calm and collected demeanor. In all honesty, a broken condom seemed like less of a problem than everything else brewing between the two of us.

"I need to clean up." I was sticky and embarrassed more so than anything else. "Unless you want to tell me that I have something to worry about health-wise, I think we can table all discussion about what's going on between us until we've had a chance to sober up. Don't worry about the broken condom. I'll handle what needs to be handled."

Zowen put himself back in his pants and helped me gather the rest of my clothing. I paused when he reached out to tuck a piece of my hair behind my ear. It was by far the gentlest touch I'd received from him tonight.

"I'm clean. Nothing happened while I was locked up, and you know I've been alone since I got out. The condom might not have broken if I were able to keep my shit together. You just need to let me know what you need me to do to help you take care of the situation. This isn't the kind of mistake someone makes on their own."

I was about to tell him there was nothing he could do to help me when his phone started to ring. The sharp sound startled us both since it was late, and the night had been quiet, other than the sounds we'd made up to that point. He picked it up from where it'd dropped when he pushed his pants down to fuck me. His expression turned serious when he saw the name on the display.

I knew exactly what the call was about as soon as he answered.

"Hyde? Is everything okay with Remy?"

Hyde was his brother-in-law, and if he was calling this late, the only reason was to let Zowen know that Remy was going into labor or that there was a complication with the pregnancy.

Zowen plowed his fingers through his already-messy hair and nodded frantically even though the person on the other side of the call couldn't see him.

"I'll book the first flight to Denver I can get out in the morning. I knew I should have tried to get home last week." He muttered a few more sentences, then hung up and looked at me with a stark apology in his eyes. "I have to get home as soon as possible. Remy's in labor. I know the timing is shit but ..."

"Go." I put my free hand on his chest and pushed him toward the still-open French doors. "Give Remy my best."

Having some time to process the swift change between us couldn't hurt anything. I told myself I didn't want him to push me away. So, this was going to have to be considered a strategic retreat on my part. Maybe when he came back from Denver, some of those sharp and deadly edges of his I'd kept bumping into would be dulled.

I wasn't scared of having to bleed for him if it meant putting the past to rest and moving forward. However, I had a feeling that once Zowen figured out he was the one holding the knife, I'd end up even farther away from him.

Why did everything between us *always* have to end up so messy and complicated?

SEVEN

Zowen

It was a strange feeling to be back in Denver after so long.

The mountains were as majestic as always, but the airport felt far more congested than I remembered, and I'd been away from the Mile High City long enough that breathing air as thin as plastic wrap wasn't as easy as it used to be.

Daire's flight from San Francisco was only forty-five minutes behind mine. I'd told her I would wait for her at baggage claim. She made the trip alone since Campbell hated flying, and she told me she wasn't sure when Ry would be able to get away from work, but he planned to visit as soon as he was free. I couldn't tell whether I was relieved or sad that a full family reunion was going to remain postponed while everyone managed their busy lives and burgeoning careers. I knew I was happy I was about to be reunited with my sister and my nieces. Plural since the new addition had made her appearance while I was in the air. And I was relieved I would get to check on my dad's health, but I was also anxious to see my parents outside of the prison visitors center. When I had been locked up, it was easy to process their sadness and disappointment in me. I had known I deserved their disdain and more. Now that I was out, I wasn't sure if I had strong enough defenses to protect myself from whatever I might see when they looked at me.

The sloppy and heated moments with Aston before I'd had to rush off were enough proof that I was not nearly as protected from the perception of others as I'd thought I was.

Thinking about Aston had me pulling out my phone and sending her a text while I waited for Daire. Someone bumped into me and muttered an insincere apology as I scowled at them. I didn't like strangers invading my personal space. And yet I'd let Aston get as close as humanly possible, proving no matter how hard I tried to convince myself that we were strangers, it was a lie. She had still been able to get to me faster than anyone else, and all the control I'd spent years locking down and keeping within an iron fist blew away like dust as soon as she touched me and looked at me with her big doe eyes.

It was still early because I had taken the first flight available from LAX to Denver. Colorado was an hour ahead of California as well, so I didn't anticipate a response. I still wanted to make sure she was okay. It was like the universe was working against me. There couldn't have been a worse time for birth control to fail or for me to absolutely lose my mind and inhibitions. I'd had a vague idea that the first time I was with someone since my release was going to be intense and slightly unhinged. I never imagined the person on the receiving end of my pent-up lust and desire would be Aston. When I had been deep within my infatuation with her, I'd always viewed her as something delicate and fragile. Like an antique doll that might fall apart if you held it too tightly.

The reality had been nothing like what I'd had in my mind. Yes, she was small; my hands could nearly fully encircle her waist when I held her down. Her limbs were petite and pretty, but she was strong. I could feel her strength when she grabbed hold of me and when she locked her legs around me. I knew I was too rough with her, that I wasn't considerate and behaved selfishly because I was a slave to both my denied libido and long-ignored love. Once the door to having any part of Aston Wheeler had opened, my entire being could do nothing but rush through that gap.

The text message pinged into the void, and I told myself to call her later at a more reasonable time. She shouldn't have to deal with the aftermath alone, but circumstances and the universe were determined to work against me—against us.

"Zowen!"

I heard my name and turned to watch Daire bounce her way through the crowd of travelers. Her white-blonde hair was hard to miss. So were the way heads swiveled to watch her move. Daire always carried herself with purpose, like she was the main event. And ever since she had gotten together with Campbell, her presence had intensified, her aura darkened. She was still playful and liked to cause mischief. She forever wanted to have her own way regardless of the circumstances, but she was more willing to yield now that Campbell was there for her to consider. The family always referred to her as the Archer princess, but these days, she was more like a dragon. She could breathe fire when she wanted to, and I had no problem envisioning her laying waste to those who threatened what she might consider her own. It was easy imagining Daire wiping out an entire empire if it meant keeping her man and her family safe.

"How is the airport this busy so early in the morning?" she complained as she grabbed my arm and hauled me toward the pickup area. "Uncle Benny is coming to get us. I didn't want to ask your parents or Hyde's folks to leave the hospital. It's going to be weird to be here while my parents are overseas. I don't know if I want to stay in their house all alone." She shook her head and gave me a look. "You can come and keep me company if it gets to be too much at your parents' house. I shouldn't say that. I know how long they've been waiting for you to be back home." She nudged me with her elbow. "I'm Team Zowen though. Don't forget that."

I snorted and pulled her to the side to avoid a collision with a young family pushing a tower of luggage taller than she was. "If you were Team Zowen, you wouldn't have blindsided me with that reunion with Aston."

She laughed and looked up at me with sparkling green eyes. "I could've told you, but then you would have refused even though staying with her is the best option. Plus, she's my bestie. I know exactly how long she's regretted the way things played out between the two of you. If there was even a slim chance that being forced together could finally get the two of you on the same page, I wasn't going to miss the opportunity."

It was on the tip of my tongue to tell her she wouldn't think that way if she knew I'd drunkenly fucked her best friend with zero resolution between the two of us. Sure, Aston had told me she liked me the way I liked her, but the guy who'd always liked her was long gone. I had no idea if the man I was now was capable of something as simple and innocent as falling for his first love all over again. The way I'd felt about her before was pure and untainted. The way I felt about everything now seemed to be dirty and dark.

We waited for an extremely expensive luxury car to pull to a stop in front of us at the curb. There were long-established rumors within the family circle that Benny had had an entirely different life before he moved to Denver and married Hyde's aunt. The older members of the family whispered that he had two different names and was initially part of the witness protection program, but no one ever verified the truth of the matter. Which was probably for the best.

Daire took the front seat, and I slid into the back. I met Uncle Benny's gaze in the rearview mirror.

One of his dark eyebrows winged upward, and the corner of his mouth hooked up in a grin. "Welcome home, kid."

I tried to give him a grin in return, but like everything else in my life now, it held little joy. "Glad to be back."

He chuckled and merged with the heavy flow of traffic. "It takes time to adjust. Don't beat yourself up if it feels difficult to walk back into the life you left behind."

Daire turned her head and asked the older man, "Are you speaking from experience?"

The two of them had grown much closer while I was away. Campbell considered Benny his mentor, and he was the reason the redheaded man had moved to Denver. Campbell's family situation was hazy—another topic no one probed too deeply into. Benny was the closest thing Daire had to an in-law.

Benny gave her a narrow-eyed look and shrugged his shoulder. He was dressed better than most of the men walking the streets of LA. And regardless of how old he was, he appeared ageless. He was a man full of mystery. A stint in jail wasn't beyond the realm of possibility for him. Besides, he had a wicked scar that encircled his neck, like someone had tried to choke him out with a thin wire. An explanation had never been offered for the distinct mark, but now that I'd spent time behind bars, I knew what it looked like when someone had been attacked with a garrote.

"Let's just say I know enough about being in prison to know it's not a place I want anyone I care about to spend any amount of time. So, you keep an eye on Campbell and make sure he always stays on the right side of things."

"I'll do my best." She turned to look out the window. "Any word on how Remy and the baby are doing? It was so quick. I thought she would still be in labor by the time we landed."

"Mom and baby are fine. Everyone is happy and healthy. Dad is the one having a hard time. You would think Hyde had never been through all of this before, as nervous and worried as he was. Both sets of grandpar-ents are over the moon.

"Zowen, your mom and dad are excited to see you. Whatever worst-case scenario you have playing in your head, stop it. All they want to do is give you a hug and feed you a home-cooked meal. They want you there for this huge moment for your sister and family. They want everyone together. Whatever execution or reckoning you're expecting, I promise it's not on the agenda."

Some of the tension squeezing my chest eased at his reassurance. "I could use both the hug and the food. I wanted to be here sooner, but everything is pretty com-plicated."

Benny nodded as we drove deeper into the city. I barely noticed that I wasn't nearly as nervous or scared of being a passenger when the older man was in control of the car. I had a lot of faith in Benny. I trusted him with my life. Literally. He was the reason my incarceration had gone smoothly and I'd made it out physically intact. I knew he wouldn't risk my life by being a reckless driver when he'd spent so much effort to save it over the last five years.

It wasn't that I didn't trust Daire or thought she wanted to harm me. I simply didn't know her capabil-ities behind the wheel. She hadn't had enough time to become as steadfast and in control the way Benny was. There was no doubt, given enough time, she would be someone I relied on just as much as Uncle Benny.

I sent a text to let my mom know we were almost at the hospital. While I had my phone in my hand, I noticed there was no response from Aston. She should be up and on her way to work around this time. I sent her another message, this time telling her to call me when she got a chance. A sliver of unease slipped down my spine.

"Who are you texting? Did you make some new friends in LA?" Daire's tone was taunting because she knew the last thing I had on my mind was making friends.

"No new friends. I texted my mom. Figured my folks would appreciate a heads-up I was almost there."

Daire sniffed and exchanged a look with Benny. "Oh. I thought maybe it was Aston. I keep hoping you'll tell me you've buried the hatchet."

No. I'd buried something much more dangerous than a hatchet when it came to her. However, I'd rather serve another year in jail than tell Daire that. She would be insufferable if she knew her plan to throw the two of us together had worked out exactly as she'd anticipated.

Benny pulled to the front of the hospital, and I stilled because my parents were already waiting outside. Daire threw herself out of the car and hugged them both while gesturing wildly. I took a deep breath and braced myself. They both looked tired, and it was obvious my father had lost weight post-medical emergency. They suddenly seemed so much older than I remembered, and I felt like every wrinkle and new gray hair was related to me. I'd always envisioned my parents as indomitable and unbreakable. Individually, they were strong people. Together, they were an indestructible unit. But now, they were so obviously battered and broken.

"It'll be fine." Benny's deep voice was low and soothing. "They love you. They missed you. All they want is the best for you. The only person who wants you to suffer any kind of retribution is *you*, Zowen. No one can move forward until you do. Keep that in mind while you're here."

I dipped my chin in silent acknowledgment and stepped out of the car.

Immediately, I was wrapped in a warm embrace. He might've gotten skinnier, but my dad was still a giant. His embrace always felt like it was the safest place in the entire world. I felt his chin rest on the top of my head and heard his heartbeat, strong and steady in my ear. I closed my eyes and let out a sigh that felt like it had come from the bottom of my soul.

"Hi, Dad."

"Zowen."

I passed over to my mom, who was much smaller. It was my turn to wrap her in a hug that fully enveloped her tiny frame. I wasn't surprised when she started crying. I was, however, taken aback that her tears made my eyes sting and burn. I was on the verge of tears. I was close to actually allowing myself to cry. Which meant I would be shedding more tears in the last couple of weeks than I had in my entire life.

"Don't cry, Mom." My voice was husky as I patted her back.

"I'm not crying because I'm sad. I'm crying because I'm so happy you're home." She huffed and pulled back so she could put her palms on my cheeks and squeeze my face, like she used to do when I was little. "And because I'm so proud of my kids."

Of course, I wanted to argue and tell her I hadn't done anything to make her proud. I bit the words back.

My mom wasn't the type to say what she thought some-one needed to hear. She never spoke with insincerity. If she said she was proud, then she was proud. I had to take her words to heart.

"I'm sorry I wasn't here sooner." It was an apology beyond not making it for the actual birth.

"You're here now. That's what matters." My father's voice was serious and brooked no argument. "Remy's been waiting for you. I think she's more excited to intro-duce you to your niece than she was the grandparents. For the last three hours, Hyde's been asking how much longer until you got here."

"Isn't she exhausted?" I couldn't imagine bringing a whole new life into the world and still having the where-withal to worry about anyone else.

"She's tired. But she's holding on because she wants to share this moment with her baby brother. Go up and meet your niece so your sister can get some rest." My dad put a hand on my back and gave me a little push toward the entrance.

I followed the directions my mom had given me and made my way to Remy's room. Daire was waiting outside the door, talking to Hyde. The man looked like he'd been hit by a truck—in a good way. He was obviously running on fumes, but the smile on his handsome face could be seen from the moon. Last time I had seen him, he had been clean-shaven and looked very much like a former military man. Today, he had a beard and looked so much like his old man that it was uncanny.

I stuck out my hand and offered sincere congratula-tions. My sister had really found her perfect partner. She and I shared a similar obsession with our first loves. It was one of the things that bonded us so tightly together. We understood each other's heartache. Only Remy was lucky, and as soon as Hyde had come back into her life, the tables turned, and the man she'd always wanted fell head over heels in love with her. In fact, he returned to Denver in large part because of his memories of her.

Hyde told me Remy was struggling to stay awake and urged me to keep the visit short. He told Daire he needed to pick up Hollyn, their other daughter, from his parents. We all agreed to touch base later, and then I quietly walked into the maternity room.

The lights were dim, and my sister looked even tinier than normal on the hospital bed. I never liked to see her laid out and drained, but when our eyes met, I knew I'd never seen her look happier or more fulfilled.

"I can't believe you just had a baby." I laughed, and the first real smile since I had been released crossed my face.

"You and me both." Remy sounded tired, but she motioned me closer to the bed and inclined her chin toward a medical bassinet. "But I did have a baby, and she's perfect. I can't wait for you to meet her."

I looked down at the newborn. She had a tuft of white hair on top of her head, and she was a small, squishy, wrinkled ball of cuteness. Logically, I knew it was impossible to say which parent she favored, but to me, she looked like Remy.

"What's her name?" I kept my voice quiet, so I didn't wake the baby up.

"Coraline."

I lifted my surprised gaze to my sister. "You named her after Mom?"

Remy nodded, her blonde curls drooping around her face. "Hollyn is named after her mom. It felt appropriate to keep the tradition."

"Did Mom cry when you told her?" I mean, how could she not? I was moved, and the name had nothing to do with me.

Remy snorted, and her eyes drifted closed. "Of course she did. I'd made her cry for all the wrong reasons, growing up. It was nice to have her crying over something good for a change. When the baby wakes up, you can hold her."

"Remy ..." I was about to tell her that my holding her baby wasn't a great idea. I didn't know how. And my hands—they shouldn't touch things as precious and delicate as a baby.

My sister's eyes popped open, and she gave me a stern look. "When she's awake, you're going to hold your niece and show her that you love her. And when you see Hollyn, you're going to treat her exactly the same. She was so young when you left. She doesn't have a real memory of you, which means you get to start fresh. I *want* you here, Zowen. I want you to hold your niece. I want you to hug me and tell me I did a wonderful job. You are a huge part of my family. Nothing will ever change that."

I held up my hands in a gesture of surrender. They were sparkling clean even though they felt dirty whenever I looked at them. "I will hold the baby when she wakes up."

"Damn right you will." She sighed softly, and I could tell she was ready to fall asleep.

It felt so much better than good to be back home.

chapter EIGHT

Aston

It was a good thing Zowen had refused my offer to take him to the airport. Almost as soon as I got out of the shower and started getting ready for bed, my boss called and issued an all-hands-on-deck meeting for one of our corporate clients.

The CEO had been caught sexually harassing a young intern at a company function, and the video was already making the rounds on the internet. The call for his resignation and the threat of an impending lawsuit were trending. Obviously, there was no way to spin a situation with such damning evidence. Our job was to be the intermediary between the company and the media. We were there to ensure that the rest of the employees of the business and their clientele survived the downfall of their leader. This type of project was my least favorite part of my job. Who wanted to be a mouthpiece for terrible men who thought their money and influence entitled them to anything with no recourse?

Not me.

Fortunately, I received another late-night call from Cassio's team, requesting an early morning meeting. I had to accommodate the outrageous time difference since Cassio and the team were back in Italy. They were very vague about what their concerns were, but I could tell the tone was tense and urgent. I was informed I would have everything I needed sent to my email, but I was way too tired to scan through it.

I barely got any sleep that night and was off rushing to work when the sun was still rising in the sky. I yawned long and loud. My jaw popped at the motion, and my eyes watered because they were red and dry. I was most definitely not at my best, but I got paid to put other people's problems before my own, and that was exactly what I was going to do.

I wasn't surprised to see my small office building already buzzing and busy with life. The CEO issue was already breaking on national news. The entire team was trying to put out fires, both big and small, while they waited for the company to decide if they were going to cut their losses and force the man to resign, or if they were going to try and ride out the storm with him at the helm.

It was annoying because, at the end of the day, it was unlikely he would ever have to face the type of punishment he truly deserved for being a creep. It didn't seem fair that someone who honestly deserved reformation and punishment would get to go on living their privileged life as normal, but someone like Zowen had had his entire world flipped end over end for his misjudgment. Where was the justice in any of that?

I sat at my desk and started scrolling through everything Cassio's team had sent over. It was the afternoon in Italy. There was so much information in my inbox that I could tell the team had had an extraordinarily long day. My eyes widened the deeper into the complaint and paperwork I went.

Cassio had a stalker.

An obsessive female fan who followed him to every event he participated in. She'd tracked down his address both in the States and overseas. Since the woman also lived abroad, it made getting away from her more difficult for him. She seemed to be *everywhere* he had to be. The young lady sent ridiculously expensive gifts and very inappropriate personal images. She befriended members of his team and tried to get close to him. She sent him thousands of messages through direct message and text. No one knew how she had gotten her hands on his phone number. No matter how many times he changed his contact information, she still managed to gain access to it.

The attention had escalated as of late, and Cassio's management team and his family were worried about his safety. Apparently, the woman was clever enough that she had conned her way into his hotel room while the team was in Japan. If Cassio hadn't sent his assistant in first because he had to take a call, there would be no telling how the situation might've played out.

Not only did the team want me to make a public statement declaring boundaries between Cassio and his fans, but they also wanted me to look at what their options were to legally get the woman to back off. The anti-stalking laws in California were stricter and more firmly defined than they were in Europe. They wanted her prosecuted here if there was any way to make that happen.

The sheer amount of documentation was proof the stalking had been going on long before Cassio began his move out of the amateur league. It looked like the woman had been following him online since he had just been a teenager. It must've been terrifying for him to have his every move watched and idolized at such an early age. I knew from firsthand experience that when you were viewed as a god, it made remembering you were nothing more than a normal mortal even more jarring. I'd watched Ry grapple with his morality the moment I told him we shouldn't be together.

Once I was finished reviewing all the information sent over, I hopped on the video conference call. I immediately noticed Cassio looked as tired and stressed as I felt. He was a very handsome guy. He had black hair and striking green eyes. His cheekbones looked like they had been chiseled by the gods, and his charisma was off the charts. He had a romantic and seductive vibe about him. I wasn't sure if it was because he was Italian or if it was practiced charm for his legion of admirers. Either way, it was easy to see why he had no trouble becoming a heart-throb once he was thrust into the public eye.

"I can take all of this to the company's lawyer and see what they suggest our next move should be. I don't know if we can file for a restraining order while you're overseas. You might have to wait until you're back state-side to delve deeper into this. Do you know if your stalker is in Italy now? Do you have security on staff to make sure you're safe if she tries to approach you again?"

Cassio sighed and shook his head. "Regarding that situation, she's not in Italy at the moment. She's back in the States. And that's the reason I wanted you to be aware of what is going on. Recently, she's started making threats toward any woman I have contact with. She privately contacted my older sister and made some horrifying comments. She attacked the only female member on my team on social media and even doxed her. The poor girl has gotten nothing but online hate for the last week."

He frowned while staring at me through the monitor. "I'm concerned she's going to try and contact you next, Aston. This woman is mentally ill. I know she needs help, but she's dangerous while she's out there, plotting and planning. Your company—you, in particular—needs to be on heightened alert." His faintly accented voice was more serious than I'd ever heard it. Usually, when we spoke, he sounded like he was trying to talk me into bed. "I'm very worried about you, Aston."

I nodded in understanding and waved off an assistant who whispered a reminder that I had another meeting waiting for me after this one. It was the type of day where I wouldn't get a moment to think about anything other than what was directly in front of me. Which wasn't a bad thing when I still had fragments of the previous evening with Zowen stuck in my head. Dealing with the broken condom was the top priority, but deep down inside, I was far more concerned with how our broken relationship could be repaired.

I worked from sunup until sundown and even a bit later than that. My entire office was exhausted by the time we called it a day. All I wanted to do was grab something for dinner and sleep for a solid ten hours. The back of my eyelids felt like they were coated with sandpaper, and every blink made my eyes burn. Now, when I yawned, it was a whole-body event, and I had to fight to stay on my feet. Honestly, I was in no condition to drive, but the day was almost finished, and I was determined to power through.

At least, I was until I got to my car.

All the windows were smashed to smithereens. The tires were slashed. Someone had taken a key to the side and dug deeply into the paint. The inside was ransacked, looking like a tiny tornado had ripped through the interior of the vehicle. It was such a mess; I couldn't tell if anything was missing. Completely destroyed. There was no way I would get home anytime soon.

After checking with security in the parking garage and calling the police and my insurance company, I went back up to my office to wait. I sent Cassio and the company's legal representative the pictures of my car and informed everyone I would keep them in the loop if the security cameras caught the stalker vandalizing my vehicle. Once the police arrived, they took a basic report and didn't seem overly enthused when I mentioned the damage might be related to one of my clients having a stalker. I felt very dismissed but chalked it up to it being the cherry on top of an atrociously difficult day.

I took an Uber home, planning on getting delivery for dinner and taking the hottest bubble bath known to humankind. I needed to arrange a rental car and get the situation with Cassio's stalker settled as quickly as possible.

Only the universe wasn't done throwing fastballs directly at my face for the day.

I managed to scarf down something resembling dinner and finally had a chance to drop some soothing eye drops into my tortured eyeballs. I started the bath and was just about to dip my toes into the frothy, steaming water when my phone rang.

Realizing I hadn't called or messaged Zowen back all day, I answered in a hurry, nearly falling into the tub in my haste.

"I've had a crazy day. Sorry I didn't get back to you. Hopefully, tomorrow chills out, and I'll be able to take care of our little issue from the other night." The words came out in a guilty rush.

I'd promised him I would be able to handle the repercussions of our drunken tryst on my own. I didn't want him to think I was a liar or that I was trying to trick him into a serious commitment. Yes, I wanted him and wanted him to stay with me. But I would never do anything devious and underhanded. Like I thought to myself since we had slept together, I was never going to do anything that might trap him and make him feel obligated to be with me. Not when he'd only recently regained his freedom.

"Aston?"

It wasn't Zowen's gravelly voice on the other end of the line. It was my brother's, and he sounded like he was crying.

"Royce? What's wrong? Why are you calling me so late?"

The time difference between New York and California meant it was close to the middle of the night where he was.

"Aston, my mom passed out tonight. I rushed her to the emergency room. I figured it was something related to how poorly she'd been feeling lately." He choked on his words, and I could hear him struggling to keep control of his emotions. "They ran a battery of tests and took X-rays. Something's happening in her lungs. They think it might be cancer."

He couldn't hold back the quiver in his voice any longer, and I knew he was crying. I felt my heart squeeze, and my entire body went numb.

"Okay. I'll hop on the next flight out in the morning." It didn't even occur to me that taking off work at the moment was probably the worst career move I could make. I loved my job, but nowhere near as much as I loved my brother and bonus mom. "You don't have to handle this alone."

"No. You don't have to come. I don't even know what we're looking at yet. They're admitting her into the ICU because she hit her head when she fainted, and she's got a concussion. She'll get more tests tomorrow, and once the diagnosis is clear, we'll know whether she needs to see an oncologist or not. She's always been healthy. I'm having a tough time wrapping my head around her not feeling well turning into something as big as cancer."

I shook my head and frowned at my pitiful expression in the mirror. "I'm coming. Even if it's only for a few days. I can help take care of the puppy and make it easier for you to be with your mom while she's in the hospital. Don't act all tough. I know you need someone to hold your hand, the same as I would in that situation. Besides, your mom has always treated me as her own. I want to be there for her as much as for you."

Royce caved quickly after my last argument. He knew his mom would want me there in case they were given bad news.

"I'll call Mom and Dad. I'll let them know what's going on. I wouldn't be surprised if Dad decides to fly to New York as well."

Our dad and Royce's mom had kept a very amicable relationship throughout the years. They worked hard to co-parent and make sure Royce never felt like he was lacking in love or attention from either side.

"He's going to be very worried about both of you once he knows what's going on."

Royce grunted, and I heard the rustling of fabric as he wiped his face. I knew he was crying even if I couldn't see him.

"Tell him I'll let him know whether it's a good idea to fly out or not. I don't want Mom overwhelmed even if it's with people trying to help. This is a lot to process, and she's already not feeling her best. I'll get in touch with him when I have more information."

I could tell by his voice that he was holding on to his composure by a thread. I felt so bad for him. It made my disgruntlement at having my car vandalized seem foolish.

We exchanged a few more reassurances, and then I switched back to business mode, the bubble bath long forgotten.

I sent an email to my big boss and copied my supervisor. It wasn't so much a request for time off as it was a statement of my intent to be absent from work for the rest of the week. Neither was happy with the timing, but I left no room for argument. Even if it cost me my job, I would be there for my brother whenever he needed me to be. He would do the exact same for me. Honestly, fuck that scumbag CEO anyway. He didn't deserve absolution just because he could pay for the best PR firm. I had no interest in seeing his tarnished image wiped clean by a few clever press releases and a couple of carefully crafted social media posts. Cassio's team was understanding and relieved. They thought it would be a good idea if I was out of town until it could be verified who had damaged my car.

As for Zowen, I waffled for a long time over how to respond to his messages. I wanted to tell him I had everything under control and that there was nothing to worry about, but the reality was, I had a lot of things to worry about. I was a ball of anxiety and uncertainty. I didn't want to drag him into the mire I was wading in while he was in the middle of what had to be his first happy moment with his family since he had been released from prison.

I gave my reflection in the bathroom mirror a wry smile. Everything between me and Zowen always seemed to hover between life and death. There was never a moment that felt like it was easy and effortless.

I tapped out a message, asking about Remy and the baby and letting him know I'd had a long day and run into some trouble with my car. I told him we could talk about everything when we were back in the same city, purposefully leaving out that I was leaving LA for New York as soon as possible.

Zowen's end of the message chain was silent.

I figured he was either tied up with family or already in bed. He'd left earlier than I did this morning, so it was likely he was as exhausted as I was. As abandoned my bath and forced myself to pack a carry-on to prepare for a rushed trip to my brother's side, I hoped the tension between Zowen and his family would ease. They were always such a tight-knit group and unwaveringly supportive of one another I hated that he'd tried to separate himself from them while he was away.

Even though I wasn't part of the family, I knew the Archers would never let one of their own wander too far off the right path. Everyone was allowed to forge their own way and determine the direction they wanted to walk in. But the Archers never traveled the road alone. Be it bumpy or smooth, it was a journey the entire family took together. Even when a huge detour, like serving five years in prison, was thrown down in front of them, they still made the trip hand in hand. No Archer was ever left behind.

I had been envious of that type of loyalty until I realized it didn't only apply to someone with the same last name. Ry hadn't written me off after our breakup. And Daire never walked away from me, even when I tested her very last nerve.

Even Zowen had held on to the memories that lingered between us. He might say he wanted to forget me and pretend we were strangers, but I knew there was no way he could fuck me like he hated me if a part of him still didn't love me. He wasn't hardwired that way.

Zowen

"I'm glad you're feeling better. If something had happened to you while I was away …" I shook my head and looked at my father with an expression beyond words. "I thought I was doing the right thing. I genuinely believed I should be punished for what had happened that night. When things started happening at home that I wasn't a part of"—I shook my head with deep regret—"I realized that was the actual penance for my actions."

My dad glanced at me over the rim of the coffee mug in his hand. Five years ago, this would've felt like any other morning where we sat down and caught up over breakfast, but not today. Today, this breakfast and the look on my father's face felt like a reckoning.

"I know your mom and I have never talked to you kids about what our lives were like before you were the center of them. I hardly ever mention my time in the service, so I know you and your sister don't have a firm idea of what I was like when I first met your mother."

His free hand curled into a fist on the table, and I watched as his knuckles turned white.

"I enlisted as soon as I was old enough, so I was gone when the twins graduated and for every major milestone that happened back home.. I was overseas when your grandparents started having problems with your uncle Rule. I was deployed when your uncle Remy died. It felt like the entire family was moving at warp speed and I was stuck in place. I know exactly how powerless and helpless it feels to be forcibly removed from the bad things happening to loved ones. For some reason, it's easy to forget you're also missing the good things while you're gone."

I frowned and cocked my head to the side while I considered the older man across from me. I had my dad's face and my mom's eyes. I knew exactly what I was going to look like as I got older. It was eerie how similar our expressions were as we recalled the past and our actions that had led to the current distance and tension between the two of us.

"I also know what it's like to watch an innocent person die right in front of you. I know what it's like to question every choice that led to that moment, be it yours or the command handed down by others. I know what it's like to feel like you need to blame yourself and be punished for surviving something like that. I know just how heavy the guilt can be. I know how hard it is to carry it for a lifetime. I wish I'd gotten the chance to explain all of that to you and your sister before you headed out into the world on your own. It always felt like a different life. At some point, I forgot who that man was and ignored that he might have some valuable information to pass along to his kids. Especially since his son is so damn similar to him. I should've done a better job of protecting you, Zowen."

I cleared my throat and looked away. "If I hadn't gone to the desert, the accident would've never happened. If I hadn't challenged the kid to a race, he would still be alive. I killed someone, Dad. I've had to come to terms with that, and so do you."

I was a murderer. The word echoed on repeat in my mind and throughout my life.

My father sighed and leaned forward to put his coffee down. "Look at me, son."

He waited until our eyes met before he started to ask me pointed questions I had refused to consider for the last five years. "If you killed him, then so did the drunk driver who had his lights off. And so did the truck driver who was driving well past the recommended working hours and was so tired that he could hardly keep his eyes open. And what about the kid's parents who had given him a bike he couldn't handle? Not to mention the kid's friends who not only hadn't tried to stop him that night, but also encouraged him? You were the only one who offered to call things off when you saw how nervous the kid was.

"You can't forget about the race organizers. They had decided to disqualify you unfairly. If they'd kept the race results honest and accurate, you wouldn't have been provoked in the first place. You'd traveled a long way for an event that was rigged.

"There were a lot of factors at play, and you're only seeing a small part of the big picture. It's not that different from soldiers following bad intel and misguided orders and ending up in a situation that was bound to go south. Did you react in an impulsive and hotheaded way? Absolutely. You're an Archer. I wouldn't expect any less from you. Archers have a history of suffering dire consequences when we let our temper and impulses get the better of us. You've seen that your whole life. You've more than paid the price for that lapse in judgment. You've done more than most would do in your situation, Zowen. It's time to let go. The only thing stopping you from growing into a better man who has paid his price is you."

I took a few minutes to let his words sink in.

It wasn't the first time all the others who bore blame for that tragic night were laid out in front of me. My lawyer wanted to use everyone else as part of my defense for my criminal The biggest hindrance to that ammunition being effective in arguing my case had been me. I refused to defend myself. I hadn't uttered a word of my innocence, which inevitably led to the jury taking my silence as guilt. Which it was. However, hearing my father relate my current feelings of inadequacy to some of his own gave me new insight into the situation.

If my dad had never let go and moved on from the tragic and devastating situations he'd experienced as a young man in the service, he and my mom would've never made it. And Remy and I wouldn't even exist.

"It's hard, Dad. I've been calling myself a killer for years."

But I knew under no circumstance would I ever consider him the same. It gave me a new perspective as to how my parents and loved ones viewed the situation I'd gone through.

"I know you have. But no one else who matters has ever called you that."

I couldn't help a smirk from tugging at my mouth. "Aston told me the same thing the other day."

My father chuckled and reached for his abandoned coffee. "I always knew she was a smart girl. Timid but clever. Kind of like her mom."

It was true that Aston's mother was more subdued and reserved than any of the women in the Archer family. And while Aston might've been similar when she was younger, she was no longer shy and reserved.

I fought down a heated blush when images of our drunken night together flashed through my mind. We most definitely needed to sit down and have a serious talk when I got back to California. I owed her an apology for being so rough. She owed me an explanation as to why she had started everything in the first place.

"Aston's not very timid anymore. She seems like she's achieved a lot and is thriving with her life out in LA. I don't think she has a shy bone in her body these days." I didn't realize how fond of Aston I sounded when I spoke about the girl who was my first and only love.

My dad didn't miss the change in tone, and his dark eyebrows lifted with curiosity. "Interesting. You should take a good look at her then. It's clear people can change. They grow and evolve. That includes you, son. You don't have to be one thing forever. I was a son and a brother. I was a soldier. Then, I was a father. Eventually, I became a husband and an entrepreneur. Now, I'm a grandfather. All those identities led to being a complete man. I wouldn't let go of any one of them even if some came with moments and memories I'd rather forget. Don't let yourself get stuck on being the one and only thing you've identified with for the last five years."

I knocked my knuckles on the table and leaned back in my seat. "I'll try." It was the only time I'd said the words and meant them.

"That's all I can ask. There's an old saying that goes, *You don't raise heroes; you raise sons*. Your expectations of yourself have always been far beyond what your mom and I wanted for you, Zowen. These days, all we want is for you to be part of this family and to figure out what it is that will make you happy. I know your future ended up paused and every opportunity you expected went up in a puff of smoke. That doesn't mean there won't ever be new opportunities headed your way. You need to stop closing your eyes and ignoring them because they look different from what you imagined."

It was my turn to lift my eyebrows. "Is that what you did when Mom told you she was knocked up with Remy?"

It was no secret that my sister had been an unplanned blessing that forced our parents to accelerate every single part of their relationship. I never gave too much thought to the fact that all of that had happened when my father was out of the military for a very short amount of time. When he'd said his roles shifted dramatically and required him to be a different man for each, he'd meant it.

"It is. Your mom and sister saved my life. Even if I hadn't been shot back then, I was on an incredibly self-destructive path because I didn't know what to do with myself and all the baggage I'd carried out of the Army with me. If I overlooked all the great opportunities they brought with them when they crashed into my life, I don't want to imagine what that would've meant for me."

Speaking of him getting shot, I looked pointedly at his chest. I knew underneath the fabric of his ugly Hawaiian shirt, there was a huge scar from his recent surgery.

"Are you going to be okay? Are you going to have more issues with your heart in the future?"

Whatever his answer was, I knew I needed to get the civil trial handled and left in the past so I could move back to Denver and be close to my parents. It was hard to accept that they were getting older and that they weren't indestructible. My dad was a monolith, the pillar the entire family was built upon. If he went down, there was no question the rest of us would fall right after him.

"I'll be fine. There are no guarantees with anything in life, but I feel good, and my cardiologist is optimistic. As much as I'd like you to be back home for selfish reasons, you need to live your life, Zowen. I won't be the next reason you put everything on hold. I refuse to be another price you feel you need to pay. Focus on yourself."

I shook my head and finally unfurled my fingers. Once the fist released, most of the tension that was coiled around my spine like a hungry snake loosened. "I've got to get through the next trial. After that is finalized, I can focus on whatever comes next."

"Are you planning on getting back into racing?"

It was an innocent question, but I couldn't help but scoff when my father asked it.

"I can barely stand to be in a car. I don't know what would happen if I tried to climb back on a bike. I think racing is going to be a thing of the past." I could hear how disgruntled I sounded by the situation.

My dad hummed and tilted his head to the side as he considered me thoughtfully. "You loved it. You were always so passionate about motorcycles and racing. Can you really give it up, just like that? You don't think you'll regret it?"

I opened my mouth to retort that the past was the past and I planned on focusing on the future. However, Aston's pretty face flashed in my mind, and I bit the words back. It was easier said than done to leave the things long beloved behind.

"I don't know. If I'm supposed to end up back on a bike or involved with racing, the universe is going to have to give me a big fucking sign. For now, the job I'm doing is fine." And honorable, like Aston had been quick to remind me. It might not set fire to my blood the way racing had, but it could change lives, and that was something important to me while I tried to find my footing after serving my sentence. "I'm lucky I have people willing to help me out when I'm at my lowest."

My dad sighed and climbed to his feet. He towered over me. And when he bent down to give me a rough hug, I felt like I was a small child within the reassuring embrace.

"When you're at the bottom, the only direction left is up. Doesn't matter how slowly you climb. As long as you get on your feet and take the first step, you'll get off the bottom in no time."

He pounded me on the back to dissipate some of the heavy emotion from the conversation and the hug. I took a shaky breath and jolted in surprise when Daire suddenly burst into the kitchen. I hadn't known she was at my parents' house and wondered how much of my father's pep talk she'd overheard.

As it turned out, I didn't have to worry about her eavesdropping. She had something else on her mind entirely. She shoved her cell phone in my face and pointed at a series of unanswered calls, showing Aston's name.

"Have you talked to Aston since getting to Denver? I've called her a hundred times and texted her a thousand. She's not responding. I'm about to send Campbell down to LA to check on her."

Daire was always dramatic. However, I could tell her current concern was genuine.

"I texted with her the day I got here. She said everything was fine. She mentioned being tired from work that day. Maybe she's just busy." *With the professional racer.* I didn't add the last part, but it was my first thought, and it made me incredibly uneasy.

"Even if she were busy, she would text me to let me know. She always responds to me. She knows I worry, and when I worry, I might do something crazy. I'm about to call her office and ask them what's going on."

I pushed her hand with the phone out of my face and dug my own cell out of my pocket. "Don't do that. Aston is an adult. She probably has a very valid reason for not responding right away. You don't have to be her guard dog anymore, Daire. She's doing fine on her own."

Daire snorted and crossed her arms over her chest. "I can't believe you bought into her independent and newfound confidence act. She's still too nice and too much of a pushover. She's not as tentative about things as she was in the past, but that doesn't mean the things that make her Aston have gone away. She's too worried about you seeing her the way you did when we were kids. The truth is, she still needs someone willing to look out for her and who has her back. Until that person comes along, I'm the one who takes care of her."

I was used to the way Daire steamrolled over people, so I ignored her tirade and sent a message to Aston, asking if everything was all right. The message went unanswered, the same as Daire's. I frowned because I'd honestly expected Aston to respond to me even if she was ignoring my cousin.

Before I could try and call Aston, Daire called her brother, who had yet to put in an appearance. Ry was still tied up with his residency, but he picked up when Daire called because that was something he always did.

"What's up? If you're asking when I'll be in Denver, I still don't know. I talked to Remy yesterday, and she understands."

Daire had put the call on speaker, and I heard the sounds of a hospital in the background. Ry sounded hurried and impatient.

"Have you talked to Aston by any chance?" Daire gave me a look when I stiffened involuntarily.

Aston and Ry had been broken up for much longer than they'd been together, and I had no right to feel any form of jealousy. But I did.

"I did speak to her. She called and asked me a bunch of medical questions about a probable cancer diagnosis. She asked me to send her any recommendations I might have for an oncologist in the Brooklyn area. I didn't have much time to talk to her because she called while I was on shift. I tried to text her to follow up and ask why she needed the information. She hasn't responded. I made a note to call Royce and see if he could fill me in, but I haven't gotten around to it yet. Medical issues are touchy and need to be handled delicately. Don't give her shit if something serious is going on, Daire."

I exchanged a look with my cousin and tapped my phone against my palm.

There was a lot left up to interpretation following the call from Ry. One thing was certain though: something awful was happening, and Aston was trying to handle it all on her own.

I could tell Daire was upset.

And it definitely didn't sit right with me.

The problem was, I had no idea how to help Aston. It frustrated me because I used to be the guy who could help everyone out in my sleep. I had a solution to any and every problem without even trying.

Aston deserved more than a man who could barely remember how to help himself these days.

However, I was suddenly very motivated to get all my failures, perceived or otherwise, figured the fuck out. If I didn't, there was an Italian guy who had his life all planned out, waiting in the wings to fix all the things that might be broken in Aston's life.

I couldn't stand the thought of her turning to someone else when I was finally standing right in front of her.

chapter TEN

Aston

As soon as I stepped in the front door of my house, I dropped everything on the floor and let myself fall apart. I sobbed so hard that I fell to my knees. My head fell forward, and my entire body started to shake. I was devastated. Even more so since I'd put on a brave face and white-knuckled my way through the week after Royce and his mom, Kallie, learned her options were limited and her situation was far worse than anyone could've imagined.

She didn't only have lung cancer. It was everywhere in her body. She had been diagnosed with a small cell version of the disease that responded well to treatment if caught early, but also detrimental because it moved so quickly. Unfortunately, Kallie hadn't moved quickly when she started feeling unwell. That, combined with the complicated movements of the health-care system taking forever, did not leave her with a positive prognosis. I would never, for as long as I lived, forget the look on my brother's face when he'd told me the doctors gave his mom, conservatively, no longer than a year to live. I watched his heart break and did my best to hold him together when he collapsed both mentally and physically.

My mom and dad traveled to New York once they heard the news. I was honestly relieved to hand the task of being the strong shoulder to lean on over to my father.

I'd taught myself how to put up a good front. But what was hidden behind the tough facade was a woman who still wanted to be taken care of and held when things got to be overwhelming and emotional. Day to day, I was stronger than I'd been when I was lost and alone as a young woman. In a crisis, I could fake my way through being tough and composed for a few days, but inside, I wanted to cry and curl up in a ball of defeat. I wanted to let someone hug me so tightly that it hurt. I wanted to blame everyone and everything for how unfair life could be. I wanted to get lost in sorrow and sink into the comfort offered by others.

However, I didn't allow myself any of those things. I stayed strong for Royce and his mom. I had taken care of everything not related to the medical situation and kept their lives afloat while they figured out what they were going to do.

I dragged my hands over my wet cheeks and looked at the pet carrier that was now part of my luggage.

I'd even brought Kallie's new puppy home with me. Taking care of a baby while my brother and his mom had lives that were so chaotic and uncertain was bound to be impossible. My parents had offered to bring the dog back to Denver with them when they returned home, but I refused. I knew there wasn't much I could do for Kallie beyond offering her and my brother unconditional love and support. So, taking the puppy and promising she wouldn't have to worry about it on top of everything else had felt like the least I could do. Bringing home the dog also meant I couldn't wallow and was only allowed to be miserable and angry at the world for a short amount of time. The puppy took the focus off me and my feelings—which wasn't the world's greatest coping mechanism, but so be it.

I kicked aside my carry-on and the miscellaneous things that had tumbled out when it dropped. I took the puppy out of the carrier and buried my face in his fur. He was small and fluffy, like a stuffed animal. He was as lost and confused as I was when I took him outside to the backyard so he could do his business. The little guy was a city pup. He'd probably never seen a fenced-in yard before. He ran in happy circles, yipping and yapping his floofy little head off when he felt grass for the first time. I couldn't help but smile at his antics, even with my insides feeling like they'd spent the last week being lacerated by a razor blade.

I lifted the hem of my T-shirt to wipe my face and blew out a shaky breath. It was wild how the world kept moving and everything remained normal when a vital part of your existence was about to be ripped away. I couldn't get my head around how I was supposed to go back to work and reintegrate into my typical routine, knowing that my brother was devastated and knowing that a woman I loved like a member of my family was spending the rest of her days with a glaring countdown ticking in the background of her life. I wanted to start crying all over again when I thought about it.

I never got the chance to sob because the puppy started losing his mind. His playful yips turned frantic, and I realized I was no longer alone in the backyard.

Zowen squatted down and offered a large, tattooed hand to the puppy to sniff. Once the tiny nose touched the inked skin, he stopped barking and started to wiggle his poofy behind like he was dancing. The puppy could quite literally fit in the palm of Zowen's hand. He handled the small dog very gently as our eyes locked across the dark yard.

"Ry told me what's going on with Royce's mom. I'm sorry the news wasn't better." His voice was gruff, and I found it particularly soothing.

I liked the combination of Zowen Archer and the velvety night sky very much. When he spoke quietly and softly under the stars, it felt like this was the version of him only I got to see and hear. It was like a secret between us that no one else was in on.

"I'm sorry I didn't answer your calls or message you back. Everything has been a blur. I'm really worried about my brother. I think Kallie is taking the news better than he is. She seems more realistic about the situation than Royce and is more worried about him than herself. I'm glad my parents are there for them. And it was very nice of Ry to call his mom to get us information on who we should take Kallie to for her diagnosis and treatment. She has a really great medical team around her." I blurted out the words on autopilot. I'd uttered the same set of sentences over and over again this past week. They were nonsense platitudes I could hide behind while I kept my emotions in a choke hold.

Zowen looked at me and didn't say anything. He picked up the puppy, and my heart squeezed at the sight of the tiny, defenseless animal looking happy as could be, cuddled up to his broad chest. He walked toward me, his gaze piercing right into mine.

Once we were toe to toe, he bent down slightly so we looked directly at each other and asked, "How are you? This week had to be hard for you as well. I know you're close to Royce's mom."

How was I?

Devastated.

Exhausted.

Frustrated.

Angry.

Terrified.

I was everything. I was so many things that I couldn't start to sift through them. Which was why it was easier to pretend to be nothing.

I cleared my throat and reached for the puppy. "I'm okay. I'm tired and sad. But I know there isn't much I can do other than be there when they need me. I figured I could take at least one thing off Kallie's plate. Which is why I brought the puppy home."

A small tongue licked across my fingers, and the big, sweet eyes almost brought me to tears once again. I inhaled sharply and looked at Zowen with a hint of desperation.

"I just realized I have nothing here to take care of a puppy. No food. No crate. No toys. And I didn't think about what I'm going to do with him while I'm at work."

A spiral of panic started to encircle my throat. Everything I'd repressed while pretending to have my shit together started to choke me. My fingers shook, and I would've ended up on my knees again if Zowen hadn't shot out a hand and grabbed my arm.

"Breathe, Aston." His deep voice ran over my frayed nerves the same way his hand patted the excited puppy. "You don't have to solve every problem on your own. It's not on you to fix the things that are unfixable." His two-toned eyes were hypnotic as the glint from the stars seemingly reflected within them. "And you don't have to deal with this alone. I'm here."

He was here. He was right in front of me. Which was the only thing I'd ever wanted the entire time he was away.

I buried my nose in the puppy's fur and started to cry. It was different from my breakdown by the front door. This was the floodgates opening, and all the thoughts and feelings I'd refused to allow myself to feel for the last week broke free. I cried so deeply and so hard that I thought I might have blacked out for a moment. I lost my perception beyond the touch of the warm and wiggling puppy in my arms. At one point, the landscape tilted, and I vaguely realized Zowen had picked me up, but I couldn't see anything through the sting of tears obscuring my vision. I was aware of being placed on a soft surface and the puppy whimpering in my too-tight hold, but everything after that was a total blur. It was easier to shut my eyes and drown in all the emotions flooding out of me than it was to act like I could control anything at that moment.

I must've fallen asleep because when I opened my eyes, I could see hints of faint light coming through the curtains. Night was no more, and neither was my catastrophic collapse. I felt better than I had all week even if there was a haze of sadness and disbelief still covering everything. I looked at my nightstand and was surprised to see my phone already resting on the charger. Last I remembered, it had been on the floor by the front door, where I'd dumped everything.

I gave a sudden shiver of awareness, thinking about the poor puppy I'd dragged home. I climbed out of bed and planned to run across the yard to see if he was with Zowen. I knew he was the one who had put me to bed last night, and I couldn't imagine him doing anything other than taking in the dog once I proved incapable of being able to take care of anything. Myself being at the top of the list.

I skidded to a halt cartoon-style when I reached the open area near the kitchen where the French doors leading outside were located.

Not only was Zowen standing in my kitchen, cooking something that smelled like bacon and eggs, but there was also a little nook set up off the living room that had everything the puppy would need. There was a cute crate. Potty pads. Matching food and water dishes. A dog bed that looked more comfortable than my couch and enough toys that there was no way the puppy could ever play with them all.

I blinked stupidly and noticed the little ball of fluff asleep at Zowen's bare feet.

"What's his name?" Zowen turned to me and cocked an eyebrow. "I've been calling him Hey You, and I think it hurt his feelings."

I lifted my hand to my mouth and coughed. I couldn't decide if I was embarrassed about falling apart all over him or ecstatic that he'd not only taken care of me when I needed him, but the puppy too. I figured I was probably both and a little bit more in love with him than I already had been because he did what needed to be done without being asked. It was exactly what the old Zowen would've done. It made me feel like the man I'd waited desperately for wasn't so far gone as I'd started to believe.

"Koons. He's named after the artist who's famous for the big balloon-dog sculptures."

Zowen lifted an eyebrow, but didn't comment on the unusual moniker. "I made breakfast. I didn't know if you were planning on going in to work today, so I asked my supervisor if I could work remotely for this shift. I'll watch the puppy for you. Even if you aren't going to work, I'll keep an eye on him. You need a day to decompress and get yourself in order before getting back to the real world."

I shifted my weight and pushed my sleep-tangled hair away from my face. "Thank you, Zowen. For everything."

I honestly didn't know what I would've done without him.

He reached out to turn off the stove and moved to pick the puppy up, so he was out of the way and didn't get stepped on. "You don't have to thank me. But it would be nice if you considered this my apology for the way things had gone down between us the other night. I've been thinking a lot about my behavior and my actions since I left. I'm not going to make excuses. I just need you to know that it won't happen again." He put the puppy in his kennel and motioned to the dining table. The table I wasn't sure I could ever look at the same way again. "Come and eat something. You look like a strong wind will knock you over."

I was still wearing the clothes from my flight. I hadn't brushed my hair in who knew how long. My teeth were fuzzy enough to compete with the puppy's fluff. And I was sure the excessive crying hadn't done my face any favors. "Let me take a quick shower, and then I'll eat. You don't have to wait for me."

He paused and seemed to ponder something before saying, "I don't mind waiting for you."

Why did those words feel like they had a double, triple, quadruple meaning behind them?

I shook my head to get rid of the winsome thoughts and practically ran back to my room. I rushed through my morning routine, returning to the kitchen with wet hair but everything else looked presentable. I picked up a fork and looked at the overflowing plate with wide eyes. This was more of a breakfast than I ever made for myself. I usually ran out the door with a cup of coffee and a squeezable yogurt.

"I wasn't sure whether your tastes had changed or not. You've lived in California for so long, and I was wondering if you'd started eating like a stereotypical Californian." Zowen chomped on a piece of bacon and watched me start to work on the mountain of food in front of me.

"I'm not picky. I eat whatever. California is huge. All the different regions have unique types of food they're known for. I don't think there really is a typical Californian diet when you get right down to it. There are a lot of good places to eat out wherever you go. But if you ask Royce, he'll tell you everything here sucks compared to New York. He's an East Coast superiority elitest." I felt a pang when I mentioned my brother, but the sensation wasn't overwhelming, the way it had been last night.

Sensing my shift in mood, Zowen told me, "This is going to be hard for him. For both of you. Keep a tight hold on him. That's the best advice I can give you. That's what I did with Remy for all those years she was dancing on the edge of destruction. Regardless of how bad things got, I never let go of her."

I nodded and looked at him over a forkful of fluffy eggs. "Did she hold on to you in return? Did you let her hold on while you were away?"

I had been secretly jealous that he only let a handful of his family members visit him over the last five years. It felt like he was deciding who could handle seeing him in the prison environment without any input from the other party. It'd always irritated me that he deemed me as one of the people too weak or too fragile to adapt to his circumstances.

"You know Remy. No one *lets* her do a goddamn thing. If she decides she's going to do something, she just does it. Hyde must have the patience of a saint."

I shrugged. "He loves her. He knows exactly who it is he fell in love with. I don't think it has anything to do with him having unlimited patience or not." I dropped the fork and leaned on the edge of the table, focusing all my attention on him. "Speaking of knowing exactly who someone is ... you don't have to apologize for the other night. I was an active participant. I was more sober than you were. I don't think any of it was a mistake, and I don't regret it. I've known you most of my life, Zowen. Regardless of how you might feel about me, I know under no circumstances would you do anything to hurt me. We're both guilty of losing control and getting caught up in the moment." I wasn't going to scare him off by admitting I was waiting for him to do both of those things again though.

He didn't say anything for a drawn-out period of time. I could see the wheels turning in his handsome head. We'd called somewhat of a silent truce since returning to LA, and I hoped he didn't do something to blow it up.

"Okay. I won't be overly apologetic. I still feel bad about the timing. You shouldn't have had to deal with the aftermath of a broken condom while everything else with your family was going on."

I gave a slight shrug. It was just a dirty little detail of real life that needed to be dealt with, no matter what else happened to be occurring. I didn't bother to tell him that I'd only gotten around to getting to a pharmacy in New York around seventy-two hours after the incident. It was a miracle I'd found time at all. I wasn't too worried about addressing the situation later than I normally would, but that was merely because I had other gigantic concerns looming. Thinking of those concerns, I reached out and grabbed his hand to make sure his attention was focused on me.

"One of my clients has a stalker. Cassio, the motorcycle racer, is in the middle of gathering evidence to try and get a restraining order against her. Right before I left for New York, his team called and warned me that she might be dangerous. That night, my car was vandalized. That's why it's not parked out front." Crap. I'd totally forgotten I needed to arrange a rental car while mine was in the shop. I shook my head to keep my train of thought in line. "I don't know for sure it was his stalker, but the timing is too coincidental. If she knows what car I drive and she went through everything in the glove box, she might know where I live." My eyes widened when I thought about the house being empty for a week. "She could've been here while we were away."

Zowen turned his hand over so our palms were clasped together. The warmth of his touch immediately sank into my skin.

He gave me a reassuring look., "No one was here while we were away. My current employer takes security very seriously. He knows the work we do can be dangerous. He's aware that powerful people don't like having their secrets—especially when they're related to children—exposed. Since I occasionally work remotely from the guesthouse and my computer is here, he has his security team keep an eye on this place. I would have known if anyone suspicious had been lurking around while we were away.

I breathed a sigh of relief and squeezed his fingers. "Thank goodness. Now, all I need to do is figure out the rental car and learn how to potty train a puppy."

Koons yipped from his kennel as if he understood he was about to be put through puppy boot camp.

Zowen stood to clear the table. "You can take the Bronco. I don't even have my license yet. I know Daire meant well, but it's just going to sit there for now."

I blinked and felt my entire body go limp with relief. I watched his broad back as he moved through my house and whispered under my breath, "My life is so much better with you in it."

It would be so easy to let him take care of me forever.

I needed to brand the fact that I was supposed to be the one taking care of him into my brain.

If I wanted to make up for the mistakes made in the past, I needed him to see that I wanted him and could care for him the way he had always done for me. I had to be as good to him—and for him—as he was to me.

It was one hell of a tall order. Especially after his recent performance.

He made the way he cared for me seem absolutely effortless. Which made the work I had to do feel daunting. I wondered if he knew his competition had never been Ry or anyone else, because he was the standard I held everyone else up to in comparison.

Zowen

"I wish you had shown this level of interest during your criminal trial. I probably could've kept you out of jail back then if you'd put up even a little bit of a fight."

Hayes Lawtons one of the best defense lawyers in all of California. He'd represented me since the beginning of my legal troubles. Under normal circumstances, I would never be able to afford his services, but my dad knew someone who knew Hayes's father. The expensive attorney had agreed to represent me at a discounted friends-and-family rate. He was a stern, no-nonsense type of man. He had a faint Southern drawl when he spoke, and more than once, he'd worn a cowboy hat and high-end Western boots during our meetings.

My first impression had been that he should be riding a bull in a rodeo, not arguing a criminal case in front of a judge. But he was smart and well spoken. He was confident and saw right through my self-deprecations with no effort. I knew he was originally from Texas and that his family had a long history of working within the legal system and law enforcement. At one point, I'd asked how a former football player from a small town in Texas ended up in LA, and he'd laughed and quipped that love made people do crazy things. It didn't seem proper to pry into the older man's private life, but I had to admit that I was curious about his story.

I'd also landed here because I foolishly followed my heart instead of listening to any other vital organ that might've had an opinion. Not that the rest of me had been making great choices where Aston Wheeler was involved as of late. My cock definitely had no chill where she was concerned. And my brain tended to short-circuit and relinquish control to my more demanding body parts when I got too close to her.

"We have evidence that shows the driver of the SUV and the driver of the semitruck were the ones directly involved in the accident is going to work well in our favor. The family settled both their suits against the other individuals without going to trial. They're going to expect you to do the same. Which is still an option if you think you want to offer a sum of money to make this all go away. I'm sure you're ready to get back to your normal life."

I grunted in agreement. "Not too long ago, I was ready to let them drag me over the coals in court. I would've agreed to pay whatever the judge decided. Recently, I realized I can't take full responsibility for everything that happened that night. There is plenty of blame to go around, and I'm the only one who gave up my freedom to show how deeply I regretted any part I'd played in the accident. Everyone else just moved on as if nothing had happened."

"You think too highly of other people. There aren't a lot of individuals with the kind of integrity you exhibited at such a young age. I was raised by one of the most upright and honest men you'll ever meet, and I don't think I'd be able to make the type of sacrifice you made, Zowen."

I felt a hint of a smile tug at the corners of my mouth. "My dad recently reminded me that he was raising a son, not a hero. The only person who appreciates the fact that I gave up a huge chunk of my life to prove how sincerely I regretted my decision is me."

Hayes chuckled and spun an obviously expensive silver pen between his fingers. "My dad used to tell me something similar. Only he told me he was trying his best to raise a good son, not a future villain. We have a lot of relatives in our bloodline who came into the world with highly questionable ethics. He about had an aneurysm when I told him I was going to work for the defense instead of the prosecution. He still gives me a hard time about keeping the kind of people he used to arrest out of prison."

"Why did you decide to work for the defense?"

I knew this side of the table made more money than working for the state, and it meant he could pick and choose his own clients. Neither of those reasons fit with my impression of the not-quite-a-cowboy lawyer.

"I want to keep good people out of jail. There are a lot of dirty tricks in the legal system. My father was the victim of those tricks when I was a young man, growing up. I don't care what happens to the actual criminals whose cases come across my desk, but I am deeply invested in those who truly need someone to stand between them and the sharp teeth of the judicial process."

"Sounds very altruistic." And maybe a bit naïve.

"So does serving a five-year sentence for an accident where you were basically nothing more than a bystander. Why do you think I was angry when you tanked the trial?"

He dropped the pen and climbed to his feet. His belt buckle was the size of a salad plate and inlaid with gold and silver. It looked like there was a bucking horse and a cowboy in the center of it.

Hayes chuckled when he saw my horrified expression at his fashion choice. He tapped the gaudy belt buckle with a finger and grinned. "It's a custom prize buckle from the professional rodeo association. My uncle used to be a competitive rider. He's also someone who's had to take advantage of the friends-and-family legal services discount on more than one occasion. Only my stepmom is the unfortunate one who gets to represent him.

"Now, get out of here, or I'll have to charge you for another hour."

I shook the older man's hand and showed myself out of his office. His assistant told me she would get in touch if there was any follow-up needed before my first court date. I told her that was fine and walked out of the upscale, modern office building.

I was instantly hit by the heat reflecting off the windows and blinded by the sun. I still hadn't adjusted to the perpetually sunny skies of LA. It was different from the ever-changing weather patterns in Colorado. I had to admit, I missed the frequent afternoon rain and cooler weather in the evenings that were common in Denver. I couldn't picture the holidays with palm trees instead of snow.

My new boss designated a personal driver for me until I was ready to take myself to and from work. Fortunately, he didn't mind when I used the benefit for personal matters.

I went back to the Hollywood Hills bungalow, thinking I would let the puppy out and take him for a walk before going back to work. I was surprised to see the blue Bronco parked on the hill in front of the house when I arrived. I told the driver to go ahead and head back to the office. I was worried something bad had happened with Kallie or Royce, and that was why Aston was home in the middle of the workday.

There was no answer when I knocked on the front door, but I could hear a commotion coming from inside. Frowning because Aston's warning about the racer's stalker was still in the forefront of my mind, I went around the house to the big French doors, thinking I could break the glass and enter if need be.

The sight that greeted me when I approached the doors was like one of those viral mishap clips that traveled like lightning across social media when they were caught on camera.

Remnants of chewed-up plants and soil were all over the living room and dining room. A roll of toilet paper was shredded and spread from one end of the house to the other. Stuffing from one of the couch cushions clung to every available surface. Little brown nuggets of dog food were scattered across the floor, and it looked like the curtains covering the front window had been pulled down.

Koons was running around happily, a toy in his mouth as he dived and dodged Aston's frantic attempts to grab him. She was scolding the puppy in a helpless manner, and she looked completely frazzled because her hair was soaking wet, and she still had bubbles of soap clinging to her skin. All she was wearing was a tiny towel that barely covered the important parts. I couldn't help but chuckle while letting my gaze rove all over her exposed skin.

I'd always thought she was the most beautiful girl I'd ever laid eyes on.

She was small and fairy-like. I liked her wavy hair with the hidden hints of fire within the darkness and her unfathomable eyes. Before, I wanted to hold her in the palm of my hand and protect her.

Aston no longer looked like a fairy. She looked like a temptress.

And I didn't want to coddle her and hold her in my hand like a doll. I wanted to hold her against me and touch her all over like a lover.

I blew out a breath that fogged up the glass on the door. I knocked so I didn't scare her before turning the handle and letting myself inside. The door should've been locked while she was in the shower. However, it was obvious the last thing she needed at the moment was a lecture on safety.

"I accidentally left the kennel door open when I took a shower. I can't believe he made this much of a mess in five minutes. I need to google if those plants he shredded are dangerous." Aston didn't even bother with a greeting. She just launched into a panicked tirade about the puppy.

I bent down to grab the fluffy, wiggling body and told her, "I'll take him outside and clean up. Finish your shower." I lifted an eyebrow and looked over her almost-naked form. "Why are you home from work in the middle of the day?"

Aston shoved her soggy hair out of her face and looked around the destroyed house with bewildered eyes. "I wasn't feeling so great, so I asked for the afternoon off. I was going to take a shower and catch a quick nap, then look into hiring a dog walker to check on Koons throughout the day. How did something so small make such a big mess?"

My heart squeezed and asked the same question. How did someone so tiny make everything inside of me feel like it was no longer within my control? She, too, was capable of doing a lot of damage while being so small.

"Are you getting sick?"

It wouldn't surprise me if she was run-down. She'd been going nonstop since returning from New York. The stress of everything was finally getting to her.

She shrugged and almost lost the towel. The puppy yelped when I accidentally held it a bit too tight.

"I'm not sure. I'm tired and achy. Maybe it's the start of the flu." She swore. "I don't have the time to get sick."

"Go finish your shower. You have to take care of yourself before you can take care of anyone else." I waved to the hallway and turned my back to let the puppy run around outside.

It was going to take some serious elbow grease to get the house back in order, and Aston didn't seem like she was up to the job. I didn't mind setting things right while she rested and regained her energy. After all, I still owed her for putting a roof over my head and being an ungrateful bastard about the situation that had thrown us together.

After taking care of the puppy, I made sure to put him back in his crate to keep him out of the way while I picked up all the evidence of his rampage. He sat quietly, almost like he knew he was in the wrong. I got all the debris picked up and in trash bags and put the curtains back on over the windows. I searched for the plants and did a visual comparison to make sure Koons hadn't accidentally poisoned himself. As long as he didn't start vomiting or showing any concerning signs, he should be all right. I was looking for a broom and mop to take care of the floor but kept coming up empty regardless of where I looked. After ten minutes of searching, I gave up and went to ask Aston where they were stashed.

The door to the bathroom was open, and steam was coming out. I didn't know which room was hers, so I called her name and walked toward the sound of her voice when she responded.

I didn't expect the door to her bedroom to be opened wide enough that I got a clear view of her naked body when she dropped the towel and reached for the clothing laid out on her bed. Our eyes locked. Hers were full of surprise and mild embarrassment.

While I couldn't see my eyes, I was sure there was nothing more than a possessive gleam radiating from both colors.

All I could think, all I could feel, was, *Mine.*

I wanted—no, needed—Aston Wheeler to belong to me.

For my entire life, that had been the one desire, the one wish, the one dream that never wavered. I'd tried to talk myself out of how deeply ingrained she was into my very core, but it didn't worked. As we stared at each other, the chasm of time and wasted opportunity began slowly shrinking. I understood if I let her slip through my fingers again, the only person I could blame this time was myself.

Aston was right in front of me, right in the middle of my path because she'd put herself there. Why did I keep trying to walk around her instead of running to meet her? How had I let myself be detoured for five years?

It was past time I got myself back on the road I'd always wanted to walk.

I stepped into the room, my gaze pinning her in place. I saw her hand freeze while reaching for her clothes, and a delicate blush crawled across her chest. Her nipples tightened while I watched, and her breath made an audible sound when it caught.

I stopped right in front of her and tilted her chin up with my fingertip. I lowered my head slowly. Giving her plenty of time to pull away or tell me to stop. She didn't utter a word. Instead, her eyes darkened, and she lifted up on her toes so her hands could rest on my shoulders and her lips would meet mine halfway when I bent down to kiss her.

Instead of cinnamon liquor and sweet soda, she tasted like minty toothpaste, super fresh and clean. Her hair was cool from being wet, but her naked skin was warm. Her breath was hot when it touched my mouth, but nowhere near as scalding as her tongue when it clashed with mine.

We were much better kissers when we were sober and aware.

There was still a touch of desperation in both our movements, but the anger and regret seemed to be gone.

This was the kind of kiss you shared with the girl you'd always been in love with. Not to say the other kinds of kisses were bad—those were the kinds of kisses you shared with the girls you'd always wanted to fuck.

For me, Aston was the girl who had *always* been everything. Which meant she was the girl I was going to kiss in as many different ways as I could conceive for as long as I could.

Lips sucked lazily as our tongues twisted around. My hands landed on her bare waist and maneuvered her back to the bed. When she sat on the edge, I stared down at her when she suddenly put a hand on the center of my chest and grabbed a handful of my T-shirt.

"What if I'm getting sick? I don't want to infect you." Her dark eyes were worried, but the way her hands held on to me told me she didn't really want to pump the brakes on whatever was about to happen.

"I have a strong immune system. I'll be fine." I smoothed my palm over her wet hair and pushed it away from her face. "But you should dry your hair. If you aren't sick, you will be, running around with wet hair."

Her mahogany eyebrows furrowed, and she started to tug the fabric clenched in her hand upward until my shirt was yanked over my head.

"I'll dry it after. I don't want to give you time to change your mind." Aston reached for the button on my jeans and started working on stripping the lower half of my body.

I tilted her head back so she was looking at me while her busy fingers worked on my zipper. I bit back a swear word when I felt her fingers brush against the underneath side of my cock. Even through the fabric of my underwear, the barely there caress felt like fire on my most sensitive spot.

"I won't change my mind. I can wait for...." The words trailed off when I felt her lips touch my stomach right above my now-bared belly button.

"No more waiting. I'm sick and tired of it." Aston's voice was firm, and so was her grip as her fingers wrapped around my erection.

Any argument I wanted to make flew out the window, along with my sanity, when the tip of her tongue darted out and licked across the tip of my cock.

My entire being tensed, and all my attention and awareness narrowed to the point where her mouth moved over my body. My abs locked, and my fingers tightened in her slippery hair. I wanted to close my eyes and toss my head back to savor the sensation, but I didn't even dare blink. I'd envisioned moments like this since I'd understood what sex was, and there was no way in hell I was going to miss a second of it.

Aston moved her mouth tentatively. It was cute and the total opposite of the way we'd devoured each other the previous time we were intimate with one another. I wouldn't call the way she worked me over shy, but there was an exploratory sweetness to her touch that made me feel like this was something she wanted to make sure she never forgot.

Her tongue licked and swirled around the length of my pulsing erection, and her fingertips skimmed over my skin and between my parted legs. Every time she exhaled, I felt tiny bumps of excitement scatter across my flesh. I was overly aroused. Not because my body had been deprived of this kind of attention for so long—though it had been—but more because it was Aston who had her head bent and was sucking me like it was the sole reason for her existence. Whatever was related to her, it affected me more deeply.

She'd always been my greatest weakness. Fortunately, the time we had spent apart taught me that being someone who was always strong, who refused to have anything or anyone in his life that made him soft and weak, was not the man I wanted to be. I didn't want to carry the struggles and shadows of the man I'd been while I was locked up with me forever. He would always be part of my past, but I was no longer willing to surrender my entire future to him.

I was much more interested in handing it over to the woman who was currently doing her best to shove my entire dick down her throat.

I chuckled because her struggle was honestly adorable. I pulled my hips back and shallowly thrust against her face and along the surface of her slippery tongue.

"You don't have to take the whole thing. Use your hands."

The last time we had been together, I had been so rough and unforgiving with her. I didn't want that to be her only impression of what it was like when we went to bed together. I could be sweet too.

Well, maybe not sweet. I'd been alone for five years after all, but I could handle her with more care than I'd previously shown her.

She took my advice and backed off a bit. One of her hands wrapped around the base of my cock and touched her lips each time I thrust toward her face. I was breathing hard and could feel pleasure coiling at the lowest point of my spine. My balls ached painfully, and my thoughts started to get fuzzy as the desire for release swirled throughout my brain. I knew I was going to come at any second and fought the urge to shove my cock as far into her mouth as it would go.

I curled my palms around the sides of her face and rubbed the pads of my thumbs along her hollowed-out cheeks. I could feel myself through the soft skin. It made my dick pulse even harder.

"I'm close."

I moved to pull away, but Aston pulled me closer.

I felt the tip of her tongue dip into the leaking slit at the head of my cock. The sensation forced my eyes closed and made my fingers dig into the sides of her head. She tilted her head back and took my erection as far back into her throat as she could. I gasped in pleasure when I felt the sensitive tip rub against her soft palate. And when one of her small hands snaked between my legs and touched the very sensitive spot that was already drawn up with excitement, I couldn't hold back anymore.

I moaned her name and pushed myself against her pretty face. It was a release that felt like it moved from my toes all the way through my body and out the top of my head. It was the type of orgasm that made my knees weak and stole my breath.

Belatedly, I realized I was supposed to be showing her that I could handle her with care and do more than blindly fuck her into oblivion. I was starting to understand that she was the one doing the handling whenever we ended up tangled up together.

Who was holding whom in the palm of their hand?

I used my thumb to rub away some of the cloudy liquid that hadn't made it when she swallowed everything down.

"I wanted to take my time with you, Aston. You keep making me forget I have good intentions."

She leaned back on the bed in an utterly provocative pose. "Unless you knew you were going to get lucky and made proper preparations, this was the only way to make you feel *my* good intentions." She offered a slight shrug, which looked sexy with the way she was lying with me still standing between her legs. "You might be calm and patient, Zowen, but I'm well past that point."

I lifted my eyebrows and moved so I was kneeling before her. Honestly, it was a position I'd imagined myself in a million times. Usually, I was begging her to see me, to recognize how much I loved her, to understand all the reasons I believed we should be together. I must admit, being on my knees for another reason was far superior.

I kissed the inside of her thigh and sucked on the soft skin until a red mark appeared. "If I make you wait again, I promise you'll like it."

And if she begged me to hurry, all the better.

I couldn't be the only one losing my mind and getting off in a heated rush.

I was the kind of guy who always returned what I received tenfold.

That was one thing she should—and would—remember about me without question.

chapter
TWELVE

Aston

I had a headache. I was still exhausted. All day, every day for the last two weeks, it had been a struggle to get through the day without needing a nap.

For the first week, I'd attributed the fatigue to the emotional upheaval in my life. My brother wasn't doing so hot. I knew he was trying to be strong for his mom, which meant the only time he allowed himself to be vulnerable and fall apart was when he talked to me.

My father was still in New York, but my mom had returned to Denver. She called and asked if she could visit me. I guiltily told her it wasn't a good time because of work. I loved my mother dearly, but she could be suffocatingly overprotective. I knew she was worried about how I was doing after the news about Kallie and wanted to see for herself how I was holding both myself and Royce up.

My parents didn't know I was practically living with Zowen Archer.

I hadn't figured out a way to tell them we'd reconnected after he was released from prison. Not that my parents held anything against Zowen. In fact, my father was very close to him. They bonded over their love of all things fast and dangerous. My mom was a trickier case. She had been really invested in my relationship with Ry. I thought she had been more heartbroken when I broke up with him than either he or I had been. Ry was a great guy, and his mom had saved my life when I was a baby. I thought my mother had idealized how safe and perfect my life would be in the future if I stayed with Ry. He was a low-risk/high-reward partner, and there was honestly nothing more my mom wanted for me. It felt like she'd forgotten that happiness and fulfillment needed to rank somewhere very high on the list.

Zowen wasn't as much of a knight in shining armor as Ry was.

He liked to race motorcycles. He knew how to hack secure internet systems. He never hesitated to follow after his sister regardless of the danger and uncertainty. And now, he was someone who had survived a prison sentence. He was never going to be someone my mother looked at as a good bet. She's always been leery of himf. Back in the day, when he had loved me silently and from afar, my mom had warned me not to take my eyes off the Archer in front of me. Now that I was older and wiser, I understood she had known if I looked away from Ry, I would end up staring at Zowen the exact same way he watched me.

"Did you catch that, Aston?"

I blinked at the sound of my name and turned my head to look at one of my coworkers. This meeting could've been an email, and I'd zoned out within the first five minutes.

I rubbed my temples and tried to think through the fog in my brain. "No. I'm sorry. I missed whatever it was that you just went over."

My coworker frowned and patiently repeated the key point the team was currently discussing. Luckily, an assistant stuck her head into the glass meeting room and informed me there was a client waiting. Cassio and his team were finally back stateside, so we'd agreed to meet up and talk about his stalker in person.

I excused myself and got up to walk to my office.

"Whoa …" I reached out and grabbed the back of the chair in front of me as my vision started to swirl and I got lightheaded.

I waved off the concern from my coworkers. I told them I had skipped breakfast and had a headache. I thought I'd better start taking better care of myself, just like Zowen kept telling me. I wouldn't be of any use to my brother—or the man I was trying to win over—if I ended up being the one who needed to be waited on hand and foot.

Cassio immediately climbed to his feet and approached me for a hug and air kisses. I ducked my head away from the very typical European greeting and patted him on the arm.

"I think I've got a lingering cold. I don't want to get you sick."

It was a miracle Zowen was still healthy as a horse, considering the frequency we had been exchanging bodily fluids these days. He kept saying I needed to go see a doctor since I wasn't feeling well, but I kept forgetting to make an appointment with everything else going on. I didn't want to add another worry to anyone's full plate. As long as I wasn't throwing up and didn't have a sky-high fever, I figured whatever I had would go away if I toughed it out.

"You look pale, *tesoro*. Is everything okay?"

I loved Cassio's accent. It wasn't terribly heavy since he had gone to a boarding school and attended college in the UK. It was somewhat undefined and a mix of all the different places he called home. He always sounded so suave and romantic. It suited his flirty and fun personality well.

I walked around my desk and plopped heavily into my chair. Instead of sitting across from me, he propped a hip on the corner of my desk and leaned down to look at me.

"What's wrong with you?"

I grabbed an abandoned bottle of water from earlier and chugged it. "I'm not feeling well. And I'm buried in work because I had to take some personal time for a family emergency. I'm fine. I'm just tired."

Cassio's eyes drifted to the picture I had on the shelf behind me. It was a picture of me and Royce from the last time my brother had visited. My older brother had one arm wrapped around my shoulders and the other around a surfboard. He was smiling and relaxed. He looked like someone without a care in the world—the total opposite of how he looked when I saw him on video chat now.

Cassio lifted an eyebrow and asked, "Is everything all right with your family? How is your brother?"

I rubbed the spot between my eyebrows and tilted my head to the side. "You do know that you ask me about Royce every time you come into this office, don't you?"

Cassio's gaze drifted away from the family pictures, and he offered a slight smirk. "And you know that you never give me a straight answer when I ask, don't you?"

"If you want to know how he's doing, give him a call. He could use a good friend at the moment. His mom is very sick, and her prognosis isn't good."

Cassio frowned and looked back at the picture behind me. "I think we said all that there was to say the last time he and I saw each other. I'm not someone he needs popping back into his life when he's in a vulnerable state of mind."

I sighed and pushed at his strong thigh to dislodge him from my desk. "You're both ridiculously stubborn. I wonder if either of you can even see how similar the two of you are."

Cassio snorted and obediently moved to sit across from me. "Any word on my stalker? Any other incidents since your car was damaged?"

"Nothing new. No strange people around my house or here at work. And the police aren't convinced it was your stalker who trashed my car. Apparently, there have been a lot of break-ins at office parking spots in the area. It might have been a coincidence." Part of me hoped so. Dealing with a deranged fangirl was the last thing I needed.

Cassio steepled his fingers under his beautifully chiseled jawline and lifted a raven-colored eyebrow at me. "Isn't that man you've been in love with your whole life some type of computer wizard? Can't you ask him to track her down? Can't he do something to make sure she's no longer an issue?"

I swore at him and threw the empty water bottle across the desk. "Shut up. Zowen isn't doing anything that might be legally questionable ever again. I refuse to let him be snatched away when I just got him back."

Cassio chuckled and gave me a teasing grin. "I would like to meet this man you are so protective of."

I frowned. "I don't know about that. I'm worried being around you might make him uncomfortable. You're living the life that might've been his if things had gone differently. You're so close to qualifying to move up to the MotoGP, and he never got the chance to try for something that huge. He's finally starting to let go of the past. I'm not sure whether you would help or hurt that effort."

"You can't hide him away from things that might make him uncomfortable forever, Aston. By doing that, you're the one holding on to the past, not him." He dropped his hands and leaned forward. "I actually want to meet him for business reasons. I want to recruit a technical director to my team once we officially go pro. I want someone who knows computers as well as bikes. The technology used in racing is no joke. I want someone familiar with every little advancement and can adapt to it." He gave me a pointed look. "Plus, Archer was very, very good on a bike back in the day. I wouldn't mind having him as a training partner."

I balked and narrowed my eyes at him. "He can barely tolerate riding in a car. I can't imagine him getting back on a bike or going anywhere near a race."

Cassio snorted, as if in disbelief. "No one as good as he was—is—walks away entirely unless they're forced to. I have a feeling that, given the right opportunity, your man might be willing to do a lot of things he swore he would never do again."

I couldn't argue against his point. After all, I was one of the things Zowen was currently doing because the opportunity was finally right.

I purposely changed the subject and got down to work. I asked him to put me in touch with his contact person at several of his sponsors and agreed to work on a plan for the next qualifying race. Each event was bigger than the one before because he was moving closer and closer to the professional circuit. We also had to be careful because it was unknown when and where the stalker might pop up. Something like that could be a media disaster if not handled correctly. It would be very easy for people on the outside, looking in, to label Cassio as the bad guy because his reputation as a Lothario was well known.

After the official work was handled, Cassio offered to take me to dinner. I declined because my head was still killing me, and I was so tired that I could hardly see straight. I just wanted to go home and crawl into bed. Preferably with a puppy and an Archer.

As I approached the elevator to the parking garage, my phone rang. Seeing it was Zowen calling, I juggled my purse and laptop while struggling to answer the call. I scowled at the *Out of Order* sign taped on the front of the elevator doors and shot a resentful look toward the stairs.

After heaving a deep sigh into the phone, I heard Zowen ask what was wrong.

"The elevator is out. I have to take the stairs down to where I parked. Not a big deal. I'm just tired." I pushed open the door and entered the quiet stairwell. It was creepily vacant, and every step I took echoed.

"You're still not feeling well?" Zowen's voice was sharp. "I'm taking you to the doctor when you get home."

I shook my head even though he couldn't see me. "I don't think I need to see a doctor. It's only a bug."

I reached the next landing and looked down the flight of stairs. The light above my head flickered, like something had moved past it.

I frowned while glancing over my shoulder and absently muttered, "I should've made Cassio walk me out before he left."

Zowen went quiet on the other side of the call until he stiffly asked, "The racer is back in the States?"

"He is. He aced qualifying and is onto the next race." I pondered Cassio's words about Zowen while watching the steps under my feet. I had five more levels to go before I reached the parking garage. "He actually mentioned you during the meeting. He's familiar with how you used to ride and seemed a bit like a fan."

Zowen grunted, not impressed at all.

I laughed as I stumbled a bit on the next step and swore as I regained my balance. "I actually think you would like Cassio. You have a lot in common, and he's a nice guy."

Zowen grunted again and mumbled something under his breath that I didn't catch. I was about to ask him if he wanted me to bring something home for dinner when the light flashed again. I suddenly heard the sound of heavy breathing and fast-moving footsteps behind me.

I turned my head to see what was going on when I felt a force press against the center of my back. Since my hands were full and I was on the edge of a step, the momentum of the push immediately sent me flying forward. My phone went in one direction, my laptop and purse in another. I screamed, but it was cut off when I smacked into the next landing. My head bounced off the ground, and my hand bent at an unnatural angle as I tried to catch myself before smashing my face into the concrete. I vaguely heard footsteps rushing back up the stairs. There was blood dripping down my forehead, and my ears were ringing so loudly that I couldn't think.

I sucked in a deep breath and tried to pick myself up, but pain immediately shot throughout my body. I closed my eyes and waited for the dizziness to subside. The call must've stayed connected even though my phone was nowhere to be seen. I could hear Zowen calling my name through the jangle that was making it hard for me to think.

The blood on my face was obscuring my vision and dripping off my chin. I could tell my head had taken the biggest hit, and my forehead was more than likely split open. I wasn't sure how bad the overall damage was, but I didn't think anything life-threatening was going on.

I attempted to call out to Zowen. Only any direction I moved, my pounding head caused an immediate surge of bile to rise in my throat. I had to pause for a minute before I could do anything to help myself.

In hindsight, that *Out of Order* sign on the elevator should've been a clue something was wrong. As long as I'd worked in that building, there was never a handwritten sign taped up anywhere. That didn't fit the upscale aesthetic of the building. Someone had wanted to force people—more than likely me or Cassio specifically—into the stairwell.

Time lost all meaning as I waited for the pain and fuzziness to subside. Fortunately, Zowen was no dummy. Right when I was about to close my eyes and pass out, one of the security guards from the building came running down the closest flight of stairs. He looked alarmed when he saw my condition and didn't hesitate to call 911. In the haze of discomfort surrounding me, I made sure to ask him to preserve any surveillance evidence of the stairwell. It could no longer be called coincidental that bad things kept happening to me while my biggest client was dealing with a possessive stalker. The security guard collected my belongings for me, and I texted Zowen to let him know the paramedics who had arrived were taking me to the closest ER. The screen was shattered, so seeing what I sent was impossible, and there was no chance to read whatever he sent back.

The paramedics moved fast. One was an older woman who was very nice, and the other was a younger guy who was no-nonsense. They strapped me to a gurney and fired off a bunch of questions while checking my vitals. The older woman frowned when she wiggled a flashlight in front of my eyes, and she muttered under her breath as she prodded the gash on my head, which was steadily bleeding.

I was coherent enough to respond to every question. However, when the younger paramedic asked me if there was any chance I might be pregnant, I went cold all over and forgot how to speak.

With all the upheaval in my life lately, I'd let a lot of things slip by. Starting with having to wait longer than recommended to take care of the aftereffects of a broken condom. Including the fact that my period was most definitely late.

I wanted to chalk the constant fatigue up to an illness or excessive stress, but when faced with the mounting evidence, the only response I could give the expectant first responder was, "There *is* a slight possibility I could be pregnant."

Holy shit.

I might be pregnant.

chapter
THIRTEEN

Zowen

"She's in with a couple of detectives. You'll have to wait before you can see her."

I looked at the man who was guarding Aston's hospital room. He was a head shorter than me and looked light as a feather. He had an accent when he spoke, but his gaze was fiercely protective as he crossed his arms over his chest and blocked the doorway. He didn't bother to introduce himself. Tshere was no need. I knew who he was without a greeting, and the same seemed to go for him.

We sized each other up until the smaller man relented with a sigh.

"Aston has a sprained wrist and a concussion. She got a nasty cut on her forehead that needed attention. She saw a slew of doctors and had an MRI done before the police showed up. She's in a lot of pain but otherwise fine. She's very lucky her injuries are minor."

I glared at the racer, annoyed he'd beaten me to the hospital and because Aston wouldn't have been hurt if it wasn't for his interest in her.

"This was your stalker's handiwork?" It was a question, but I said it more like a statement.

Who else could have it in for Aston? The girl didn't have an enemy in the world.

The dark-haired man dipped his chin slightly, his gaze shifting toward anger. "More than likely. That person has been making threats and harassing all the women in my life. The security team at Aston's workplace have already handed over the surveillance from the stairwell. Hopefully, the stalker will have a face and name soon." He sighed. "I told Aston she had to be careful during our initial meeting about this deranged person. She shouldn't have been in the stairwell alone."

I grunted and copied his pose, crossing my arms over my chest. "She wouldn't have been a target if you weren't close to her. Your stalker wouldn't have even known what Aston looked like if you hadn't put her picture on your social media." I glared at him, anger radiating off of my body in heated waves. "This wouldn't be an issue if you behaved in a more professional manner."

Cassio snorted and rolled his dark and expressive eyes. "She's pretty. I like pretty things. That's why I posted a picture of her." His eyebrows furrowed. "For the record, Aston and I are friends. We were close long before I hired her to work for my team."

I stiffened and took a step forward, unintentionally trying to intimidate the other man. "She might be your friend, but she's my *everything*." There was a big difference.

Cassio snorted again. This time, there was a hint of laughter in the sound. "Jealous? You shouldn't be. Aston isn't my type. I love her like a little sister. There isn't anything romantic between the two of us. There never has been."

I blinked in surprise. I hadn't been prepared for his blunt denial of anything going on between him and Aston. I'd perceived him as the biggest threat to our burgeoning relationship, and to have that complication removed so effortlessly left me a bit dumbfounded. Our road had never been this clear and easy to travel, and it threw me off just a bit.

"How do you know each other if it's not through work?"

Cassio finally relaxed his stance and dropped his arms to his sides. "We know each other through Royce."

The smaller man sighed dramatically, and his expression shifted to one I was all too familiar with. It was the face of a man desperately in love with someone who didn't return the sentiment.

"When Royce was studying in Italy, he and I had a brief situationship. I met Aston while she was visiting him. Her brother and I lost touch, but Aston always made sure to keep tabs on me. She's a sweet girl, and I've enjoyed watching her grow up and come into her own."

He sniffed and gave me a pointed look. "Do you know that Aston never complained about having to wait for you to be released from prison? Not once. She told me that she made you wait for her for far longer than five years. She saw giving up a significant portion of her youth as something she owed to you. She's worked tirelessly to prove she can stand on her own two feet. To show everyone she doesn't need to be coddled and handled with kid gloves. She desperately wants you to see her as someone you can rely on, as someone who can take care of you. I hope you end up being worth the work and wait. If you're not ..." He trailed off and gave me a haughty look down his nose. "I'm happy to introduce her to any number of single, successful men in my field. You should know better than most how rare it is to find a partner who understands not only the mechanics of motorcycles and racing, but also the passion needed to compete."

I opened my mouth to retort, but never got the chance to get any words out. A young Hispanic woman and an older African American gentleman exited the hospital room. Both Cassio and I stepped aside as the two spoke to one another. One was tapping on a cell phone, and the other was pensively muttering about the insanity of modern fandoms.

The young woman pulled Cassio aside to speak about the stalker while I pushed into the hospital room without a backward glance.

Aston was propped up in the bed. She had an IV in the back of the hand that wasn't injured and a bandage on her forehead. She was alarmingly pale, and the worry in her dark eyes was easy to read. She bit her bottom lip when she saw me enter the room, and I could see tears start to gather in her eyes.

I hurried over to the bed and put a hand on the top of her head. Her hair felt dirty and sticky from all she'd been through that evening.

"You're okay. Don't cry. Everything will be fine."

I wanted to kiss her. I wanted to hold her. She seemed so fragile and unsure at the moment; it was heartbreaking.

"I'm sorry I wasn't here sooner."

If this incident had taught me anything, it was that I needed to get over my aversion to driving and being in a vehicle as soon as humanly possible. While I had been on the way to the hospital, I'd found myself longing for the days I could zip through traffic and weave in and out of a gridlock on my bike. I resented being a passenger and leaving my fate up to someone else. The fact that Cassio had beaten me to the hospital was another tick in the get-over-myself box. I didn't want anyone else to get to Aston before me when she was in danger or needed help.

Aston rocked her head to the side, like she was getting ready to shake it. However, even the bare minimum of movement caused her to gasp in pain. The fingers of her good hand tightened into a fist, and the tears started to fall.

"I'm so stupid. I should've known better. I don't know why I blindly believed some dumb, random sign taped on the elevator. If the fall had been worse ..." Her voice drifted off, and I noticed she curled in on herself and put her injured arm protectively across the middle of her body. "Zowen, we need to talk about something."

She sounded equally scared and serious.

I smoothed my hand over her hair and told her, "Sure. We can talk about whatever you want. I think it can wait until you're feeling better though."

She was already under the weather, and now, she had a concussion on top of that. There was no way she was up to the kind of come-to-Jesus conversation we needed to have about our ambiguous relationship and undefined future.

Aston sighed and lifted her watery eyes up to mine. "No. It really can't wait. We need to have a conversation right now. I'm—"

She was cut off as the hospital door opened, and a young nurse dressed in cartoon scrubs walked into the room. The new arrival offered a cheery smile while looking over Aston and then the information on her medical chart.

"Good evening. I'm Luna. I'm here to move you to the obstetrics department. We're going to do an exam and make sure everything is okay. Then, I'll bring you back to this room. I know the attending physician wants to keep you overnight for observation because of the concussion. Do you have any questions or concerns?"

The nurse appeared to belatedly realize Aston wasn't alone in the room even though I'd been standing next to her the entire time. "Oh. You can wait here for her. We won't be gone long."

She gave Aston a look. "Unless you would like him to come with you."

Aston made a choking sound as our eyes locked. "No. I can go by myself, but can you give us a minute? The detectives just left, and I haven't had a chance to fill him in on what's happening yet."

The nurse looked at her smartwatch and then back at the chart. "Sure. I'll be back in ten minutes."

She turned and left the room, leaving me and Aston in a heavy silence.

We both started talking at the same time.

"Obstetrics is the department that deals with pregnant women, isn't it?"

"Zowen, I'm pregnant."

The words smashed together and mingled. Regardless of us both being in a rush to speak, the word *pregnant* was impossible to ignore or mishear. I looked at the bandaged arm Aston was using to protect her stomach.

I'd been referred to as a genius and prodigy for most of my life. However, I felt like the most ignorant man alive right now.

The broken condom.

The delay in precautions.

Aston not feeling well and being tired all the time.

The signs had been right in front of my face, and other than mild concern the night of the incident, I'd never stopped to think we might've made a baby.

"You're pregnant?" I sounded like a broken record.

Aston tilted her chin down in a barely perceptible nod. "I'm pregnant. I just found out tonight. When the paramedics asked me if it was a possibility, I started adding all the symptoms and signs together. They did a pregnancy test when they were checking everything else out. I have to see an obstetrician to make sure the fall didn't hurt the baby. I'm so sorry to spring this on you all of a sudden."

She exhaled, and I watched her brace herself like she was getting ready to ride into battle.

"I never intended to use sex to trap you into being with me. I wasn't ever going to use your gratitude or even the fondness you used to have for me. I wanted you to choose to be with me because you could see how much I care about you. I wanted you to notice that I'm a different person than I was when we were younger. I hope it was obvious—that I finally figured out what *I* wanted. I'd stopped making choices I thought would make my parents happy the minute I moved to California. It took me longer than I want to admit to realize I had screwed up so much of my youth and would've chosen you all along if I had been more aware of what I was doing and the type of woman I wanted to be back then." Her gaze shifted into defiance. "I wish we could've learned about the baby a different way, but I refuse to feel bad that you and I created something so unbelievable together."

I touched her head again and struggled to get my bearings.

Of all the things I'd planned on happening once I was released from prison, having a baby was nowhere on the list. I'd only just recently stopped thinking of myself as a killer. It was a huge shift in gears to start thinking of myself as a father. It didn't take a genius to read between the lines of Aston's profound speech. Even if I decided I wanted nothing to do with her or the baby and didn't stick around, she was going to protect the little life growing inside of her.

It was such an Aston thing to do.

"I know what it feels like to be trapped in a situation you can't get out of, Aston. This is not like that. I think you should know me well enough to not even question whether or not I'm willing to take responsibility. You weren't alone that night. I was there every step of the way. I won't make you walk alone any longer. Okay?"

I dropped a kiss on the top of her head and carefully picked up her uninjured hand. "We'll figure this out. We just have to take things one day at a time. And right now, you and the baby need to get checked out to make sure you're both healthy."

She quietly agreed, and I could see her lower some of her mental armor. Her shoulders relaxed; her chest shuddered as she exhaled. If I was stunned to find out I was facing impending parenthood, I couldn't imagine how blindsided Aston had felt. She already had so much on her plate and was juggling the emotional turmoil of everyone around her. She probably hadn't allowed herself the time needed to process the life-altering changes that were about to take place.

"I already told you that I've *only* ever loved you, Aston. It doesn't matter if I wasn't your first choice when we were kids. What I care about is being the *right* choice for you from here on out."

I'd felt like I was the absolute worst choice anyone could make up until recently. She was one of the main reasons I'd realized that if someone loved you at your worst, they really deserved to have you at your very best. And now that I had a new lease on life and the chance to start over, my very best was yet to come.

The nurse came into the room, followed by a few other staff members dressed in scrubs. They asked Aston a bunch of questions and worked as a team to wheel her out of the room. She kept her eyes on me until the last possible second. I nodded to her to let her know I wasn't going anywhere and would be right here when she got back.

I let out a long breath and dragged my fingers through my hair. I wasn't surprised to see that they were unsteady. I had a million thoughts a minute racing through my mind, but I kept landing on the fact that I was going to have a baby.

A baby with Aston Wheeler.

If I'd really believed that serving my time in prison was paying penance and trying to do right by the universe, I would take this as a sign I was forgiven and could begin again. It felt like I shouldn't be allowed to be a part of something so monumental and magical.

"She's fine, Royce. The Archer she's obsessed with is here and watching over her like a hawk. If you want more information, you can talk to him." Cassio looked incredibly irritated as he spoke into the phone.

"Yes, I am well aware I'm at fault for putting Aston in the line of fire with my stalker. Of course, I'll take care of the medical expenses and hire whatever type of security is needed. Stop acting like I wanted this to happen just for an excuse to call you. I'm not that lonely or desperate." The man paused and hissed out a breath through his clenched teeth.

"I'm not going to argue with you. I only wanted to let you know Aston was injured and to tell you I'm sorry to hear about what is happening with your mother. It shouldn't surprise me that you still manage to hear only what you want to hear. You have not changed one bit in all these years, *amore mio*. That is such a shame."

He hung up the phone decisively a second later and took a minute to compose himself. He appeared visibly shaken after the phone call.

I lifted an eyebrow with curiosity. I wasn't very close to Royce, but I'd always known him to be a laid-back and easygoing kind of guy. He had a very artistic temperament, which was very different from mine. I knew he was under a tremendous amount of pressure because of his mother's health, but I was surprised by the clear contention and hostility between him and the racer.

"Everything all right?"

I hadn't planned on liking the man I thought I was competing with for Aston's affection. He didn't seem so bad now that I knew it was her brother he was interested in.

Cassio flashed a lopsided grin and tucked the phone away in his pocket. "Matters of the heart are always complicated, aren't they? Did they take Aston for more tests?"

"They did. They're keeping her overnight. I'm going to stay with her as long as they let me." I frowned and considered the other man carefully. "Aston has a puppy at home. Are you close enough friends that you can go take care of it until I get back to the house?"

I figured it wasn't my place to tell anyone about the baby. I was pretty ignorant of all things having to do with pregnancy since I'd been away while Remy was knocked up. I did know that there was usually a waiting period before letting friends and family in on the good news. Besides, she and I needed to adjust to the changes and discuss our relationship before bringing anyone else in on the matter.

The Italian man waved a hand and assured me, "Of course. I even have a key. I can take care of the puppy for her, no problem. Anything else you need me to do?"

I thought about it for a moment and told him, "If you don't mind, have someone from your team send me everything you have on the stalker. I can get into places the police can't to look for them" I could track them down faster than anyone else if I had the right information. "And don't worry about setting up security. I'll ask my big boss to get something in place. Whoever he has on his payroll will be more effective than anyone you hire."

Since my release, I had been determined to keep my nose clean and to stay away from anything that could be considered morally questionable.

Now that I had Aston and our child to protect, all my righteousness went out the window. The regular rules no longer applied.

I would do whatever it took and walk however far into the darkness I needed to in order to keep them safe.

FOURTEEN

Aston

"Don't tell my mom what happened." I gave the order to Daire like she would ever listen when someone told her to do something as I leaned on the edge of the tub. I was careful to keep my still-bandaged wrist out of the tepid water and glared at the video image of my best friend on my phone screen. "Royce already promised to keep this quiet until I'm ready to talk to my parents."

Daire sighed heavily and rolled her expressive eyes. "I won't say anything ... unless someone asks. When your life is in danger, I think the people who care about you have a right to know. It's not fair to keep them in the dark."

"I know that." I blew a soggy piece of hair out of my face. "I'm not going to keep it a secret forever. Right now, I think it's best that their attention is on my brother and what he needs. I have Zowen here and you and Campbell. Royce is alone." I raised my eyebrows and tried to look as confident as a grown woman in a lukewarm bath could.

I had been all set to take a warm *bubble* bath and relax, but Zowen vetoed the idea after googling if it was safe or not. Sometimes, his need to know everything was very annoying. It never occurred to me that a bubble bath would be on the list of things an expectant mother needed to avoid. And I'd made no secret that I would settle for a regular bath, but I wasn't happy about it. I missed the bubbles.

"I'm sure this whole stalker situation will be under control in no time now that the police are actively involved."

Daire snorted. "And so is Zowen. Don't think for a single second that I don't know he's done a deep dive into the darkest parts of the web, looking for this girl. He even asked Campbell if he knew anyone who could help find her." She shook her head and made a tsk sound. "If he's willing to use the kind of resources Campbell has access to, he's not playing around."

Daire didn't know about the baby. No one did. Zowen and I decided to wait until some of the danger surrounding me subsided. It would take parental concern to a whole new level if my parents were worrying about me and their unborn grandchild at the same time. Daire would also turn into an unbearable kind of paranoid and persnickety monster if she knew how drastically the situation between her cousin and me had changed.

"Zowen's taking extra precautions, and he's mostly moved into the main house. I feel like someone is always watching me. Not in a bad way though. I don't think the woman stalking Cassio can evade being caught for much longer."

Daire grumbled, "I heard she's from a very wealthy family in the UK. That's why she's been so hard to pin down. When there's a lot of money involved, it makes things a hundred times more difficult. Ask Zowen what it's like to tangle with the ultra-rich."

I didn't need to ask. I was the one who had waited for him after he was taken away because a wealthy brat had decided to rig a motorcycle race.

"I believe everything will be fine. I'm extra cautious these days. No more acting like I'm a main character in a book who is too stupid to live to the end."

I heard Campbell call Daire's name somewhere out of the screen of the video call. She answered him over her shoulder and turned back to tell me she had to go.

Before she disconnected, she wrinkled her nose and ordered, "Your hair looks gross. Make Zowen help you wash it."

If I'd had two functional hands, I would've flipped her off. "I can't get the spot where they taped the gash shut wet." So, I'd been using my weight in dry shampoo and having Zowen help me with what amounted to a birdbath to keep clean the last week.

"My cousin is very smart. I'm sure he can figure out a way to help you wash it and not get that spot wet."

I told her I would talk to her later and ended the call. I rested my chin on the edge of the tub and pouted in frustration. Now that Daire had mentioned it, my scalp felt tight and itchy. I dropped my phone to the padded bath mat and poked around the injured spot high on my forehead with a fingertip.

It'd been a little over a week since I had nearly been killed and discovered I was pregnant, all on the same day. I had to make a huge mental adjustment to come to terms with both. Fortunately, the baby and I both had gotten a clean bill of health after the concerns around the concussion subsided. Now, I was focusing on the future and moving forward as a *we* instead of a *me*. Of course, the *we* included Zowen, who had insisted he was sticking by my side, no matter what we might face. But I was still worried about him feeling trapped and stuck in a situation he hadn't asked for. While I wanted to believe him when he told me he very much wanted to be with me, I kept some reservations. I felt like he hadn't really gotten the chance to know who I was now that I was grown up and living for myself. What if he hated me when he realized I wasn't the version of Aston he always loved before? He kept telling me I was the *only* person he knew how to love. However, I knew I was no longer the same girl he had initially been so devoted to. I kept my concerns mostly to myself because I didn't want to invalidate Zowen's feelings.

I figured time would tell.

It was the great equalizer between me and him.

This was the first time since we'd been in each other's lives that time was on our side.

The bathroom door opened while I was lost in thought. Zowen stepped into the small space, dressed in sweatpants that were cutoff into shorts and a white tank top. I recognized it as his workout outfit. He must've just come back from a run or finished lifting the free weights he kept in the guest cottage. Zowen flashed a grin in my direction as he triumphantly held up something that looked like a bar of soap.

"It's a shampoo bar. I think we can wash your hair with it and avoid getting soap and water near the Steri-Strips. Figured it was worth a try."

I sat back in the tub and sent the cooling water sloshing. "Let's give it a shot. My scalp feels like ants are crawling all over it." I pointed a finger at him when he moved closer. "No making fun of how dirty the water is when you rinse it."

He chuckled lightly and lowered himself to the rim of the tub. "I'm pretty sure we got most of the blood and grime out already. It feels gross because you're used to washing it all the time."

I turned around and leaned my head back so he could take the cup that was sitting on the ledge and wet my long hair. Once the long strands were damp and he set down the cup and worked his way through the dark strands with the suds from the shampoo bar. I closed my eyes and nearly purred as he massaged my scalp. I could get used to this kind of treatment if he was planning on pampering me until I was on the mend. Or maybe he was going to handle me like I might break throughout my pregnancy. It wouldn't be too far-fetched. When we had been young, he'd often look at me like I might shatter at any given moment.

I sighed in contentment and whispered, "This feels great."

His thumbs circled along my temples and dipped down to tug on my earlobes as he rinsed everything with light movements, being careful to avoid my injury. "Your hair is still soft. It looks a lot darker when it's wet. All the red is hidden." When he was done washing my hair shifted so his lips could touch the curve of my shoulder. "It's fitting. You had a fire hidden inside of you I never noticed."

I lifted my good arm so I could curl it around the back of his head. My fingers toyed with the ends of his hair, which he still hadn't gotten around to getting cut. I was starting to grow quite fond of this new version of him.

"I had to find it for myself. It had silently been smoldering for a long time. I never let it spark to life because I was worried about how it would affect my family." I caressed his nape and let a lot of memories roll down my back.

"My parents are wonderful. I couldn't have asked for a better upbringing. I owe them everything, but it wasn't always easy, being their daughter." I let his big hands soothe me.

"My mom had a horrible childhood. Her meeting and falling in love with my dad was kind of a miracle. And I was her rainbow baby. When I was born so ill, it was extraordinarily hard for her. She's always treated me like I'm one step away from the end of everything. If there is such a thing as being loved too much, that's what my life is like.

"I didn't know how to be anything other than pampered and protected. She was always so worried about me; I did everything in my power to make sure she didn't have to be concerned. My days were a copy and paste of each other. Every choice I made was safe and made with my mother's ever-growing paranoia in mind. I didn't even recognize I had no space for myself. That's why I had to leave Denver. And why I had to leave Ry."

Because I wasn't facing Zowen, it was a lot easier to talk about the past. It was a subject we both tactfully avoided. However, there were still some sore points I felt we needed to clear up.

"It's not that I didn't love him. I did." I felt the man behind me stiffen, so I dug my fingers into the back of his neck to prevent him from pulling away. "It wasn't the kind of love you're supposed to have with the person you want to give forever to. I loved him because he was kind to me. I loved him because he listened to me and understood how hard things were at home for me. I loved him because my parents liked him so much and because he was my best friend's older brother. I loved Ry because he was the safest choice a teenage girl could make for her first boyfriend. He never pressured me. We hardly ever fought. He wanted to be perfect in his parents' eyes almost as badly as I did. All our broken pieces fit together." I laughed. "I knew he was in love with Bowe. And he knew there was someone better for me."

"You're telling me that Ry knew I was in love with you, and he dated you anyway?"

I could hear a trace of anger simmering in Zowen's voice.

"No. I don't think he knew exactly what you were feeling. He's a man, and he's not the genius in the family. Plus, he's single-minded. He tends to see only what's in front of him, which is why he and Bowe are such a good match. She's the same way. What I think he knew was that I wasn't very happy and there was nothing he could do about it. I think he understood, both now and then, that I needed to figure out what I wanted for myself. Once I did that, I would be happy, and I could find someone who was in love with the *real* me."

I let go of his neck and turned around, water sloshing everywhere. The raw hem of Zowen's shorts got damp, and he lost his light massage motion as I leaned toward him. I grabbed the front of his tank top and tugged until our noses almost touched.

"You make me happy, Zowen. You always have. I wasn't brave enough to do anything about it back then, but now ..."

I pulled until his entire body fell into the water with me. Zowen was not a small man, so obviously, he'd relented and let me tug him into the tub. There was no escaping the water going everywhere, and I belatedly sent out a prayer that my brand-new phone was out of the splash zone.

"The life I've built, the happiness I've found, those things are all mine. But I want to share them with you. I didn't get to this point all on my own. Even when you were gone, even when you were pretending like we didn't know each other, I kept moving in this direction because I knew this was where I wanted to end up. I want to be right here with you, Zowen."

I mean, the baby hadn't exactly been part of my plan. At least not this early in my efforts to show him I could love him the same way he loved me. Aside from that, I considered our reunion a smashing success.

Zowen struggled out of his wet shirt and wiggled around until I was sitting on his lap. I was suddenly aware of just how exposed and vulnerable I was.

He lifted a wet hand and rubbed it across my cheek-bone. There was still an ugly bruise covering half of my face, which made his eyebrows furrow.

"It's been a long time since I allowed myself to be happy. I honestly didn't know if I would recognize that feeling anymore." His fingertips moved to trace over the arch in my eyebrow, and the other arm wrapped around my waist. His hand splayed across the small of my back. "When I look at you, I feel what I remember happiness feeling like. And when you told me you were having my baby, I felt something bigger than happiness. I can't even explain it." He pressed the lightest kiss against my lips. "I do know that no one else in the world makes me feel the way you do, Aston. It's *always* been that way."

I kissed him.

Because I could.

Because I always wanted to.

Because it felt good.

And because it made me happy. So fucking happy. I'd waited a very long time so I could kiss him whenever and wherever I wanted.

Zowen pulled me closer and dropped a series of kisses across my chest. He was very careful with the way he held me, keeping my various bumps and bruises in mind. The tepid water didn't appear to bother him as he pulled one of my puckered nipples into the warmth of his mouth. I felt him tug on the pointed tip with the edge of his teeth as his other hand skimmed up and down my spine. I rubbed against the hardness I could feel under the thin material of his cutoffs and heard him groan against my skin. I urged him to lift up so we could maneuver out of the remainder of his wet garments. By the time it was all said and done, there was going to be more water on the bathroom floor than inside the tub.

Zowen placed my bandaged wrist around his neck and ordered, "Leave it there. Don't get it wet."

I hummed an agreement and pressed closer to his mouth. Even though the water surrounding us was dropping in temperature, he was still as hot as an inferno. I clasped the back of his head with my good hand and moved my hips so I could rub against his thickening erection. I could feel the arrowed tip drag and slide through my tender folds. Maybe it was all in my head, or maybe it was hormones, but everywhere we touched felt extra sensitive and responsive. My head was already spinning, and my nerves felt electrified.

Zowen used his tongue to trace a line to my other breast. I wondered if I tasted like the suds left in the bath. If so, it didn't seem to bother him. He nipped at the other nipple and moved one of his hands so that it was under the water and between my legs. His fingertips danced across my opening, and then his thumb of his other hand pressed down the head of his cock so just the tip was inside of me. It was a tortuous tease as he moved his fingers to play with my clit. He sucked hard on the pointed peak in his mouth, which made me gasp his name. I tossed my head back, and my hair slithered across my skin. The sensation made me shiver. Zowen pulled me closer as a result. It felt like there was no part of me that wasn't touching some part of him.

This was exactly where I wanted to be, where I couldn't tell where he started and I ended.

His fingers played with my clit as he pushed fully inside of me. I gasped and lowered my head so I could look at him. His blue eye was on fire, and the dark brown one looked like it held all his secrets ands and forbidden promises. His duality was beautiful, and I could easily picture a miniature version of him with a familiar kaleidoscope gaze.

We moved together, and Zowen kissed his way up along the column of my neck. His teeth bit into my earlobe, and his tongue swirled around the shell of my ear. My heart rate kicked into overdrive, and my insides started to flutter in anticipation.

Regardless of how fast and urgent I rose on top of him, Zowen kept the pace slow and steady. He was driving me out of my mind. We were grinding and rocking against each other as if we had all the time in the world. He played my body like an instrument, pushing and pulling in all the right places.

I could feel his breath quicken and his cock throb in time with it. He felt impossibly big, and I'd never felt so full. Both in body and spirit.

Zowen muttered that he was close as his hand tightened on my breast. His thumb circled my nipple, which was still tingling from the attention of his mouth, and the fingers of his other hand dug into one of my ass cheeks.

He finally let me move. There was no more gentle rocking. Now, he was urging me to ride up and down like his dick was an amusement park.

He tilted his head back so I could kiss him, and I nearly lost my mind when he used his tongue to mimic the motion of our bodies. Everything was hot and wet. I couldn't recall a point in time when I'd ever felt better.

Now that I was pregnant, we didn't have to be concerned about birth control. Not like taking precautions had done us any favors anyway.

Zowen came with a low groan and sent a final wave of water to the floor.

It took me a little longer to reach my completion, but Zowen kept his fingers and mouth busy until he felt my body clench around his. I collapsed on his lap and rested my forehead against his. He wrapped his arms around me in what was probably my favorite hug I'd ever received.

"Maybe when I first fell in love with you, it was because I saw you as someone who needed to be protected. I was used to taking on the role of saving someone because of Remy. It was a type of love that felt familiar to me." Zowen rubbed our noses together in a sweet move that felt completely out of character for the man who had shown up on my doorstep freshly out of prison but was just right for the guy I was going to have a baby with. "What I feel for you now is unknown. It's intense and scary. It feels more powerful than anything I've ever felt before. And since it's you who makes me feel the most, my best guess is that this is what love should've felt like all along. I've always been a smart man. But there is something about you, Aston, that makes me feel like I know nothing. I have so much to learn. I can't wait for you to teach me."

We shared another kiss, and I told him, "We're both about to get a whole new world of education together."

Neither one of us knew the first thing about being a parent. We were going to have to tackle every new experience and challenge together to be an effective team. Any knowledge gained was something we were going to have to share.

I couldn't wait. The last thing that had made me this excited was the day Zowen came home.

chapter
FIFTEEN

Zowen

"One of the first things I figured out when I was in prison is that you aren't allowed to be afraid. Nothing should scare you. And anyone who shows even a hint of fear is considered inferior. They were automatically viewed as weak and would more than likely end up the victim of any number of awful, inhumane acts. When I told you I forgot what happiness felt like, I wasn't exaggerating. I forced myself to stop feeling a lot of things the first year I was locked up."

I cast a glance at Aston, who was sitting in the passenger seat of the Bronco. My hands shook when I took the keys from her and offered to drive up to the beach now that I had my license back. Getting over my hang-up relating to being in and around any type of vehicle was a big step in the opposite direction from the past that I'd let myself get trapped in. There was more than one type of freedom I'd surrendered in the name of trying to do the right thing.

"When I got out, I channeled all the anxiety and apprehension I'd suppressed for so long into irrelevant things like driving." And being around the people I loved.

There was so much terror breaking loose; it had to find somewhere to go. All that unleashed fear had also been a factor in why I was so hesitant to help defend myself when I was first released. I could finally admit I was beyond terrified that if I pointed out I wasn't the only one at fault the night of the accident, no one would believe me.

The Bronco really was like driving a tank. It felt solid and indestructible even though it was missing the top. I was driving below the speed limit, much to the annoyance of everyone else on the road, and meticulously following every traffic law. It felt like I was learning to drive all over again, but by the time I could smell the ocean in the air, my hands stopped shaking, and my heart rate returned to normal. This ride, I appreciated the sun on my skin and the warm breeze blowing through my hair. If it wasn't for the dark sedan following us—a silent reminder that an unknown danger was still lurking about—it would've been an ideal afternoon date.

Aston had her wavy hair pulled up in a high ponytail, but the wind whipping through the Bronco pulled pieces loose, and they flew around her face. She had dark sunglasses on, and she was wearing a pretty floral sundress. Looking at her made my mouth dry. She was my teenage fantasy, all grown up.

Even with a threat looming and the complications in her family, she was still more carefree and confident than I remembered her being. Her independence was sexy. So was the way she let herself need me in rare moments. Like when she was hurting and afraid. I was glad she allowed herself to lean on me. I really appreciated that I could lean on her. She had shown me her perseverance when she took me in with no questions asked. I also watched her be an unbendable source of strength for her older brother while he navigated what was inevitably the hardest situation he'd had to face. The Aston from our youth would have never been able to withstand the emotional weight of everything she was currently carrying. I found myself being impressed by her more and more, the longer we were together.

"I want to face everything I'm afraid of. I don't want to let the things that scare me get the better of me." I almost shouted the words to be heard over the wind.

Fortunately, the beach was close, and we could park and then have a normal conversation.

Aston waited until the Bronco was stationary and we were staring at the endless ocean before she responded. "I'd much rather you have a fear of driving than other things."

She turned her head to look at me. I reached out and lifted her sunglasses to the top of her head because it bugged me that I couldn't see her eyes.

She picked a loose strand of hair out of her mouth and gave me a bright grin. "You barely blinked when I told you we were going to have a baby. You have a right to be terrified of what's waiting for us."

I tugged on the end of her ponytail and sat back in the seat of the Bronco. "There are things about the future I'm afraid of. For example, I don't know what's going to happen with the civil trial. I might be broke and unemployable for the rest of my adult life. And we've never talked about where we're going to live. Your life is here; mine is in Denver. I'm worried that we're still getting to know each other as adults, and there is a lot of uncertainty in that." I wrapped a wavy strand of hair around my finger and pulled her toward me so I could kiss her. "I'm not afraid of doing anything with you, Aston. No matter what the situation is, you are the person I'd choose to go through it with. You've always been my first choice."

She sighed lightly and lifted her hand so it was covering mine. Her voice was soft when she spoke. "You've always been the first choice I made for myself." They were significantly different but equally important choices. "As for where we live in the future, we can tackle that when the time comes. I know you would like to be closer to your family, but I've never planned on going back to Denver. Even if I don't stay in LA, I like California. I'm happy here." She lifted a hand and pointed at the view through the windshield. "I'll take the beach over the mountains any day."

I wasn't sold on sunshine every single day. I would miss the seasons changing and the snow in winter. The beach was nice, but I'd always been a mountain kind of guy. Not to say that I couldn't change. My life felt like it had been all about evolving lately. And if there was one thing all the successful relationships I'd witnessed while growing up had taught me, it was that compromise was key. It was never all or nothing.

Aston was right. Where we planned to settle down was a problem and a conversation for another time. I was stuck in California until the civil suit was over anyway. It wasn't that I hated California—even if I had some truly terrible memories attached to this place. It was more about wanting to be closer to my parents as they got older and wanting to be there for Remy now that her family was growing.

However, I had my own family that was just about to start, and I was going to have to put the wants and needs of Aston and the baby before everything.

That was what my dad did for my mom to this day. And there was no better example of someone building and taking care of a family they hadn't been prepared for than Rome Archer. I'd always done my best to follow in my father's footsteps in all the ways that mattered.

Aston gave me a soft little peck and lifted her hands to hold my face. Her eyes were intense as they stared into mine, and her tone was serious when she asked, "Did Cassio ask you about joining his team?"

I'd been spending more time than I wanted to with the Italian racer.

He hadn't been lying when he said he thought of Aston as a little sister. He often popped up at her house now that he was back in the States. Their working relationship definitely took a back seat to their genuine friendship. There was no denying he felt extremely guilty that she had been hurt because of someone's obsession with him.

There was also no ignoring the fact that the man was head over heels in love with Royce Wheeler. My preconceived image of Cassio as an international playboy had been shattered when he revealed himself to be more of a lovesick puppy dog. Aston swore it was more about Royce being the one who had gotten away than true love, but I didn't agree with her. I was all too familiar with unrequited love. Cassio looked the same way I had while I was pining for the other Wheeler sibling.

When I'd asked what went down between the two men, Aston had told me it was all a misunderstanding. She didn't dive too deep into details, but from what I gathered, Royce had caught Cassio in a compromising position with someone else while the two of them were hooking up. Royce had played it off like it was no big deal since they were only having a fling, but over the years that followed the incident, he never forgave Cassio or let the other man make any kind of amends. Apparently, Aston's long-standing friendship with the racer was a point of contention between the siblings.

Cassio had talked his way around his interest in wanting me to come check out his team. He also mentioned that when I was ready to get back on a bike, he wanted to be my first call. I'd tactfully avoided agreeing to anything. Not because I wasn't interested. Because I was afraid.

Afraid that the second I touched a bike, I wouldn't be able to let it go again.

Racing as a hobby was already risky. Doing it for a career was a whole different level of commitment and danger. I had a hard time believing that Aston would be so encouraging when it came to my getting back into the sport.

"He's never come outright and said he's offering me a job, but he's dropped some pretty heavy hints that he would like me to be involved in his team if he goes pro." I snorted and reached out to open the door. "Let's go walk on the beach."

She followed me out of the Bronco and took my hand. I sent a text to the security detail that I could handle a short walk on the shoreline without them shadowing us. I wasn't sure they would listen since they didn't technically work for me, but if they did follow, they were discreet about it.

"Cassio asked me to run a course with him. I didn't have the heart to tell him that the only reason he could beat me in a race was because I'd been off a bike for over five years. I don't know if that ego of his could take it if I got back to fighting form."

Aston took off her white sneakers and held them in her empty hand. She sighed contentedly as her painted toes sank into the sand. The sun caught the fire hidden in her hair and lit her up like a beacon. She'd always been like that for me. A guiding light I couldn't help but follow.

"I think he wants you to get back to your best. Actually, I think he wants you to be better than you were when everything went wrong. I told you, he's a fan. He admired you quite a bit before you gave it all up. He doesn't want you to be involved in his career out of pity or as a favor to me. He wants you to be part of what he does because he believes in you and your skills. He's smart enough to know you won't ever be willing to race again. But that doesn't mean you have to give up what you love. There are lots of aspects of racing besides being on the back of a bike."

I didn't know if she'd ever sounded more like her father than she did at that moment.

I threw my arm around her shoulders and pulled her to my side. Our height difference was perfect for forehead and temple kisses. I dropped one on the side of her head and gave her a little squeeze.

"Once I get comfortable being back behind the wheel of a normal vehicle, I'll attempt to get back on a bike. I don't know about working with Cassio in a formal kind of way, but I wouldn't mind running around a track with him once I get my feet back under me.

"I still have to see what happens when I go to court. If the judge finds me guilty of wrongful death and orders me to pay what the other side is asking for, I won't be able to afford the risk of wrecking a bike. My lawyer told me not to take the settlement deal since everyone else involved had already paid out. He thinks that will work in our favor."

Aston scoffed as she wrapped an arm around my waist and leaned more fully into my side. This felt like such a nice, normal couple thing to do. I savored the moment, still stunned that this was where I'd ended up once I was released from prison.

"You shouldn't settle since you already paid for your part in what had happened. No one else went to jail. No one else had their future and reputation ruined. So what if the other drivers gave the family money to appease their conscience? That's far easier to do than sacrificing your youth for the one that was lost." She sniffed in aggravation and wrinkled her nose like an irritated bunny. The sight made my heart clench.

"I looked over the court records. The modifications to that kid's bike were not something a novice rider should've been on the street with. If he knew what he was dealing with, he would've won the actual race fair and square. Money can buy a lot of things, but skill and experience are not on the list. He was set up to fail before that night began."

I hummed in acknowledgment and looked out over the water. The waves hitting the shore made a soothing sound. I heard the sound of childish laughter from somewhere ahead of us and watched a woman with a big dog go running by. I reminded myself to be more aware of our surroundings. Even though this was supposed to be a relaxing afternoon at the beach, there was no guarantee the stalker wasn't mixed in with the innocent beachgoers.

"All of that is true. But he was still just a kid." I told her the issue that always stuck with me. Not that I'd been much older than him. However, I had definitely been wiser. I would never let go of the reality that every ounce of intelligence I'd possessed disappeared that night while I operated purely on emotion. I never wanted to end up in that situation again.

Aston's elbow dug into my side. "So is Cassio's stalker. She's very young, but that doesn't excuse the fact that she pushed me down the stairs. It also doesn't excuse her family for using their wealth and connections to protect her. She's hurting others. She's affecting other peoples' lives and livelihoods. She clearly needs help she's not getting. Youth can't be an excuse for everything."

It was true. We finally had a name and physical ID on the stalker. She was a nineteen-year-old girl from England. Her family was rich. Old-money rich. She'd gone to the same boarding school as Cassio, but she was a decade younger. Apparently, he'd left a legacy, and the girl became obsessed with him after hearing others talk about his wild days spent at the school. She'd moved from online stalking to in-person stalking after she went to see one of his races in Monaco.

The police had yet to locate her, but my boss and whoever Campbell had asked to look into the situation assured me she was still in California. Tracking her down was infinitely harder, considering her family's money and connections. According to Campbell, there was someone working on the UK side, burying any information about the girl and blocking any inquiry made into her. It was so frustrating. I hated getting close and then getting shut down because someone had enough money to make the situation disappear. It made the danger to Aston even more heightened.

"You're right. Youth can't excuse everything. I just think it's sad when it's wasted on foolish things." I chuckled when she tilted her head to glare up in my direction. "I don't consider loving you from afar a foolish thing. It was the correct choice at the time. I never wanted to get between you and Ry. I wouldn't hurt him that way. And"—I bumped her with a hip, which made her laugh—"it sounds like you would've never been able to bring me home to your folks anyway."

She let out a long breath and reached up to hold my hand that was dangling over her shoulder. "My dad has always adored you. He was devastated when you got arrested. He was so angry you didn't defend yourself at all. He always said, 'Anyone who races knows the risks.' My mom was the problem. It's not that she didn't like you or think you were a good guy. You were just too unpredictable back then. No one knew if you were going to hack into NASA or end up laid out after a race. Not to mention, you were right there in the middle of the mess every single time Remy did something outrageous and unhinged. You never thought of yourself. All you wanted to do was save her. My mom is the type who would rather have the kind of life where no one ever needed saving in the first place. She's cautious and careful to a fault."

A silence fell over us as we both got lost in our thoughts. I started to guide Aston back toward the Bronco while adding a new worry to the list of the ones we would have to face when the time came.

"What's she going to say when she finds out you and I are together now?" I didn't bother to ask how she was going to react to the news of the baby. I couldn't even picture my mom's response, and she was used to big surprises after raising my sister.

Aston was quiet, but she didn't let go of my hand. "Whatever she says, it won't change anything. I let her have her hands all over my past. I can't let the things she went through shape my future. She'll understand that— eventually."

I hoped so.

It was hard to understand that our parents had had entire lives full of triumphs and traumas before we were in the picture. They'd also had a youth they had to survive and learn how to grow from. It had to be impossibly difficult for them to let go and watch their children take the same steps that had tripped them up.

Ultimately, I had to believe that as long as Aston and I were happy, our parents would be as well.

That was all any of us could ask for.

SIXTEEN

Aston

After we walked on the beach, Zowen took me for Mexican food. We found a little hole-in-the-wall that wasn't crowded and spent the rest of the afternoon talking and getting reacquainted with one another in all the non-carnal ways we probably should've tackled before having sex. The more time I spent with him, the more I recognized the significant changes in his personality and demeanor.

When he had been a kid, he had been smart and kind of quiet. Out of all the Archer kids, Zowen was the only one who managed to blend into the background and not stand out. It wasn't because he was any less extraordinary than his cousins and his sister. It was because he had to be the voice of reason. He had to be reliable. He had to be steadfast and predictable. He was the only Archer who didn't mind being boring. Or rather, he didn't mind being perceived as being the boring Archer by others.

The truth was, Zowen was quiet and didn't create chaos because he was sneakier and craftier than his relatives. Daire caused trouble for attention. Ry was a peacock who proudly paraded around his talent and skill because he *had* to be the best at everything. His entire identity was wrapped up in being number one. Remy caused crisis after crisis because she couldn't help herself. Her brain chemistry was always working against her, often leading her to be the loudest and most outrageous of the entire bunch.

Zowen wasn't someone who needed the validation of others. He wasn't seeking all eyes on him because, quietly and persistently, he was holding everyone together by the skin of his teeth. It was no wonder his interests when he was young were dangerous and bordered on being illegal. Racing and hacking into digital places he wasn't supposed to be were his way of rebelling. He acted just as outrageous as the rest of the Archers. Only he had done that where no one could see.

Now, he was much more defiant. He wasn't as quiet. He didn't seem to hesitate when it came to taking up the space in his life. Before, he had been squeezed into a corner by the other Archers, and now, he had room to move. He was also sharper and meaner than before he was arrested. I always remembered Zowen being low-key and calm. He'd rarely gotten rattled or lost his temper. Now, he was quick to anger, but also quick to find a resolution to whatever had triggered his emotions. I could tell he was tiptoeing through an emotional minefield. He'd told me he forgot how to feel happy. It was clear happiness wasn't the only feeling he needed to relearn.

Zowen was also frighteningly alert. Wherever we went, he treated it like we were about to head into battle.

I knew safety was important, especially with the current circumstances, but I wanted Zowen to be able to relax when we did something as simple as walking on the beach. It became glaringly obvious that he never stopped watching his back for a hidden attack. Even after the prison gates closed behind him. No one would call him chill or calm these days.

My favorite change was the wide-eyed surprise on his face anytime he discovered something new or improved. Since Zowen was a tech guy, there was no end to the advancements made over the five years he had been away. He was like a kid on Christmas morning every single time he came across a new technology he'd never seen before. Those were the infrequent times when the fierce and furious Archer looked adorable. I would never tell Zowen how cute I thought he was, but my heart melted every time his two-toned eyes lit up.

There were other smaller changes as well. Aside from his hesitation to be in the car, regardless of being the passenger or driver, he also hated crowds. He was nervous around strangers, and he didn't have a lot of patience for questions and other people's curiosity. He was definitely more jaded and cynical than he'd been when he was young.

One thing that hadn't changed was the way he looked at me.

Zowen's whole heart was in his gaze whenever I caught him staring at me or at my still-flat belly. He never managed to hide his feelings when they were related to me. His eyes made his infatuation the worst-kept secret anyone had ever tried to keep. He used to try and hide his reaction from others, namely Ry. But he no longer dropped the shutters when there were others around. Anyone who happened to catch sight of the way Zowen watched me would know within seconds how deeply devoted he was.

I silently hoped how I felt about him was reflected back to him when he looked at me. I'd never had to guess where I stood with him, and I wanted the same for him. I wanted him to know every single time our eyes met that he was the man I wanted to be with. Come hell or high water, before or after all the changes in our lives, he was mine just as much as I was his.

After the Mexican food, I was tired and wanted to take a nap. Zowen took us back to the bungalow, and I noticed that his hands barely shook when he got behind the wheel this time. It gave me hope that, eventually, he might find his way back to his other love—motorcycles.

He'd given up so much in the name of guilt. I wanted him to get everything that belonged to him back.

When we pulled up to a stop in front of the house, I was surprised to see someone sitting on the steps that led to the front door. Zowen and I exchanged a look, and I saw him glance over his shoulder at the nondescript sedan that had been following us all day. I knew he was worried about someone being at the house because we'd been gone all day, and the security detail was with us. The person stood up, coming fully into view, and I belatedly noticed the suitcase by her feet. I groaned and pushed out of the Bronco and rushed toward the woman. I heard Zowen call my name, but I didn't stop until I reached the spot where my mother was waiting.

She moved to hug me, but I evaded her hold and caught her hands in mine.

"What are you doing here, Mom?"

I'd specifically told her it wasn't a good time to visit. There was so much going on; I couldn't begin to think about how to explain everything to her.

My mom shook my hands loose and lifted her fingers to touch the still-bandaged spot on my forehead. Thankfully, I'd put on makeup for my date with Zowen, or the bruise on the side of my face would've given her a heart attack.

"Your brother told his mom that someone pushed you down the stairs. Kallie told your dad because she thought he should know, and your father told me. Last time we spoke on the phone, I asked you if everything was okay, and you lied to me, Aston. If you aren't going to be honest, my only option is to see for myself what's going on with you."

I gritted my teeth and silently cursed my brother. I couldn't believe he'd ratted me out after all the things I'd kept quiet for him over the years. I also couldn't believe my mom was still talking to me like I was a wayward teenager.

Sensing my irritation, she patted my head like she used to do when I was a child. "Don't be angry with Royce. He's having a hard time right now. He's worried about you, and the only person he could talk to was his mom. I think he forgot that Kallie also had a hand in raising you and would be just as concerned about you as I am. You should've told us what was happening out here, Aston."

Poppy Wheeler was one of the most stunning women on the planet. I took after her in a lot of ways. Both good and bad. She was soft-spoken and rarely acted as any type of disciplinarian. Her heart was as big as the whole sky, and she carried more empathy within it than imaginable. I could count on one hand the number of times she'd scolded me, today included. It very much felt like being killed with kindness.

Zowen walked up behind us and reached for my mom's suitcase. He lifted it easily and pushed open the front door with his free hand. Without looking at either of us, he said, "I'm going to take the puppy for a walk and give you two time to talk."

He gave my mother a polite greeting, but my mom didn't offer any type of response. I would have to explain to Zowen later that the reason she was being so rude had nothing to do with him. In her mind, he was an accomplice who had helped keep my recent secrets from her since he knew I was injured and didn't tell anyone back home. The tension was high, and it made my tummy hurt. I was already tired. Now, I felt the start of a headache building right in the center of my forehead.

My mom frowned and watched as Zowen walked into the house. She turned to look at me, her gaze full of questions. "He seems quite at home in your house, Aston."

I sighed and ushered her through the door. "That's because it's his home too. He's been living with me since he was released from prison."

"Whose idea was that? Daire's?"

My mom walked into the living room and looked around the small home. I could tell she was looking for signs of Zowen in my space, but other than the bedroom, most of his stuff was still out in the guesthouse.

I shook my head and asked her if she wanted anything to drink. I realized she looked tired, and I could tell she was incredibly tense. We rarely argued, but that was only because I never let her see the picture of my entire life. I only let her peek at the parts I knew wouldn't upset her or trigger her. I told myself I was being respectful of my mom's previous trauma, but what I really was doing was playing a huge game of hide-and-seek with my own issues. I was hiding all the important parts of myself and forcing her to seek out what little information she could glean from our short interactions.

"I wanted him to stay with me when he was released. He was one of the main reasons I'd decided to transfer from San Francisco down to LA. Daire didn't have anything to do with it." I sighed and handed my mom a glass of juice, which she clenched in shaking hands. "I have my own mind, Mom. I outgrew letting other people force me into things I didn't want to do a long time ago."

My mother blinked and gave me a pointed look. "You're talking about me, aren't you?"

I took a seat next to her on the couch and leaned forward to rest my elbows on my knees so I could hold my aching head in my hands. "No, I'm not talking about you specifically. When I was younger, I had a bad habit of doing things to make everyone around me happy while I was miserable. I'm not like that anymore. I know how to focus on myself and how to make choices that will make me happy.

"Zowen is the choice that makes me the happiest. I was going to tell you and Dad that he was staying with me and that I had feelings for him once our relationship was more clearly defined. I didn't think you needed to know when we didn't even know ourselves.

"The same thing is true with being hurt. It isn't anything majorly serious, and the situation involves a client and the police. It's not that big of a deal." I waved my sprained wrist around to make my point. "I didn't call Royce. My client did. I would prefer that no one knows what's was going on until the stalker is behind bars. It's better to keep our attention on Royce and Kallie. That's a circumstance that deserves the whole family's attention, not my bumps and bruises."

"You don't get to decide what your father and I worry about, Aston. You're our child. Big or small, if it affects you, it affects us."

I swore under my breath and turned my head to look at her. "I don't get to decide what makes you worry, but I *do* get to decide what I share with you. My life is not an open book for you to edit and leave notes in the margins, Mom. I'm living it for me, not you, like I did for so long."

Typically, I wouldn't be so harsh, but she'd ambushed me, and my hormones were all over the place.

My mom blinked, and her mouth opened in an O of surprise. I'd never responded to her concern so bluntly before. It was obvious she was taken aback.

"All I've ever wanted is for your life to be easier than mine was. I've never intended for you to sacrifice your own wants and needs in order to please me and your father."

"Mom ..." I pushed my thumbs against my forehead and prayed for the throbbing to stop. "I did what I thought was right when I was younger. Now that I'm an adult, what's right looks a lot different. No one will ever love and care for me the way you and Dad do. I am so lucky to have you both. I hope I'm capable of giving someone else the kind of security and unwavering support you've given me. But you have to let me *live*.

"I know you almost lost me when I was a baby, and you've always been terrified of me being taken away from you. There is no room in that fear for me to have any kind of fulfilling existence. That's why I had to leave Denver. Your fear was big, and it left no space for me."

I turned my head to look at her and noticed she was crying. Her tears made me feel awful, but they didn't change the fact that I was telling her my truth for the first time in my entire life.

"Be nice to Zowen, Mom. He's a good guy. He is the only person on the planet to come close to loving me as much as you do. If you removed your blinders, you would see there is no better choice for me than him." I let out a dry chuckle. "And even if you don't approve, I'm not letting him go."

We were tied together for the foreseeable future, no matter what. It would be nice if my parents jumped on board before they knew about the baby. I didn't want Zowen to feel like they were forced to accept him for the baby's sake.

My mom reached out and put the untouched juice on the table in front of her. At least her hands weren't shaking any longer. "To be honest with you, I've known everything you're saying about Zowen since you were kids. One of the reasons I encouraged you to date Ry and not him is because I always knew that if you returned Zowen's feelings, you would know that it was possible to find someone who loved you just as much as your family did. I knew you wouldn't need your dad and me as much if he was the one you decided to be with. I've always felt this relationship was inevitable. If he hadn't gotten caught up in that accident when he first came to California, I bet the two of you would've found your way to each other a long time ago. Your dad has always told me he felt that Zowen was the right Archer for you. As usual, he was right."

Her eyes roved over my face and landed on my injured wrist. "I understand you don't want your parents prying into every corner of your life. I can also admit I'm too invasive and too demanding with you now that you're an adult. However, I think you need to put yourself in my shoes in some instances as well. What if you had a child who lived thousands of miles away and they were hurt badly enough to require an overnight hospital stay and you knew nothing about it? You would be as concerned as I am. You would also want to see that your child was fine with your own two eyes. You'll understand if you ever decide to be a parent down the road."

I stilled and felt my heart drop. She was right. I was going to have to see things from the perspective of a concerned parent. Much sooner than she realized.

I leaned my entire body against hers and let her wrap her arm around my shoulders in a tight hug. "I'll do better in the future." I made the promise quietly but with determination threaded throughout every word.

"I'll do better too. It's not fair that you've had to hold one side of my baggage your entire life. That isn't a weight you deserved to drag around with you all this time." She gave a wry laugh and shook her head. "If you were one of my patients and not my daughter, I would've been able to see I was transferring my issues onto you instead of doing the work to deal with them myself. Sometimes, you end up too close to the problem to see it clearly."

As a domestic abuse survivor, my mom took her job as a victims' advocate and counselor very seriously. Her whole life, all she'd ever wanted was to keep people safe and save them from relationships that might end with them losing their lives. She was actually one of the most sensitive and compassionate women I'd ever had the pleasure of having in my life, but like she'd said, we were too close to see what was happening deep within our complicated dynamic clearly.

"How long are you staying for? Since I had no idea you were coming, I have to work."

I'd also have to buy groceries and act like a real adult was staying in the house. My mom would be appalled if she knew how much I spent on takeout and delivery per week. I placed a hand on my tummy and told myself I was going to have to do a better job of acting like a grown-up, considering I was going to be responsible for the health and well-being of an entire human being.

"I'll only be here for a few days. Your dad has to go back to work, so I'm going to New York to stay with Kallie for a few weeks. Royce has to get back to work on a big commission, and he won't be able to concentrate if his mom is by herself while he's busy." She sighed and wrapped a strand of my hair around her finger. "It's such a sad situation."

I nodded. "It is. He's lucky to have you at a time like this."

She knocked the sides of our heads together and let out a soft sigh. "We're all lucky to have each other."

That was the key to family. Regardless of wins and losses, ups and downs, missteps and leaps forward, tragedy and triumph, we *always* had each other.

chapter SEVENTEEN

Zowen

I finally got a haircut. I also bought a suit and tie. I drew the line at putting on shiny dress shoes, so polished black combat boots would have to suffice. I wanted to look reformed, but not like a pushover. It was a tricky balance to find.

Aston had offered to take off work so she could go with me for the deposition with the other side. I'd declined and told her I didn't want her anywhere near the mess from my past. It was hard enough for me to relive the events of that ill-fated weekend. She didn't need to share in the nightmare of that night. I could tell she was disappointed I wanted to go alone, but I truthfully believed it was for the best. This was my battle to win or lose. I'd refused to fight before, but now, I had too much on the line to give up and let myself be railroaded. I would never deny the family their right to grieve and seek some type of solace for their lost loved one. But giving my life in exchange for his was no longer a feasible solution to the problem.

The civil suit was churning its way through the system. If I didn't agree to pay out a settlement, we would go in front of a judge within the next few months. My lawyer's advice was not to settle. He was convinced any seasoned judge who'd been on the bench for a while would see the suit for the cash grab that it was. I hadn't decided one way or the other yet. Part of me was ready for the entire situation to be in the past. I was tired of living my whole life around that disastrous night. I didn't have the kind of money they were asking for. Which Hayes had told me the other side was counting on. They were hoping my friends and family would liquidate their assets and help me pay the settlement. My father had several profitable businesses, including the one he ran with Aston's dad. If he sold them off, it would be more than enough to make the other side go away.

I would never let that happen.

I was a grown man, responsible for my actions. Any consequences left to bear were mine and mine alone.

I was lucky Hayes could see the big picture and had no intention of letting me give up more than I already had. He might look flashy with his cowboy hat and snakeskin cowboy boots, but the man was sharper than a tack and had no problem putting up one hell of a fight.

In fact, the opposing lawyer looked downright annoyed when Hayes followed me into the meeting room. The older man took off his cowboy hat and offered a charming smile. The flash of teeth and hint of ruthlessness hidden within the grin reminded me a lot of Uncle Benny. There were some men you simply didn't want to underestimate.

Hayes motioned for me to take a seat next to him as we both faced the other lawyer. The family wasn't present, which I was thankful for. I'd tried to apologize in person before the criminal trial started, and they'd accused me of harassment. I couldn't blame them for not wanting to hear what I had to say, and I understood an apology did nothing to ease the loss of a loved one. Especially one so young. No one owed me acceptance or forgiveness.

"Good afternoon, Mr. Lawton, Mr. Archer. I assume you've carefully considered our last and final offer to settle this case out of court."

Hayes made himself comfortable and crossed one booted foot so it was resting on his knee. He looked more like a gunslinger about to face off with an opponent at high noon than an attorney.

"We considered it. I told my client to sit with it for a couple of weeks before making a firm decision. After a lot of thought, Mr. Archer has decided to proceed with the trial. We'll let a judge hear both sides and determine whether Mr. Archer should be implicated in the wrongful death suit."

"The judges have already ruled in favor of the family in the previous civil cases. Are you certain your client wants to risk it?" The opposing attorney sounded cocky and cast a smug look in my direction.

I didn't say a word. After all, I was paying Hayes a fortune to speak for me.

"The previous cases involved a driver who was under the influence and a driver working past the recommended driving hours for a professional trucker. The case against my client has no legal legs to stand on. My client had nothing to do with the accident. He's the only one who tried to stop the race from happening. Your client's son was on a vehicle he had no business being on—a vehicle your client facilitated getting into his hands. Your client's son streamed the entirety of the accident, including where my client urged the deceased to stop the race. The footage provided by him shows my client was a hundred yards away upon the initial collision. It's going to be a hard sell to any judge worth his salt that my client was the one responsible for any part of the actual crash, which ultimately caused the death."

The opposing lawyer frowned at the mention of the footage from the live stream and stiffened. He cleared his throat and started tapping the tip of his pen on the conference room table. "Your client is the one who initiated the race. An illegal race. If your client hadn't challenged my client's son, he wouldn't have been traveling at such a high speed on a public road. Your client instigated the events leading up to the accident. He's very much responsible for the events that followed."

I opened my mouth to argue that the kid could've played fair at the official event and to remind the lawyer that the kid could've always turned down the challenge. He'd targeted me that weekend and wanted to start something. No one had known the final outcome would be so devastating and tragic.

Hayes put a hand on my arm as a sign to keep quiet. I bit back the words of self-defense and clenched my hands into fists under the table. It was frustrating, being talked about like I wasn't in the room. When I'd resigned myself to going to prison because I knew I deserved some form of punishment, it had been scarily easy to stay silent while others decided my fate. I didn't have that kind of luxury anymore. I had to get back to Aston, and I needed to be around for my baby in the future. I'd already let the other side own my past. I wasn't willing to surrender my future to them as well.

"What if I tell you I have chat records from the night of the race, indicating your client's son targeted my client? I can prove their son spoke to multiple people involved with the event about getting my client disqualified that weekend and egging him on. He *wanted* to race against my client illegally. Which was why he was wearing a body camera and filming that night. He was looking for engagement and followers on social media. Even before the invite had been sent out for the weekend event, your client's son had been instrumental in orchestrating that my client was present at the event.

"I also have various emails from the event coordinators and friends of the deceased, warning him that he needed more practice with his motorcycle, the more he modified it. In fact, the deceased made modifications the day before the illegal race that he hadn't had time to test out or practice riding with. Your client's son knew the risks involved. He ignored any and all warnings given.

"My client was baited and acted exactly how the deceased had expected. I think once all of this is laid out in front of a judge, there will be no question about my client's culpability."

Hayes dropped his foot and leaned forward. I saw the other lawyer tense up and lean back in his leather chair.

"Not to mention, my client has already been criminally convicted for his actions that night. He served the time handed down by the justice system. He accepted responsibility for his part in what had occurred without complaint. Asking for more"—Hayes shook his head and frowned—"is going too far."

The other lawyer froze and stopped tapping his pen. He gave me a look, then scribbled something on the notebook in front of him. "I'll go back to my client and let them know you aren't interested in a settlement and prepare them for trial, moving forward. Have one of your paralegals send the conversations you have between my client's son and anyone else who might have knowledge about what transpired that night. I'll summarize everything for them and get back to you once they are aware of this new information."

Hayes lifted his eyebrows, and the sinister smirk was back on his face. "You do that. I'll be looking forward to hearing from you after you speak with them." He patted me on the shoulder and told me, "Let's go, kid."

The entire meeting had taken less than twenty minutes, and I hadn't uttered a single word.

"Do you really have all that stuff?" I was curious about Hayes's sudden ace in the hole.

We stepped into a glass elevator and started to descend.

"I do have it. I started digging around during your first trial, but didn't have anything conclusive until recently. No one had been willing to talk back then because they were worried about getting the event shut down and having their own illegal activities discovered. I've had a few of the kids who work for me monitoring several con-versations pertaining to the race and the accident that weekend on social media." He gave me a hard look. "It's stuff you probably could've found without any effort if you were interested in saving your own ass back then. I put some pressure in the right places and managed to make some progress. Since this is a civil trial and it's not as daunting as a criminal one, I found a few people will-ing to talk.

"The kid who died had it out for you from the jump. Even if you hadn't challenged him to a race, he was going to manipulate the situation so there was a head-to-head showdown regardless. He paid enough people off; you were trapped the second you hit the desert. He saw you as a surefire way to boost his cred within the circuit and got in way over his head. You were as much of a victim as he was."

We walked out of the building, and I squinted up at the sun. It was really bright, and for once, that felt like something to be celebrated. I'd lived in the dark and cold for so long; I'd adjusted to the idea of never feeling warm again.

"I haven't been on a bike since that night. It fucking terrifies me."

Hayes snorted and slapped his cowboy hat back on his head. "Not to be cliché, but you know what they say where I come from. *When you fall off a horse …*"

I chuckled and turned my head to look at him. "Su-perbikes go a lot faster than a horse."

"True. But if you handle them with care and take things one step at a time, you can successfully get back on whatever type of beast threw you off. No one is making you ride. You should do it because you love it."

"And to prove to myself that I still can."

Ultimately, I wanted to overcome the fears holding me back, and currently, riding was at the top of the list. I was doing better behind the wheel of a car, but it didn't come without struggle. I had to give myself a pep talk every time I went to drive somewhere, and I still moved at the pace of a turtle. I was fortunate I hadn't been run off the road by an angry and impatient driver yet.

That sharp smile that felt like a threat was back on Hayes's handsome face. "Or you can get back to it out of pure spite. Don't give away important things, like passion and skill, to unnecessary people. Whatever motivation you use, I think it's past time you let the clock restart on your life."

"What happens now? Do we wait and do nothing until the trial? Do you think they'll come back with another settlement offer now that they know it's unlikely I'm going to be found at fault?"

"I doubt this will go to trial. They might be bold enough to come back with a lower settlement offer, thinking you'll pay it just to make them go away, but it's doubtful. If they're any kind of parents at all, they'll let this vendetta go and let their son rest in peace. What kind of parent would parade their child's culpability in such a tragic accident in front of the whole world? As of now, he's been viewed as a saint who was in the wrong place at the wrong time. If it gets out he was the puppeteer behind the scenes, the narrative changes, and so will the public perception of them. In any other city, that might not mean anything, but this is LA. Image is everything."

We shook hands, and Hayes told me he would keep me updated on the next steps. I sent a text to my dad, letting him know the deposition went well. I told him I would call later to fill him in on the exact details of what went down today. I also thanked him for finding and hiring Hayes. It was reassuring to have a man like him watching my back.

Just as I was getting to the Bronco and about to call Aston, she called me instead. I answered, not even realizing how big I smiled at her name on my caller ID.

"What's up? I'm headed back to the house now. Do you need me to grab anything on the way?"

Aston's mom, Poppy, had left for New York yesterday morning, so the house was back to being only the two of us and Koons.

I had done my best to stay out of sight and mind while Aston had a visitor, but much to my surprise, Poppy had extended an olive branch and made inroads to getting to know me. She was careful with her questions and avoided anything that might cause conflict. I could tell right away why Aston had felt she had to protect her mother and made choices in an effort to appease her back in the day. Poppy was on the opposite end of the personality spectrum from the women in my family. It had taken a bit of adjusting, but I felt like her surprise visit was mostly successful, and some progress had been made toward getting her to approve of me as Aston's partner.

However, now that she was on her way to see Royce, Aston and I were back to fending for ourselves in the kitchen. Neither one of us knew how to cook beyond the basics. Aston had mentioned taking a cooking class so we could learn together. She'd reminded me that we were going to have a small human we were going to have to teach good, healthy eating habits. It was wild to think about all the responsibilities approaching us.

"I'm going to make dinner tonight." Aston sounded a bit hesitant. "Correction: I'm going to attempt to make dinner tonight. It might end up being inedible."

I laughed as she sighed.

"I'm actually calling to tell you that I'm leaving work early. My car is finally ready to be picked up from the body shop. I didn't want you to worry if the security guys told you I was leaving all of a sudden."

"How are you getting to the body shop?" I tapped the steering wheel with my fingers and squinted against the reflection of the sun off the hood of the Bronco.

"Cassio said he would drop me off. He was here for a meeting." She told someone in the office she was leaving, and I heard the sounds of her gathering her things.

"I can come and get you."

We were both surprised by my offhand offer.

"Are you sure? That's a lot of LA traffic you would have to deal with. I know you were already stressed about the deposition. It's fine if Cassio drops me off."

"I can do it." I cleared my throat and tried again because the words sounded weak. "I'm happy to do it. I'm not that far away from your office. The deposition was a piece of cake. I'm perfectly fine."

"Okay. Let me text Cassio and tell him he doesn't have to wait for me."

The other end of the call went quiet for a minute until Aston came back and told me she would wait for me in the lobby of her office building.

Before I started the car and merged into traffic, I told her, "You don't have to shield me from things that might be challenging, Aston. You can't protect me from life. No one can. It's okay to ask me to do things that are hard."

She made a soft sound, and I could clearly picture the look of contemplation on her face even though I couldn't see her. "Don't you want to protect me, Zowen?"

I balked for a second but had to answer honestly. "I do." I always had. Wanting to protect her felt like it was as much a part of me as breathing was.

"We are on equal footing in this relationship. There isn't one set of rules for you and another set for me. We have to watch out for each other. We have to challenge each other. It's a two-way street."

I grunted in agreement since her point was incredibly valid. "All right. I'll do my best not to get all prickly when you're just trying to look out for me in the future."

I'd gotten used to being alone and taking care of myself. I was still adjusting to having someone in my life who wanted to take care of me.

I was used to being the caretaker. The hero. The savior.

It was an entirely different experience, being the one who was repeatedly saved.

Aston laughed. "You can be prickly. I don't mind it. You're kind of like a cute little hedgehog when I accidentally poke one of your sore spots."

No one had ever called me cute or compared me to a hedgehog before. Aston seemed determined to own more and more of my firsts.

"I'll see you shortly. Wait for me."

Before I disconnected the call, I heard her whisper, *"Always."*

chapter EIGHTEEN

Aston

I was not a good cook. It wasn't something I had an innate talent for, as I had hoped.

My mom had tried to teach me a few of my childhood favorites during her short visit, but I could tell by her reaction to anything I'd made that the verdict wasn't great. I'd ruined more than one pot, and Zowen had put out a small fire I'd started in the oven. The timing and temps were confusing. And once one thing went wrong, I became so frazzled that I couldn't save anything that might've still been edible. After a week of attempting to feed both Zowen and myself, I was ready to throw in the towel. I figured that if I'd managed to survive on takeout and delivery, so could a child.

Fortunately, Zowen was more levelheaded and picked up the basics much faster than I had. He wasn't up to making anything overly fancy, but he could put a meal on the table. If he had a recipe in front of him, nine times out of ten, whatever he made was a perfect replica. It was obvious that once he had more time, he would be excellent in the kitchen. I mean, he would be an excellent *cook* in the kitchen. He was already amazing at other things in the kitchen.

Currently, we had settled into a pattern where he cooked and I cleaned up as long as I didn't have to work late or go out with a client. It felt seamless and effortless. A big part of me wondered how we had integrated our lives so easily after all the time and distance that spanned our ill-fated relationship. I wondered if all star-crossed lovers managed to fit together so well once those same stars aligned. I believed we were extraordinarily lucky that neither one of us was willing to give up on the other after a lifetime of not being the right choice at the right time. It was a miracle that we'd finally found something that was not only right, but damn near perfect too.

"Why are you staring at me?"

Zowen was sitting on the floor, playing tug-of-war with the puppy. The small ball of fluff had gotten much bigger, but he was still tiny enough to fit in one of Zowen's hands. The little guy had gotten very attached to the tattooed man since Zowen was the one who had taken on the responsibility of walking him every day. It was adorable to see such a big, tough-looking man handling a little and cute animal.

Now that Zowen had cut his hair short, he looked more like a badass biker and less like a surfer boy. I wasn't the only one who enjoyed the contrast between man and puppy. I noticed several of my female neighbors conveniently had work to do in their yards right around the time Zowen typically went running. I couldn't blame them. All that muscle, covered in bright tattoo designs, combined with the gray-sweatpants allure, made watching Zowen run a delightful hobby for the neighborhood to have.

"I'm still getting used to your short hair. It makes you look younger."

It reminded me of how he'd looked in high school. He always kept his hair buzzed down close to his scalp. I thought it was a style he'd adopted because his father, Rome, also rocked a buzz cut from his time in the military.

He rubbed a hand over the shorn locks and lifted his eyebrows in my direction. "Do you like it? My attorney told me I look like I just got out of boot camp."

I laughed. "You look good regardless of what kind of haircut you have."

Those Archer genetics were really something. My baby was blessed to have those genes in the mix.

Zowen patted the puppy on its head and handed it a chew toy to keep it occupied.

He lifted to his feet in a smooth motion and walked over to sit next to me on the couch. He tossed out a muscular arm and hooked my neck, pulling me close enough that he could kiss my temple. It was one of his favorite signs of affection. It highlighted how much smaller I was when compared to him. However, it never intimidated me. It made me feel cherished and protected.

"I feel the same way about you. I've always thought you were the prettiest girl I ever laid eyes on. I still do." One of his hands reached out to rest on my still-flat tummy. "I think you'll be even more beautiful as time goes on."

I had no doubt he would feel that way. I could tell by the way he looked at me that he wasn't only infatuated with me; he was falling in love with the life we would build together. Some of the shadows that always haunted his gaze were beginning to fade. He wasn't the same as he had been before the accident by any means, but I felt that he was starting to move beyond the man who had spent five years in prison and given up on everything.

I turned my head and lifted my face, tapping my lips with a finger to indicate I wanted a real kiss. He complied by lowering his head and brushing his lips over mine. It didn't matter how lightly any kiss started; it always seemed to turn into something heated and hungry after a couple of seconds. He slipped his tongue between my parted lips and flicked the tip against mine. I sighed in contentment and lifted a hand to wrap around his neck.

I did miss him having longer hair when it came to giving me something to grasp and run my fingers through. My emotions often got the best of me and ratcheted up to the point of being overwhelming. It was nice to have some part of him to anchor myself to. For now, I had to settle for digging my short fingernails into his skin. He didn't seem to mind the leftover marks that were scattered across his flesh.

I nipped at his lower lip and kissed my way across his handsome face. A moment later, I rubbed the tip of my nose along the high arch of his cheekbone and nuzzled against his ear. He grunted when I bit his earlobe and gave it a tug before licking my way down the side of his neck. His skin had a slightly salty tang, and his pulse thumped under the damp caress.

I guided a hand down and across his broad chest and felt his muscles tense in response. His eyes glittered with interest when I lifted the hem of his T-shirt. I scratched the tips of my nails through his dark happy trail and watched as the thin material of his track pants started to lift with his erection. It was always a thrill to know at a base level that his body was going to respond to my slightest touch.

Zowen raked his fingers through my hair and gave me a lopsided grin. "We shouldn't take this any further in front of the puppy."

I let out a yelp of surprise when he climbed to his feet and reached out to pick me up. He carried me princess-style back to my bedroom.

That was another new thing I'd learned about him since being reunited. He was shy when it came to some things. I didn't know whether it was a holdover from being constantly watched while in prison or if it had always been one of his quirks. Either way, it was another new trait about him I found utterly endearing. I especially liked this side of him because he'd told me one of the reasons he liked me so much when I was younger was because I was on the quiet and reserved side. That wasn't who I really was, but it was who *he* actually was. It was a fun surprise for both of us as the contrast between imagination and reality became evident.

When I broke it down, I realized I was his first real relationship. He might've hooked up on and off when he was younger, but he was never serious about anyone until we recently got together. He had no experience at being a boyfriend, so watching him figure it out was one of the highlights of being with him. Plus, the boy was brilliant and a fast learner. He was better at being a boyfriend than a lot of men who had years of experience under their belt.

He left the bedroom door cracked so he could hear Koons if he started to cause trouble and placed me on the bed like I was made of glass.

I grabbed a handful of his shirt and pulled him down on top of me. He caught his weight on his hands so he didn't crush me and lowered his head to kiss me. I wanted as much of him touching me as possible, so I wrapped my legs around his lean waist and dug my heels into his firm ass. He landed with a grunt and used his teeth to nibble on my bottom lip. One of his hands skimmed along my rib cage, taking the fabric of my loose top with him.

We'd undressed each other so many times; it was like a practiced dance. Things that were in the way of having bare skin against bare skin were quickly discarded. I was intimately familiar with every inch of his tattooed and non-tattooed skin. I could tell he had leaned down some since he had first shown up on my doorstep. He still had carved muscles and obvious strength, but he wasn't as bulky as when he had first arrived. It was another change that reminded me of the teenage version of himself. He'd always been fit because he played soccer, but wasn't jacked like a professional athlete or like Ry was in high school. Either way, he was sexy as hell, but I appreciated that he didn't feel like he needed to keep the body of a Spartan warrior any longer because he didn't have to be the biggest, scariest guy around to ensure his survival.

I dragged my nipples across his warm chest and lifted my hips to nudge impatiently at the hardness between his legs. His cock slid across my center, the skin hard and warm as it pulsed with excitement and arousal. He growled into my ear and thrust his hips just enough to brush the tip of his cock against my opening. My body clenched with anticipation as I squeezed him with my thighs.

Zowen lifted himself back up so he could get his mouth around one of the puckered peaks on my breasts. I felt the edge of his teeth and let out a soft moan in response. He was very good at finding the perfect balance between pleasure and pain.

He put the hand he wasn't using to hold himself aloft on my backside. He held me in position so that he could guide his cock through my quickly dampening folds. I rocked with him, chasing the faint sensation, and told him I wanted more. He sucked harder on the nipple that was trapped within the warm cavern of his mouth.

Since our first time together had been a frenzied clash of bodies, Zowen went out of his way to prove he could take things slow and be gentle. He'd gotten even more considerate since we'd found out about the baby. Sometimes, I appreciated it because it was nice to be treated like I was the most special person in his whole world, but sometimes, I wanted the rush and heat from our first night together. I wanted to know that I could make him go out of his mind with desire. I wanted him to see that I wouldn't break, no matter how intense things got between us in bed. Foreplay was fun, but there were instances when I just wanted to fuck.

This would be one of those times.

I caught hold of his ears and tugged until he looked at me with his dual-colored eyes. "I want you inside of me. Stop playing around."

His eyebrows winged upward, and the corner of his mouth lifted in a sexy smirk. "A gentleman always gives a lady what she asks for."

He shifted position and clasped one of my thighs so he could hitch my leg higher on his hip. A moment later, I felt his length press into my body. It was a long, deep thrust. The feeling that followed made my eyes widen, then immediately slam shut. Pleasure coursed through me as the temperature between us built with each of his deliberately rough movements. Flesh dragged against flesh, moans mingled, nerves sizzled, and arousal heightened. He had me wet and wanting with little effort. I wrapped myself around him as much as I could and tried to absorb every sensation and feeling radiating between the two of us.

Zowen told me repeatedly that he could *only* love me. But he'd yet to tell me he *loved* me. Fortunately, I could feel it in the way he touched me and in the hurried way we moved together. It was easy to see it in his magnetic gaze and hear it between every heavy breath he took.

I hadn't told him how I felt either. Not because I was afraid he wouldn't return the sentiment, but because I didn't want him to feel like he had to be responsible for my emotions. I still harbored some fear that he wouldn't walk away from me only because we were going to have a baby together. I didn't want to add another link in the chain that tied him to me just yet. He had to know he was free to make choices for himself. Hopefully, they were decisions that would lead him to me. Besides, if I could feel how he felt about me, he had to be able to tell by my actions and unbridled response to him that I felt the same. Our bodies were having entire conversations while we remained mostly silent.

Zowen must've sensed my impatience and my need. He picked up the pace of his movements so that he was practically pounding into me. I gasped as his cock pressed against the tiny spot hidden within the damp, clenching walls. He relentlessly hammered at the same location while I tossed my head from side to side. Everything behind my eyelids burst white, and his name caught on a strangled sound in the back of my throat. He kept up the heavy thrusts, even as my body clamped down on his. I could feel the rush of my release surrounding him as he grunted his pleasure in response.

It didn't take much longer for him to find his own finish line. When he did, he was flushed, and his eyes were very bright. He looked like a man who had just won first place in the biggest race of his life.

He opened his mouth to say something but was drowned out by a loud crash from the living room. A second later, the puppy barked, and there was the sound of tiny paws racing across the hardwood floors.

Zowen groaned and rested his forehead against mine as Koons burst into the bedroom. He yipped and yapped at the side of the bed until Zowen reached down to scoop him up.

He held the puppy eye to eye and scolded, "You couldn't have waited five more minutes?"

The dog tilted his fluffy head in confusion and shot his tongue out to lick Zowen's hand.

I laughed and wiggled out from underneath him, wondering what he was about to say before the puppy caused chaos. "You'd better get used to it. Being interrupted is going to be a big part of our lives once this baby is born."

A complicated mix of emotions flashed through his eyes. They were too quick to identify, but his smile was enough to melt my heart as he said, "Then, we have to make the most of the time we have before we're constantly interrupted, don't we?"

I'd always known he was a very smart man.

chapter
NINETEEN

Zowen

The sun was scalding, but I was shivering.

I stood on the asphalt and watched the set of brightly colored motorcycles whip around the turns as they circled the track in front of me. Cassio was good. My heart raced every time his body came within inches of touching the ground as he followed the momentum of the bike around different turns. His training partner was also pretty good, but not in the same league as Cassio. It was easy to see why one was on his way to the pros, and the other was stuck at the amateur level.

The sound of motors revving, the smell of gasoline and oil, the feel of heavy riding gear—they were all famil-iar yet foreign as well. I'd never thought I would be this close to a motorcycle or racetrack ever again. Not that I'd ever reached the point of standing on a legit track or seeing how a real race team operated.

After weeks of Cassio pestering me to come and watch him do a practice run, I'd finally caved. Deep down, I'd always wanted to get close to the thing I still feared most. It felt like the final hurdle I had to cross before being able to fully move on with my life. I felt like I was going to throw up the entire drive to the track. When Cassio and his team rolled the bikes off their trailer, I wanted to turn around and drive back to Aston's house. It took all my self-control not to bolt as soon as the motorcycles were fired up. And watching Cassio put on his riding gear had sent my whole body into a cold sweat.

Memories from the night of the accident flooded my mind. They were different motorcycles with different riders; however, I kept seeing myself and that kid instead of Cassio and his partner. I didn't realize I was frozen in place and fully zoned out until one of Cassio's team members shoved a helmet in my hands and told me to suit up if I wanted to ride. Apparently, Cassio had already had a full set of gear ready for me to use if I decided to ride today. He hadn't mentioned the preparation to me. But the more I got to know the Italian, I was learning that he was full of surprises and often two or three steps ahead of everyone else when it came to understanding complicated emotions. He was as empathetic as he was showy.

It was easy to see why he was such a popular figure in the industry.

With the helmet tucked in the crook of my arm, I squinted against the sun and watched as Cassio and his partner pulled into the pit area after their last lap. The two men bumped fists, and the other rider climbed off his bike. Cassio made a motion that indicated he wanted me to approach where he was parked. I had to steel my nerves the closer I got to the bike because as much as I wanted to reach out and touch the sleek machine, I also wanted to spin on my heel and run away. The steps I took were slow and steady. Feeling fear was fine, as long as I didn't let it control me. That was the thought that kept running through my head.

I set the helmet down on the seat of the abandoned bike and looked at Cassio through the visor of his helmet. He flipped the protective layer up and winked at me. It was hard to talk with a helmet on, so he simply tilted his head toward the other bike and raised his eyebrows in question.

I stood there for a solid ten minutes while Cassio watched me silently. There was no pressure from the other side. Which I greatly appreciated. If I did this, it had to be because I wanted to. The only person I needed to prove something to was myself. That was the main reason I hadn't asked Aston to come with me to the track. If she were waiting and watching with anticipation, I had known it would be enough motivation for me to get back on a bike even if I wasn't ready.

With a deep sigh and a litany of swear words repeating in my mind, I picked the helmet up and put it on. I closed my eyes as I adjusted to the feeling of having my entire head encased in a protective layer. I tightened the gloves on my hands and swung a leg over the powerful machine. It was mostly identical to the bike Cassio was riding, which meant it was a lot faster and handled differently than a stock bike. Probably not the best choice for my first time getting back on the horse after so long, but beggars couldn't be choosers.

Cassio closed the visor on his helmet and slowly started to roll out in front of me. It took me a lot longer to get used to the feeling of having a land rocket ship between my legs. He was already halfway around the track before I started to slowly exit the pit area. Cassio must've told his crew something about my situation before I arrived because they all quietly found something else to do as I lightly hit the throttle. No one was watching me or judging me. It was just me and the bike and a long-forgotten thrill that started to electrify my entire body.

The phrase *it's like riding a bike* really had a lot of merit to it. Even though I hadn't been on a motorcycle in years, my body's muscle memory kicked in to seamlessly operate the clutch, gas, and brake out of ingrained habit. My instincts and balance weren't lost either. Even though the bike was supercharged, I handled it easily as I puttered behind Cassio on the track. I was still sweaty and felt like a nervous wreck, but I couldn't ignore the zing in my blood and the adrenaline making my heart pound.

I felt so alive.

So free.

It felt like a large chunk of the man I used to be, before he was thrown away and forgotten, finally found his way back to where he was supposed to be.

On the second lap, I was comfortable enough to crank the throttle. I couldn't go as fast as Cassio, but it was more than a slow puttering. The bike jumped underneath me, and the scenery around me started to blur as I picked up speed. My heart was racing—in a good way.

By the fifth lap, I forgot I was afraid. Without realizing it, I was actively chasing Cassio around the track, annoyed that he was faster and handled the bike better than me. He was also smaller and lighter than I was. Around lap ten or eleven, I caught up to him. And while I couldn't pass him because he was so much better at cornering than I was, we finished neck and neck on the final lap. If I had more time to practice, I figured I could beat him in a real race within the next four or five months.

We pulled to a stop next to each other and removed our helmets.

Cassio took off his racing gloves and smirked at me. "You are still worthy of being one of my favorite riders. I'm selfish enough to admit that I'm glad you don't have any interest in getting back into racing. I don't think anyone will be able to catch you once you've had enough practice. I much prefer having you as a colleague than as my competition."

I snorted and peeled the top of the racing suit down to my waist. The T-shirt underneath was soaked with sweat, so I pulled that off over my head as well. I watched as Cassio's gaze roved over my tattooed torso.

His smirk turned into a grin as he teased, "Aston has good taste. I can't say the same for that brother of hers though."

I hopped off the bike and rolled it to where one of the mechanics was waiting for it. Cassio coasted closely behind. Someone came over and handed us bottled water. I followed Cassio's lead and took a seat on the edge of the hauling trailer. I was happy to see that only a couple of fingers were left shaking and not my entire hand, like it had been when I first approached the bike.

"You're better than good. I can see why you're knocking on MotoGP's door." I begrudgingly admitted that Cassio was a superior rider. He really did need a better training partner.

"I started late. I didn't know what I wanted to do when I was younger. My parents expected me to take over the family business once I was old enough. That's what all the children have done for generations. I had no interest in making wine or tending to vineyards. I wasn't even interested in staying in Italy. I technically ran away from home after I graduated from secondary school.

"While traveling through Japan, I met a boy who was big into all different kinds of racing. I stayed in Tokyo for three years and fell in love with both the boy and racing. I figured out what I wanted to do, but had no idea how to go about getting started."

He took a drink of water and turned his head to look at me. "Royce and Aston were the ones who pointed me in the right direction after we connected in Italy. Their dad opened a lot of doors I hadn't realized were closed. He put me in touch with the person who customized my first bike. When I made the amateur league, he was my first sponsor. I owe the Wheeler family more than I can ever repay. Getting you back to where you belong is the biggest way I can thank Aston for all she's done for me. Plus, I'm greedy. I want the best for my team, and that is you, Zowen."

I chugged the rest of the water in the bottle and leaned forward to rest my arms on my knees. "I was the best a long time ago. Now ..." I had no idea what I was. But at least I wasn't as terrified as I used to be at the thought of getting back on a bike.

"Now, you're a guy who needs to be reminded that he's the best. I'm not asking you to jump back into the industry with both feet. I don't want someone on my team who is giving their all while I'm still pushing to advance classes. There's time for you to get your feet wet and feel things out. There's time for you to get your own bike and practice riding. You're definitely rusty." He chuckled. "When you can beat me in a full-out race, then I'll know you're ready to take the next step." He stretched his legs out in front of him and tilted his head back.

He closed his eyes and asked, "How are things going on your end with the stalker? She's been quiet ever since the police identified her."

"There's a security detail following Aston everywhere. It looks like she's surrounded by the Secret Service most of the time. And I moved into the main house with her. She's rarely alone, so there hasn't been an opportunity for the stalker to get close to her."

Which was both a good and bad thing. Aston was safe, but the stalker was in hiding. A threat you couldn't see coming was always worse than one that was anticipated.

"She's alert and aware of her surroundings. Getting pushed down the stairs was a real eye-opener for her."

Cassio sighed. "Don't you have any connections that can do something about this girl? I thought the people you work for have some questionable tactics they like to use to solve problems."

I snorted. "They do. But your stalker also seems to have those types of tactics working for her on her side. She is mostly a ghost. Any progress we make in trying to locate her is being derailed by the other side. Rich people are better criminals and have more connections than the actual bad guys in most situations. I'm still looking. She'll have to show her face eventually."

Cassio nodded. "I have a race coming up. The police think she'll definitely put in an appearance for it. She hasn't missed one yet."

"I'll make sure to keep Aston away then." It would be best for her and the baby, obviously.

"You might not be able to. Since it's a local event, she'll have to manage all the press and media. I doubt her boss will let her skip it." Cassio frowned. "I can't ask for another PR rep. If I do that, it'll make Aston look bad. She's already missed so much work because of Royce and being injured from the fall. She's very good at her job. I don't want to be the reason she loses it." He sounded genuinely concerned about the prospect of Aston getting fired.

I swore and leaned my head back against the trailer. The metal was hot against my head since my hair was so short. "I guess we'll have to amp up the security around her for the event then."

Thank goodness my boss didn't bat an eye at deploying his personal army when I asked him for the favor. I was pretty sure it was actually Benny he was doing the favor for, but I didn't care as long as Aston's safety was guaranteed.

"Speaking of Royce, are you planning on going to see him at any point in the future? You know he's struggling. He could use a friend." Or something more, if the two of them could figure out how to bury the hatchet and make amends.

Cassio laughed, but it was a dry and brittle sound. "Royce Wheeler and I were never friends." He scoffed and lifted a hand to ruffle his hair. "We were lovers who turned into enemies, who then turned into strangers. I'm not someone he would find any comfort in. There was nothing soft or reassuring when we were together."

"He has enough people around him who offer comfort. He's got Aston and his parents. He even has his mom. Aston said she's doing her best to make sure he knows she's not leaving this world with regrets. Maybe he needs someone who can offer him something else."

Cassio laughed again and turned to look at me. "Sex? You think he needs someone he can hate fuck out all his frustrations with?"

I shrugged. "I think he could use a distraction. I think he could use someone who can tolerate him being mean and nasty." I gave him a pointed look. "When I first got out of jail, I was really angry. It was difficult to put on a happy face when my life was in the toilet. I needed someone who let me feel bad while trying to make me feel better."

The Italian man fell silent and seemed to contemplate my words.

The silence was broken when my cell phone rang.

Seeing Aston's name on the screen, I slid to answer the call with a soft smile on my face. "What's up?"

"Did you leave the gate in the yard open when you left to meet Cassio?" Aston sounded a little panicked, which made me sit up straight and narrow my eyes.

"I left through the front. Why? Has someone been at the house while we weren't there?"

"Maybe the dog walker left the gate open. I let Koons out when I got home and didn't realize the gate was open. He ran out the back. I need to go find him. He's so small, and there're all kinds of wildlife back in the Hills behind the house."

I could hear her moving, and every few steps, she called the puppy's name.

"Aston, wait for me to get back. Or go grab one of the security guys from in front of the house. Don't go looking for the puppy alone."

"He couldn't have gone far. I have to find him." I heard her sniff and could tell she started crying. "I promised to take care of the puppy for my brother, Zowen. I can't let anything happen to him. I can't let Royce and Kallie down. This was the *one* thing I could do to actually help them."

"I understand that." I got up and moved toward the Bronco. Realizing it would take forever to get home if I drove the big blue beast, I stuck out a hand and motioned for Cassio to give me the keys to his street bike. I needed to get back to Aston as quickly as possible, and a bike was the only option. "But it's not safe for you to wander around without someone watching you. You don't know that the stalker didn't open the gate specifically for this reason, like with that elevator sign. You might be walking into a trap."

She sniffed again. "I don't care. I have to find Koons."

I ran toward the bike, Cassio hot on my heels. He shoved a helmet in my hand and told me he would meet me at the house. I asked him to alert someone on the security team to let them know that Aston left the backyard alone.

"He has a GPS tracker on his collar. Open the app it's attached to and see if it shows you where he is. Wait for one of the security guys to come find you, Aston. I'm serious." We used the tracker to see where the dog walker took him during the day in case there was an emergency. "I'll be there in fifteen minutes." Even though it was a thirty-minute drive. "Just wait for me."

I waited for her to whisper, *Always*, but it never came. Instead, the call went dead, and when I tried to call her back, there was no response.

I climbed on the bike like I'd never been afraid and cranked the ignition.

I was about to be faster than I'd ever been before. I had known all along that she would be the motivation I needed to conquer all my fears.

chapter
TWENTY

Aston

I lost service as I climbed higher on the trails that twisted and turned around the hills behind the bungalow. It
happened occasionally when I came hiking out here, and
Zowen complained the service was spotty every time he
ran back in this direction instead of on the street. I knew
it was a dumb idea to blindly follow in the direction the
puppy tracking app told me to go, but I couldn't stop myself from putting one foot in front of another.

I couldn't let anything happen to Kallie's dog. I'd
promised Royce I would protect Koons and make sure
the little fluff ball would have the best little doggy life
possible. I couldn't bear the thought of letting my brother
down. My heart also clenched painfully when I thought
of something bad happening to the puppy. He was so little and defenseless. There were a lot of unknown dan-
gers beyond the fenced-in yard that he wouldn't stand a
chance against.

I'd heard Zowen order me to grab one of the security
guys, but I had already been halfway up the trail when I

realized I'd left through the back of the house and not told them.

Maybe I was actually too stupid to live because I just kept going, calling the puppy's name at the top of my lungs.

I had to find the dog.

There was no other option. It wasn't rational, and my emotions felt like they were all over the place. All I could see in my mind's eye was the distressed look on Royce's face when he'd thought about how difficult taking care of a puppy would be for his mother in the future. I hadn't seen him cry often, but he'd sobbed with his entire body while talking about the puppy.

I knew Zowen was going to worry and that he had every right to be unhappy with the choice I was making, but none of that was enough to stop me from huffing and puffing up the tree-lined trail that zigzagged behind my house. I wondered if this was how Daire felt every time she jumped into a situation without a thought to the consequences or her own safety. I was not a risk-taker by nature. I'd spent too long trying to mitigate any danger or disruption I might encounter. Being reckless didn't come naturally to me, and the farther away from my house I got, the more I realized I was probably making the situation worse. However, I couldn't force myself to turn around.

This was a defining moment, where I understood I'd really left the girl behind who couldn't think for herself because she was so worried about her actions hurting others. My life and choices were my own. Even if I wasn't being as smart as I should be with either.

Right now, only Koons was missing and in danger. If I kept going, I was putting not only myself, but also the unborn baby I was carrying in peril.

I shouldn't be that selfish.

I looked at my phone, and there was still no service. I was getting ready to turn around and head back to my house to alert the security guys and grab someone to accompany me when two teenage girls came around the corner on the trail. I paused and waved at them to stop. They exchanged worried looks, and I realized how frantic I must appear. I caught my breath and ordered myself to calm down so I could ask them if they saw the small, fluffy puppy somewhere along the trail.

The girl closest to me nodded and told me, "I've seen that cute puppy before. Usually, the lady who walks him back here lets me and my sister play with him for a while. We tried to pet him today, and the person walking him today yelled at us to leave her alone. She picked him up and ran in the direction of the overlook. We thought it was hella weird. We thought about following her, but she was acting super sketchy. I was going to post about it on the neighborhood app once I got service on my phone and see if anyone local knew who she was." The teenager sounded shocked and afraid after the encounter.

The overlook was a scenic spot on the trail that offered clear views the skyline of LA. It also had a great view of the Hollywood sign. It was a popular spot. Some of my anxiety lessened as I thought that whoever had taken Koons probably wouldn't hurt him in front of an audience.

"That's my puppy. He got out of the yard. The person you saw shouldn't have him. She stole him." I blew out a breath and asked, "On your way back down the trail, if you run into anyone who appears to be looking for me, can you point them in the direction of the overlook? They shouldn't be too far behind me."

The teen girls exchanged another look, but they both nodded in agreement. I thanked them for being observant and took off in the direction of the overlook.

Any of the anxiety I managed to hold at bay broke free when I caught sight of a *Trail Closed for Maintenance* sign hanging on a chained gate that led to the scenic spot. The teens hadn't mentioned this part of the trail was closed. It meant if I crossed the barrier, I was going to have to face the person who had stolen Koons on my own.

I knew it had to be Cassio's stalker who was behind this stunt. The young woman had already proven she wasn't afraid to harm me when she pushed me down the stairs. That knowledge only served to make me more nervous. If she had no qualms about hurting a human, there was no telling what she might do to the poor puppy.

Swearing out loud in a long litany, I climbed over the rickety gate and made my way farther along the path that would take me to the overlook. I glanced at my phone and noticed I had a single bar of service. It didn't seem like enough to get a call or text through because there was nothing on the display from Zowen. I was sure he was losing his mind, and there was no way he wasn't trying to get ahold of me.

I sent him a couple of messages, letting him know exactly where I was on the trail and telling him that I thought Cassio's stalker had our puppy. I told him the security detail was right behind me even though I didn't know for certain if that was true. I watched the notification ping and tell me the message failed to send over and over. Getting a text to go through seemed futile.

Knowing the situation I was walking into might go horribly wrong, I sent him one last message before making my way out into the clearing, where a young woman stood precariously close to the edge of the path, holding a frantically barking Koons.

I love you, Zowen. I've always loved you.

I wanted to tell him to his face. However, if I didn't get the chance because things went south, he needed to know how I felt. He deserved to know he owned my heart and he was no longer alone when it came to the feelings that flowed between us. In fact, I was pretty sure I was the one who was over-the-top infatuated these days. He brought so much into my life that I'd never thought was possible.

I put a hand on my tummy and squared my shoulders. I needed to believe I could keep myself and the baby safe. This wasn't the same as being attacked from behind because I wasn't paying attention. This was facing an ongoing problem head-on.

It occurred to me after I took a couple of steps toward the young woman that if she was armed with a gun, facing off with her was the last thing I should do. I tried to calm my racing heart by telling myself if she had access to a gun, she would've used it by now.

The puppy barked and wiggled even more violently when he caught sight of me. The girl holding him screamed at the dog to stop and squeezed the small body tightly enough that he yelped in pain.

"Hi. Your name is Sophie, right? Do you mind if I call you Sophie? I know you're very angry with me, but can you let the puppy go? He's just a baby, and he doesn't deserve to be hurt."

I hoped she didn't think that I was using her name to trick her or something more sinister. I just wanted her to know I saw her as a person, not as a monster who had tried to kill me. She looked so much younger than nineteen. It was such a shame she was willing to throw her entire life away because of some man she didn't even know. I hoped someone in her life would get her the help she needed instead of sheltering her from her mistakes and misdeeds, as if they didn't matter and had no consequences.

The young woman glared at me and held the puppy even tighter. Koons tried to bite her, and she screamed in response.

"Why won't he look at me the way he looks at you? Why does he smile at you all the time? Even when you started seeing someone else, he's always around you. What makes you so special to him?" Each question was shouted louder than the one before it. Her eyes were wild, and she was breathing like she'd just finished running a marathon.

I didn't see a weapon, but she was standing close to the edge of a huge drop-off. If she took one wrong step or let go of the puppy while he was held aloft, he wouldn't survive the fall that followed.

"You're talking about Cassio, right? He and I are friends. We've known each other for a long time. And we work together. That's it. You know I have someone else who is very important to me. There is no need to be jealous."

I didn't have a degree in psychology, but I was pretty good at reading people's reactions. It was part of my job. I could tell by the way her face tightened that whatever I'd said had no impact on her.

"I'm not jealous. I don't lack in any department when compared to you. I'm better than everyone who is close to Cassio. He needs me. I just want a chance to show him how much I love him. We're perfect for one another."

It wasn't my place to out Cassio and disclose his sexual orientation. I doubted this obsessed young woman would believe me if I told her Cassio only dated men anyway. I noticed the longer we spoke, the less focused she was on holding the puppy. Koons seemed to be aware that she wasn't as intent on hurting him and quieted down significantly.

"It takes two people to be in a relationship. I know you're young, but you must realize that. Even if you love someone with your whole heart and they don't return those feelings, there is no way for the relationship to get off the ground. It's like beating your head against a brick wall." I sighed and watched her closely. "I had someone who loved me like that when I was your age. I didn't know how to return his feelings at the time. I could see how much I hurt him, but there was nothing I could do about it back then. It was impossible for us to be together. I think the situation between you and Cassio is similar. You might not know him as well as you think you do. Trust me when I tell you, he can't be in a relationship with you.."

I wanted to tell her she should concentrate on herself. I wanted to tell her puppy love felt like the most painful thing you were ever going to go through, but it wasn't. I wanted to tell her she deserved so much more than a one-sided infatuation.

I didn't get the chance to say anything because she started screaming at me in an incomprehensible tirade. She backed up a step and jerked forward as she wobbled on the edge of the drop-off. I wanted to rush forward and grab her. I refrained as she screamed that I had ruined her life and deserved to die. She was getting more and more agitated, the longer we faced off. I heard someone calling my name and figured the security detail had finally caught up. I was worried that when they broke into the clearing, she was really going to freak out and go over the edge.

I held my hands out in front of me and continued to try and reason with her. "I told you, Cassio and I are friends. We're practically like family. He treats me like a little sister. I know you tried to talk to his real sister, and it upset him a lot. If you keep confronting people he cares about, he's going to keep misunderstanding your intentions.

"You can't use force to make yourself part of someone's life. They have to welcome you in with open arms.

If you let my puppy go and calm down, maybe I can help you have a conversation with Cassio where you can explain yourself better."

I sighed and gave her a weak grin. "I want to help you. The people coming to find me since you lured me away from home won't feel the same. They don't care what happens to you as long as I'm safe."

The young woman gritted her teeth and once again squeezed the puppy tight enough that he yelped. I couldn't stand it anymore and moved closer to her. I just needed to get her to step away from the edge. Even if it was a couple of inches, it would be enough to give me room to work with.

"You don't want to help me. No one does. Everyone thinks I'm crazy. That I'm too young to know what or who I want. No one ever supports me." Her voice broke, and I realized she was crying.

I hated that I felt sympathy for someone who had hurt me. She really needed someone who cared enough to hear her cries for help.

I carefully walked closer to where she was standing. "I don't think you're crazy. I think you have a lot of big feelings you don't know what to do with and you're letting them get you in trouble. I think you're impulsive and angry. I also think you might have the right to be mad, but not at me. And definitely not at my puppy. Please let him go."

Time was up. Several men, dressed in dark colors, burst into the clearing. More than one had a weapon drawn. I saw the young woman's eyes widen, and panic flashed across her face. She took another precarious step back, and I watched her struggle to keep her balance. I screamed a warning at the top of my lungs, but it was too late. She was too close to the edge and too startled by the appearance of my rescuers.

I ran forward as she started to fall. There was no chance I would reach her in time, but as our eyes locked, she loosened her hold on Koons, and the small dog dropped to the ground before she disappeared from sight. I heard her shout split the air until it suddenly stopped.

I raced to grab the puppy, who rushed into my arms. His entire body was vibrating, and as I picked him up to cuddle to my chest, his whimpers broke my heart. Poor little thing was probably traumatized. I kissed his head and accepted his frantic licks on my face.

I maneuvered to the edge of the drop, followed by a couple of the guys on the security detail. I could tell they were all annoyed with me. Their boss was rumored to be pretty scary, and they were no doubt going to be read the riot act when they reported on the events of today.

Glancing down into the valley below the overlook, I saw the young woman sprawled at a very painful-looking angle on a small outcropping of rocks and bushes. She'd fallen several feet, but not to the bottom of the hill and not far enough that sending someone down to help her would be difficult. I heard her moan and saw one of her twisted limbs twitch. She was clearly still alive, which had everyone hovering above her breathing a sigh of relief.

"We need to call the police and find a way to get her back up here." I looked at the men surrounding me, and the one who was in charge nodded.

They assured me they would handle the rescue effort, and one of the men offered to walk me back to the house. I was about to agree when someone else crash into the clearing. I had no clue how Zowen had made it all the way here from the racetrack out in the desert this fast, but I was so happy to see him that I didn't ask any questions.

I ran into his arms, and he embraced both me and the puppy with a tight hold. He was violently shaking, and I could feel how tense his big body was. I buried my head against his chest and wrapped an arm around his lean waist. I felt that if I held on to him tightly enough, he wouldn't push me away and tell me how angry he was with me.

"I'm sorry. I know I made you worry." My voice was soft and honestly apologetic.

"What if she'd had a gun, Aston? What if she hadn't been alone? She'd already tried to kill you once." He broke off, and I could sense him trying to control his temper. "You're more careful than this."

I *was* normally more careful than this. Or at least, I always had been. It seemed that part of growing into the woman I wanted to be also included acting recklessly when it involved the people I loved.

"I don't think she wants to hurt anyone. I think she's ill and she doesn't have anyone to help her. I know she's not harmless, but I don't think she's as dangerous as we initially thought." I kept the words quiet and held him even closer. "Did any of the messages I sent you get through? I lost service the farther up on the trail I hiked." I didn't forget that I'd told him I loved him.

He wrapped his arms around me even tighter and rested his chin on the top of my head. "I love you too, Aston. *Only* you. I've never been so scared of anything in my life as when that call was dropped. I wanted to strangle you and teleport to your side at the same time."

He loved me. I had known it. I'd known it since we were kids. But hearing him tell me directly for the first time was something entirely new. The words wrapped around my heart like a warm hug. I felt them float through my veins and tickle the tiny life that was sheltered inside of me.

"I love you too, Zowen." A real love that was just for him. *Only* for him. It was the same kind of love he'd *always* had for me.

I pulled back so I could look at his face and asked, "How did you get here so quickly?"

He gave me an impenetrable look and took a step back so he could run his hand across the back of his neck. "I stole Cassio's bike."

I blinked in surprise and tilted my head to give him a confused look. "You rode his bike on the highway? With all that traffic? Weren't you afraid?"

He grabbed my face and squeezed my cheeks together. "Yes, I was scared out of my mind. But nowhere near as frightened as I was that something was going to happen to you and the baby. I had to do it. It was the fastest way to reach you."

I puffed my cheeks out against his palms and reached up with the hand not holding Koons to grasp his wrist. "I'm very proud of you."

He was doing so well at overcoming all his fears.

He was an inspiration in his own way.

"I'm proud of you too. But next time I ask you to wait for me, do it." He bent down and kissed my forehead, then took Koons from me so he could guide me back down the trail.

I held his hand tightly and told him, "*Always.*"

chapter TWENTY-ONE

Zowen

"The family is dropping the case against you. Their attorney talked them out of bringing forward another settlement offer. He explained the plethora of evidence that pointed to their son being actively culpable in the events that had happened that night. You're in the clear, kiddo."

I let out a long, slow breath and felt the final link of the chain tying me to the past snap and break.

"Can they refile a civil complaint once they drop one?"

I should've spent more time studying the basics of law while I was locked up. It was knowledge that would benefit me the most post-prison.

"They can. But they won't. Not with the evidence we have. They already got their payday from the other people they'd sued. They won't risk endangering the victories they already won by chasing after a guaranteed loss."

Hayes sounded so certain that I chose to believe him. Mostly, I didn't want to worry about the lawsuit any longer. It was time to focus on the future.

"Thank you. Not only for handling the civil suit, but also for never making me feel like I was the bad guy. You've always had more faith in my innocence and intentions than I ever did. I don't know how I would've survived any of the things I've been through without your help and guidance."

Hayes laughed as he twirled his pen between his fingers. It moved so fast that it was nothing more than a silver flash in the sunlight. "I told you, I want to keep the good guys out of jail. It really pissed me off that you wouldn't help yourself at the criminal trial. Not only do I believe that you never belonged behind bars, but that loss on my record also irritates me to no end. I'm a winner, kid."

I knew he was. That was why my family had hired him in the first place.

Before I could apologize for tainting his acquittal rate, he gave me a serious look and asked, "Do you want to put me on retainer? It seems your days of breaking the law are far from over, Mr. Archer."

I narrowed my eyes and stiffened in the fancy leather chair across from his massive desk. I felt like I was getting scolded by a principal or reprimanded by a parent. I cleared my throat and looked away from that penetrating gaze. "I have no idea what you're talking about."

Hayes chuckled and tapped on the tablet in front of him. In no time, a viral video showing a street bike outrunning a police cruiser played in front of me.

"You're going to try and tell me that isn't you on the bike?"

I blinked and refused to incriminate myself. "I do believe that bike was reported stolen by the owner. I'm pretty sure I read that on a post somewhere."

The bike was recognizable, but the rider was covered from head to toe in riding gear, and the black helmet obscured any identifying features. The bike was moving so fast, and a lot of the video was a blur. It was easy to see the cop car had no chance of catching up to the rider.

"If they had gotten a chopper in the air or managed to track the chase with drones, there would have been no way for the thief to outrun the cops. That's one brazen criminal."

I lifted a shoulder and let it fall in a fake nonchalant shrug. "Maybe it wasn't a criminal. Maybe it was someone who needed to be somewhere in a hurry and the cops got in the way."

Hayes hummed an amused sound and turned the tablet back around. "I guess it doesn't matter. The motorcycle belongs to some famous racer. The authorities tracked it to a sketchy suburb in Northern California. It had already been stripped for parts."

I raised my eyebrows and coughed into my hand. "That's a shame. It was a nice bike."

Hayes snorted and tapped on the tablet again. This time, when he turned it around to face me, there was a news article about the rescue of a young woman off a hillside on a popular hiking trail. The details were vague, and the headline was flashy. My name didn't appear anywhere in the article. I was stunned that Hayes knew I had been involved in the incident.

"I'm not going to ask you about the backstory of this. I do find it very interesting though that the same famous racer whose bike was stolen is also the main focus in this stalking case. Do you know that those who practice law often say there is no such thing as a coincidence?"

I shook my head and kept my mouth sealed shut.

"I'm still your attorney. Anything you say to me is privileged information. It doesn't leave this office."

"I don't have anything to say. Other than I'm glad no one was seriously injured on that overlook. That girl was lucky she landed where she did. She's also lucky the woman she lured up there has a soft heart and doesn't know the definition of the word *malice*. Things could've gone very differently."

Hayes gave a faint nod and rose to his feet. "I like you, Zowen. You seem like a good kid. You've got a stronger sense of justice than I do. Stay out of trouble. Don't get yourself into another situation where you feel like you have to take the fall to make things right. I won't represent you again if you're going to refuse to fight for yourself."

He stuck out his hand, and we exchanged a firm handshake. As different as this man was from my father, my uncle ... and, well, pretty much all the male influences I had in my life, he felt like one of the best mentors a guy could have. His advice was always straightforward, and I felt like he could fully see the kind of man I wanted to be. I promised the next time we saw each other, it would be for personal reasons, not professional ones.

When I left Hayes's office, I got in the Bronco and headed to the last place I needed to visit to fully put the past to rest. I stopped along the way and bought a bouquet of flowers. It felt silly, buying such a thing for someone I didn't really know, but I couldn't show up with nothing.

The cemetery was huge. I needed a map to guide me to the resting place I was looking for. The property was meticulously maintained. It looked like an extremely expensive spot to spend all of eternity. I took a deep breath to steady myself and walked through the rolling green landscaping until I found the headstone I was looking for.

It was a strange sensation to grieve for someone you didn't know. It was like the sadness was hollow and empty. Staring down at the grave, I felt my heart constrict and all the guilt and remorse I'd struggled with since that night try to rise up and choke me. I bent down so I could put the colorful flowers into the small brass holder attached to the headstone.

I stayed hunched down and lowered my head. "I know this apology is a long time coming, and it doesn't change anything, but I am sorry. I regret everything that happened that night. I regret letting my emotions get the better of me. I regret not seeing the provocation for what it was. I regret thinking that a race was so important that I couldn't handle losing. I don't care if it was rigged; my pride was not worth the price you paid."

My chest shuddered as my breath caught. A ball of emotions tangled in the back of my throat.

"I believed I was the only reason you had died that night. I considered myself a murderer for a long time. I went to prison because I truly believed I belonged there after what had happened to you. I was ready to give my life up for yours."

I rubbed a hand across my face and looked down at the artfully carved marble headstone. "Someone showed me that even a life that was tainted, like mine, was still worth living. The best person in the world loved me when I was at my worst. I'd never thought something like that was possible. I'm sorry you won't get the chance to experience what that feels like. I'm sorry for all the things you're going to miss out on. I don't know that I'll ever be able to fully forgive myself for having a part in taking those opportunities away from you." I gulped and clenched my hands into tight fists. "I think the best thing I can do is maybe share all the big things that happen in my life with you."

The least I could do would be to walk away from this pristine resting place and never look back. I could forget this arrogant kid had ever existed and move on with my life as if that night had never occurred. But I wouldn't do that. I no longer felt like the past was pulling me under and tossing me around like an undertow. Now, it was more or less a lesson I needed to remember anytime I started to act before my mind caught up to my instincts. It was a warning that things could go very wrong in a heartbeat, so I needed to be present and accountable. I was no longer a man living for himself and driven by my own wants and needs. I had to take Aston and the baby into consideration with every step I took.

Speaking of the baby ...

I got to my feet and shoved my hands deep into my pockets. "I'm going to be a father. Once the baby is born, I'll bring it by so you can meet the little nugget."

Aston was still a few months away from being able to determine the sex of the fetus, so we were alternating cutesy nicknames until we knew what we were having.

"No one knows about the baby. You're the first person I've told." Because I'd planned on sharing this major moment in my life with the kid who never got to experience his own.

Aston and I were actually planning on flying to Denver at the end of the month. It was finally time to share our good news with our loved ones. We'd timed it after Royce told his sister that Kallie wanted to travel to Colorado while she was still able. We were going to break the news while everyone was in one place.

I sighed after moving so I could knock my knuckles on the tombstone. "I'll be back."

It was supposed to be a promise, but it sounded slightly like a threat.

I left the cemetery and headed back to the bungalow. Aston had had a doctor's appointment and told me she would be home early. She'd also said she wanted to take care of dinner. Her cooking skills were still highly questionable, but the only way to learn was to try and fail or to try and succeed. She'd been particularly domestic after the shared *I love you* and the excitement on the overlook.

I thought she knew I was still upset about her taking an unnecessary risk. I was also annoyed that she'd gone out of her way to advocate for the young girl who was stalking Cassio. She wanted the girl in a psychiatric center, not behind bars. Unfortunately, there were a litany of charges the girl was facing that wouldn't be so easy to navigate. Her empathy was a point of contention between the two of us, but I understood her stance slightly better after my visit to the cemetery. It was hard to watch a kid throw their entire life away.

I parked on the hill in front of the house. It was nice to no longer have black sedans and men in dark sunglasses watching every move we made. I owed my boss a lot, so I was sticking at my current job at least until the baby was born. I needed something safe and stable, but I'd started to admit to myself that working for Cassio's team was very appealing. I wondered if there was a way I could juggle both since I was very good at each specialty individually. Either way, it meant I was staying in California for the foreseeable future. Which was a whole other conversation I needed to have with my family. Once they found out about the baby, they would understand my decision to stay on the West Coast even if they didn't love the idea.

As soon as I hit the front door, I heard the smoke alarm going off.

I chuckled under my breath and walked into the house, covering my ears to block the shrill sound. The back door was open to let out the puffs of smoke, and Aston was standing on one of the dining room chairs, waving a dish towel in front of the alarm to try and get it to stop screaming. Koons was running around the dining room table, barking his tiny head off. Aston gave me a pleading look for help when she caught sight of me.

After I washed my hands, watching the water and the last remnants of feelings from the cemetery go down the drain, the first thing I did was wrap an arm around her waist and guide her off the chair. We were really going to have to have a talk about her deciding that she actually was a risk-taker. My heart could only handle so much. Then, I took the puppy into the back bedroom and closed the door, hoping the sound was less intense. With the puppy secure, I opened the front door and flipped the switch to turn on the ceiling fan.

Aston swore and looked at the smoke detector that finally went quiet. "I was going to do all of that if the towel didn't work." She sighed and looked at the kitchen with regret. "Dinner is a no-go. I burned everything." She turned her head and gave me a sheepish grin. "I think I even burned the water I was going to use to cook the pasta."

I stepped closer to her and backed her up until she bumped into the dining table. I put my hands on either side of her so her body was caged by mine. I bent down and brushed the tip of my nose against her soft cheek.

"I can eat something else." The offer was sultry and full of innuendo.

Aston wrapped her arms around my neck and cocked her head to the side as she playfully asked, "Are you hungry?"

"Very." I grasped her hips and picked her up to place her on the table.

She was wearing one of the flowy, flowery sundresses she seemed to prefer, so most of her bare legs were exposed in this position. The fabric of her dress was great at concealing the tiny hint of a bump that was just starting to show. Aston had mentioned that Cassio asked her if she was gaining weight. She told him she was but attributed it to my cooking skills. Cassio was smart. He had taken her word at face value, but every time I saw him, he gave me a knowing look.

I pulled her to the edge of the table and skimmed my hands up the outside of her thighs. I felt her flesh tremble as I hooked the band of her underwear with my fingers and guided it down her legs. Aston fell back on the table as I dropped to my knees in front of her. I moved her legs so they were resting on my shoulders and kissed my way up the inside of her thigh. The material of her dress slithered along my forearms, and I reached my hands out so I could hold her ass and keep her pinned where I wanted her. I couldn't see her face with the fabric obscuring my view. It somehow heightened the emotion. She had no idea where I was going to touch her or how I was going to taste her. Every move was a surprise, followed by the shock of sensation.

Even before I got my tongue anywhere near her opening, I felt her body clench and quiver with anticipation. By the time I swiped the length of her pussy, the delicate folds were wet, and Aston was moaning. She shifted above me and moved her hands from where they had been holding my head to touching herself. I couldn't see what she was doing, but I could imagine her elegant fingers caressing and teasing her nipples after she lowered the top of her dress. I could envision the tightened points begging for my mouth and the flush that would cover her heaving chest. My imagination was enough to get me hard. Aston's taste was enough to keep me that way as my tongue licked into her most private place. I swirled it around her opening, then dipped it into her hidden sweetness. I loved the way she throbbed as I darted the tip in and out of her. I could easily lose it over the passionate sounds she made while I feasted on her. The wetter and hotter she became, the harder and more impatient my dick was.

I removed one of the hands holding her in place and added a couple of fingers to the mix. She writhed under the stimulation and called out my name. Her legs clamped around my head and squeezed. I laughed, and the vibration against her hot center had Aston practically screaming with pleasure. I used my fingers to toy with her inner heat and to slick across all the excited places that were pulsating. I moved my tongue to lightly lick around her distended clit and watched her back bow off the table in response. I could hear her gasping for air, and every pant and sigh sent my arousal soaring.

As I lapped at her clit and used my fingers to thrust and twist inside of her, it didn't take very long for her to come. Aston let out a breathless sound and rocked against my face. She was chasing after all the different types of satisfaction awaiting her. It was sexy to watch her fall apart under my mouth and hands. Even more so because I couldn't see her face or her expressive eyes. All I had to go on to know that I was making her feel good were the sounds she was making and the reaction of her body. There was no way for her to hide how beautifully she responded to me.

I wiped my wet mouth on the inside of her thigh in a teasing manner and climbed to my feet. My eyes immediately went to where her hands were covering her bare breasts. She looked thoroughly debauched and happily loved within an inch of her life.

Her gaze shifted to the bulge behind my zipper as she lifted a knee and pressed against the rigid erection. I hissed through my teeth and reached out to smooth her dress down so the places on her body only I was allowed to have access to were covered.

"What if I want to eat too?" One of Aston's eyebrows lifted as she smirked at me.

I leaned over the table and braced myself over her languid body. "I'll feed you whatever you want." I touched the tip of my nose against hers. "But you have to eat something real first." I cast a look down at the barely rounded belly behind her dress. "I want you to have enough energy for whatever comes next."

She chuckled and allowed me to pull her up so she was sitting on the edge of the table. "We appreciate your sacrifice."

I gave her a hard kiss on the mouth, knowing she was going to taste herself on my lips. I wiggled my eyebrows at her and stepped away to figure out if I could salvage something for dinner. My dick might be screaming in protest, but my heart flipped at being able to come back to her and do something as simple as cook for her.

"It's not a sacrifice if it's something I love doing." And taking care of this woman and the life we were building together was what I loved most.

chapter
TWENTY-TWO

Aston

It felt strange to be back in Denver when it wasn't a holiday.

Though it was nice to have my entire family under one roof for the first time in ages, the visit was tinged with sorrow because it was clear to see that Kallie wasn't feeling well. She'd lost so much weight, and she barely had any appetite, but she looked very happy, seeing the whole family gathered in one place. My brother didn't look much better. The guy who was always the life of the party and was so carefree had grown sullen and solemn. He didn't laugh. He didn't smile. He didn't entertain everyone with tales about living in New York or reminisce about the days when life had been easier. All he did was watch his mom like a hawk and urge her to eat and sleep well.

I knew the circle of life meant children would eventually end up as the caretakers for those who had given them life, but it was a touch disconcerting to witness the change in dynamic. Royce was never serious unless it came to his art. Seeing him act so reserved and mature was like having a stranger for an older brother. And since Zowen and I decided to spend the first few days of our trip with our respective families, I didn't have anyone I could express my concerns to. I knew my parents were as worried about my brother as I was, but no one could quite figure out how to help him. Even Kallie seemed at a loss as to what to do about his shift in personality.

Tonight, Remy was hosting a large dinner party. My family and most of Zowen's were going to be there. His aunt and uncle were back from Europe, but Ry was still stuck working in Texas. Daire was supposed to show today, but the weather was bad, and her flight had been canceled. I'd told her I would touch base after dinner was done and she didn't need to make the trip if she didn't want to. After all, once the news got out tonight, there was no real need for her to travel to Denver. She was going to be furious when she found out she wasn't the first person I told about the baby. Zowen and had I toyed with the idea of letting her know before talking to the family, but ultimately decided it was easier to pull the Band-Aid off with one yank than trying to tiptoe around the subject if only a few family members knew about the situation.

After dinner, Zowen and I were going to spend the rest of the week at his sister's place. Zowen wanted to spend time with his nieces, and neither one of us was ready for our parents to go into full-on grandparent mode.

I had a feeling my mom was going to want to wrap me up in bubble wrap and keep me from leaving the house. Her first pregnancy had been so difficult and complicated, and she'd suffered so much after the miscarriage; I knew once she found out about the baby, she was going to expect me to be extra cautious and careful.

Zowen didn't have the same concerns with his parents, but he did mention he was worried they were going to be upset when they found out he was planning on relocating to California permanently. He'd told me they were going to have a hard time with it mostly because he'd been locked away in California for all those years. There was a psychological shadow left by them only getting to see him in a prison visiting center. They wanted to make up for lost time, but that was hard to do if he lived halfway across the country. Instead of staying with them and letting them try to convince him to come home, he opted to avoid the pressure and conflict by crashing with his sister.

Was it the most mature response from either of us when it came to approaching a very adult problem? No. However, when we were together, we felt a lot more invincible and a lot less likely to cave under the force of familial pressure.

At the moment, I was chased out of the kitchen and told not to step back in. Remy gave me a bewildered look and asked how I could be such a bad cook. I heard Zowen laugh from where he was gently holding his newest family member. The infant already had a head of curly blond hair, and while it was too early to tell, it appeared one of her blue eyes was going to be a darker shade than the other. Zowen was delighted at the idea of his mother's two-toned gaze being passed along to the next generation.

Fortunately, Hyde, Remy's partner, was handy in the kitchen. He helped her assemble all the side dishes that went with the main course. He even set the table and offered to play bartender. I noticed Remy's curious look when both Zowen and I turned down a drink. I couldn't have one, and he was being supportive by not drinking until I was able to have a cocktail with him. Zowen's sister watched him closely for the rest of the night, and every time our eyes locked, I felt like she could see right through me. Maybe it was because she'd recently given birth, but she seemed to know the big secret before either Zowen or I said a word.

Soon, all the Archers arrived, followed by my family. Even though she wasn't feeling well, Kallie's eyes lit up at the large, warm gathering. Her reaction was a good reminder that families didn't need a reason to celebrate. They should get together and enjoy each other simply because no one knew how long we would get with one another. Life was unpredictable, and not having enough moments and memories with loved ones would be the biggest regret any of us would have.

Zowen had clearly filled his family members in on Kallie's health situation. Collectively, everyone seemed to decide no one was going to mention her illness or offer useless platitudes. Instead, the atmosphere was joyous and celebratory. She was still with us, and every minute with her was a gift.

Zowen's aunt and uncle chatted with my brother about all the places they'd recently traveled to, and finally, some of the tension in his face lessened. His uncle Rule was a tattoo artist, one who had successfully branched out into other mediums. He and my brother had a lot in common, just like Zowen and my father did. Zowen's mom and his aunt Shaw jumped in to help Remy finish dinner while my mom took a seat next to me and watched the interaction with a small smile on her face.

"You must have big news to have asked Remy to orchestrate this get-together." She let her gaze rove over my face. "Is there something you should've told me while I was in California?"

I nearly choked on the glass of water I had been sipping from. I turned my head to look at her and shrugged. "It's something you'll know when the time is right."

She laughed softly and reached out to pat me on the back as I continued to cough. "Okay. Zowen's parents know you're dating at least, right? You need to explain that you're in a relationship and living together, so whatever follows doesn't land Rome back in the hospital."

I looked at her out of the corner of my eye. "He told them we were together after we decided to come and visit. He said they didn't have much of a reaction. They had known about his crush on me from when we were kids. He hinted that they weren't exactly over the moon, but that's because they know if we're together, he's going to stay in LA with me."

My mom sighed and tilted her head so it could rest on my shoulder. "That makes me sad too. You really won't consider moving closer to home? It's already hard, having your brother so far away. It's like you both picked the farthest place away from one another to settle down."

I stroked her head in a comforting manner. "Royce needs to be where he is for his career. You and Dad are lucky he stayed in the States. If Kallie wasn't in New York, he would more than likely be living somewhere overseas."

We both made a distraught sound when we realized that there wouldn't be anyone tying my brother to the States when his mother's illness ran its course. There was so much to be heartbroken about; it was hard to keep the sorrow in check and not bring the mood down.

My mom reached for my hand and gave it a little pat. "As long as you're happy. That's all your dad and I want for both of you." She chuckled. "Well, that and for your brother to find someone and stick with them for more than a couple of months. He needs someone to remind him to take care of himself. He's going to need that even more in the future."

My thoughts immediately went to Cassio. I'd always thought they were nothing more than a passionate fling. Cassio was flirty and fun, and my brother refused to be tied down by anyone. However, now that Royce was facing a true crisis, I could see the way Cassio worried about him. I could tell that whatever feelings he harbored for my brother ran deep. He had always told me that he understood what it was like while I waited anxiously for Zowen's return. I'd never put together that the person Cassio was waiting for was my older brother.

"Maybe the right person for him is someone who's been there all along."

My mom lifted her head and gave me a probing look. "Are you keeping even more secrets than I thought you were?"

I shook my head and tilted it to the side, and it bumped lightly into hers. "No. That's not a secret. But it's also not my story to tell. If you can get Royce to talk, ask him about Italy."

"Now, you're speaking in riddles." She pouted, and it made me laugh.

I got to my feet as Remy started to move the food from the kitchen into the dining area.

All the men moved to help her haul everything, and I noticed that her mother was beaming with pride.

When she caught me watching her, she winked and said, "I'm really proud of Remy. She used to forget to go grocery shopping for months on end. She lived on cereal and ice cream. She's come a long way from her barren-cupboard days. Not only is she taking care of herself, but she's also feeding the whole family. I'm so glad we get to share moments like this."

Remy rolled her eyes dramatically behind her mother's back, but she also blushed hotly, and there was no hiding the raw happiness in her eyes. Hearing her mother's praise obviously meant more to her than she was willing to let on.

Once everyone sat around the large table, conversation flowed, and the food was plentiful. Hyde's parents, who showed up late, played with the kids while several of the other parents grilled me and Zowen about the situation with the stalker. Out of the corner of my eye, I noticed that Royce finally seemed interested in the conversation going on around him once Cassio was mentioned. I kicked Zowen under the table and inclined my head in my brother's direction. He lifted his eyebrows and dipped his chin in a slight nod. I made a silent vow to try and rebuild the burned bridge between the two of them.

Once dinner was done and everyone was ready to move on to dessert, Zowen cleared his throat and said, "Before we dive into dessert, Aston and I want to tell everyone something. I'm sure you all have an idea why we asked for this get-together out of the blue."

Zowen's mother, Cora, leaned forward and rested her arms on the table in front of her. If she wasn't such a small woman, the motion would've been intimidating.

"You're staying in LA. Your father and I figured that you would decide to do that when you told us you were dating."

Zowen cleared his throat and reached up to rub the back of his neck. It was a nervous tic that his family members immediately noticed.

"I'm staying in LA, but it's not only because Aston and I are dating."

He gave me a helpless look and reached for my hand. I watched as Remy smiled knowingly while my parents stared at me in anticipation.

"Aston and I are going to have a baby."

There was a round of gasps, a shout, and Remy cheering, "I knew it!"

Both our parents went still and exchanged wide-eyed looks with one another.

"I'm staying in LA because that's where Aston wants to be and for work. The job I have now is something I'm good at, and it makes a difference. In the future, if I want to do something with bikes, that opportunity is also in California. It's where our family needs to be."

"I know all of this seems fast. It's not. Zowen and I have been waiting for each other and the right time to be together since we were kids. We're both very excited about the life we're building with one another, and we want our families to be excited with us." I blew out a breath and looked at my mom. She had tears in her eyes. I couldn't tell if they were tears of sadness or joy. "This is all I've ever wanted."

Remy jumped to her feet and clapped her hands. Of course, Zowen's sister would be the one to break the awkward tension and silence.

"I knew it was either a baby or an engagement." She walked around behind her brother and wrapped her arms around his neck in a hug that made him choke. "I'm so glad it's a baby. Engagements are boring." She turned her head and gave me a smacking kiss on the cheek. "Weddings are overrated. I can't wait to throw you a baby shower and for our kids to grow up together. Congratulations! I'd welcome you to the family, but it feels like you're already one of us."

Her reaction was so very Remy and eased some of the worry I held in my heart. However, Remy was never the one I was worried about convincing that I knew what I was doing and that Zowen and I were going to be okay regardless of the challenges ahead.

Zowen's mom also blinked the obvious shock out of her eyes and offered a weak congratulations. His dad was staring at him with an intense look while my parents were watching one another.

Royce also got up and came over to give me a hug. "Why do I feel like you're suddenly so much more grown up than me? I'm very happy for you, Aston." He looked at Zowen. "You too, Archer. If you're going to be her family, you have to make sure she stays safe and happy from here on out."

Zowen nodded as if he took Royce's words to heart. "I will. Aston and the baby are my first priority." There was no missing that he really meant every word he said.

Finally, Zowen's dad reached out and slapped him on the back. "You've always been brighter than anyone else in the family, Zowen. If you're ready for the challenge of being a father, I'm not going to tell you any differently. I do think you should reconsider starting your family closer to home so you have a support system to navigate things when they get tricky, but you're grown. We can't make those kinds of choices for you." He cleared his throat in a manner that was so similar to his son's that it was uncanny. "I'm happy for you both."

Cora echoed the sentiment.

My parents took much longer to respond.

Eventually, my dad came to my side and gave me a big hug. I could feel him shaking, and his voice cracked when he told me, "It's hard when your baby gets to the point in life where they're having their own babies. Your mom and I just need a minute to adjust to the fact that you're no longer the little girl who asks for permission before doing the slightest thing. I'm proud of the woman you've become, Aston. I'm glad you know what you want for yourself and are unapologetic about it."

"Thanks, Dad." I blinked away tears and continued to watch my mom.

It felt like there was a thin wire connecting the two of us, and if her response to the news that she was going to be a grandparent was wrong, the wire would snap, and our relationship might never recover.

When my mom realized all eyes were on her, she composed herself and forced a weak smile. She wasn't someone who ever liked to be the center of attention.

Her words were quiet and her demeanor was reserved when she spoke. "Like Remy, I also already had a hunch about what you wanted us all to gather for. I could tell there was something different about you when I visited you in LA. I knew there had to be more than you and Zowen living together for you to suddenly be interested in learning to cook."

A round of laughter went around the large table, and my mom and I stared at each other.

"You'll be a great mother, Aston. I have no doubt you are going to give your child the best life possible." She sighed and closed her eyes.

She leaned against my dad when he stepped behind her to offer his silent support. It was a gesture I'd witnessed throughout my childhood. My parents were always giving and taking strength from one another. It was truly beautiful and something I hoped would happen naturally the longer Zowen and I were together.

"Being someone's mom is hard. You're going to make mistakes. Don't beat yourself up too much when things don't go the way you anticipated." She lifted her eyebrows and opened her eyes as a smile finally broke free on her beautiful face. "I'm still making mistakes, and you haven't been a baby in a very long time. Don't be afraid to ask for help. You are never alone."

Her eyes drifted over to Cora, and the two women shared a look that was too deep to fathom. Maybe after I'd been a mom for more than a few months, I would understand.

"You have this entire family at your disposal. We're here for whatever you might need." She smiled at Zowen, and I felt him melt with relief. I thought he had been just as nervous about my mother's response as I had been. "We're here for both of you."

Every single person around the big table shouted their agreement.

We were all family. Some were family we shared blood ties with. The one we'd created in our own vision. Some were family we'd found, and some were the family who had found us. It didn't matter if we were wayward or exactly where we were supposed to be; at the end of the day, we loved and cherished each other. Whether the occasion was a celebration of new life and the family growing and thriving, or it was a gathering cloaked in sorrow because we had lost someone irreplaceable and there would forever be a hole left in the fabric of our unity, we cheered and grieved together.

Good or bad, we never had to face anything alone.

Because that was what *this* family was all about.

EPILOGUE

Aston

Funerals were dark and bleak.

Not this one. This one was full of color and warmth. It was packed with fond stories and family members offering solace to one another. This was a celebration of the life Royce's mom had lived. It was an affirmation that her memory was going to last forever within those who loved her. While there were a lot of tears and endless condolences, there was also a sense of remembrance because this one tragic event wasn't allowed to overshadow all the bright spots Kallie had brought into the world.

I kept an eagle eye on my brother. He was the only one not able to shift his grief into something more positive. He was a shell of his former self. I hadn't seen him smile or laugh in months. Every time I laid eyes on him, he looked more haggard and less like the outrageous and fun-loving brother I'd always known. He hadn't even made an effort to meet his new nephew.

Kallie had managed to hang on to the last bit of her health until I gave birth. Shortly after our son, Zephyr, was born, Kallie entered into hospice. She left New York when it was obvious she could no longer care for herself, even with Royce's help, and moved south to live with her sister, Dixie, and her large family. Royce had gone to be with her as soon as he finished up his lingering commission.

Since Kallie's wishes were to have her ashes scattered somewhere in the world she'd never been before, my brother was taking off for parts unknown to fulfill his mother's final wish in just a couple of days. Because Kallie's parents lived in Denver, and she still had strong ties to the city, they decided to hold a wake and small service there before Royce departed. It was a central location that all the different people whose lives she touched could travel to in order to say goodbye. The small service turned into a large one, but there were no complaints. I wanted to go with him, but it was too soon after giving birth. Just traveling to Denver from LA had almost been too much with a newborn.

Even now, Zowen was watching the baby while I played host and mingled with the large crowd. Zephyr was too little to be fully vaccinated, which meant we had to limit his contact. It was hard because everyone would much rather have their attention on an adorable newborn rather than the silent urn that seemed too small and sterile to contain a life as big as Kallie's.

"Your brother looks like the smallest thing is going to shatter him." Daire whispered the words in my ear as she twisted the black diamond ring around her finger.

I was pretty sure she was going to stay engaged forever and never actually have a wedding. Every time

I asked her about it, she would shrug and say the time wasn't right. It was like the entire event was deemed unnecessary to her. I often wondered what Campbell had to say about the situation, but the reality was that he would do whatever Daire wanted. If Daire decided she was ready to walk down the aisle tomorrow, Campbell would have the whole ceremony planned out in a single afternoon. As long as she was happy, so was he. She was much more direct when I asked her if she thought about having kids with Campbell.

She always looked at me like I'd lost my mind and said, "Hell no."

It was odd since they were both good with little ones. They were even lil' Zee's godparents. Daire was the one who had shortened the baby's name, saying Zephyr was too much for such a small body to bear. She never elaborated on her answer as to why she didn't see kids in her future, but she had mentioned more than once that Campbell had raised his siblings and the children of the family that fostered him when he was nothing more than a kid himself. She told me they both were more content with things the way they were.

"He's not doing so hot. I'm worried about him."

Especially since he was about to disappear on a plane halfway around the world and would be too far away if he finally collapsed under the grief weighing down on him. No one would be there to pick him back up and force him to move forward.

Daire put her arm around my shoulders and pulled me in for a hug. "He'll be okay. Royce is a sensitive guy. He feels things bigger and more intensely than the rest of us. Once he gets to say goodbye in his own way, he'll be able to start to heal."

I hoped so. It hurt my heart to watch him be inconsolable and miserable. I could tell my parents were deeply worried about him, but Royce seemed immune to their concern.

I looked over as Daire's brother and sister-in-law took a seat next to her. Ry and I exchanged sad smiles while Bowe gave me a brief nod. It'd been long enough that I thought all the teenage angst and awkwardness would disappear between Ry's first and final love, but Bowe was still very leery around me. It was kind of cute, and I could tell Ry enjoyed her obvious jealousy. Bowe wore a wedding set with a rock that was the size of Rhode Island. It was clear I was no longer any type of threat to her relationship and happiness. Zowen acted similarly around his cousin, but since the two of them were best friends, Ry refused to let any harbored resentment linger.

"I just saw your baby. He already looks like an Archer." Ry sounded proud, but he wasn't wrong.

Zephyr did look more like Zowen than like me. And one of his dark brown eyes looked like it was going to have blue within it. It was unlikely that either of the Archer grandchildren were going to have the full two-toned effect, but they were both going to end up with a uniquely beautiful color.

"That name is a mouthful. Did you let Zowen convince you to name him that so his son would have the same initials?"

I shook my head and hid a grin because both brother and sister had said the same thing about the baby's name. "No. I'm the one who came up with it. I wanted to name him after a car brand, like Royce and me." It was a nod to my father. "It just so happens that Zephyr also starts with a Z."

Zowen hadn't loved the choice at first, but now, he appreciated the way it represented both of us.

"Everyone just calls him Zee."

All the conversation stopped when Royce got up and stood at the front of the reception room. His aunt Dixie was on one side of him, my dad on the other. It looked like they were holding him up. My heart squeezed in response, and I had to blink against the tears flooding my vision.

"Thank you all for coming. My mom loved every person in this room. I know she was deeply touched and greatly appreciated how hard you worked to make her last moments the happiest and most memorable they could be."

Tears rolled down my brother's face, and I watched his chest heave as he tried to control his emotions. There wasn't a dry eye in the brightly decorated room.

"I'm going to take her to see all the places she dreamed of. I'm going to see every famous artwork she told me about when I was growing up. I'm going to eat delicious food and meet interesting people. I'm going to be open to any experience that might teach me something. All the things my mom encouraged me to do and all the things she was afraid to do herself, I will tackle them all."

He choked on a sob and nearly fell to his knees. My father reached out to hold him upright. My dad wrapped my brother in a tight hug and tucked his head down as everyone started to clear out of the reception hall. I blew my nose and let Daire hold me as the only sounds in the room became my brother's anguish.

"Let's give him some space and get you back to your baby." Daire pulled me to my feet and guided me toward the aisle.

Just as I was about to step out, the doors at the back of the reception hall opened, and a familiar figure appeared. I blinked as Cassio marched toward the front of the room, a fully loaded backpack resting on his shoulders. The dwindling family members looked at the young man in confusion. My brother's expression shifted from sorrow to surprise in the blink of an eye. Cassio looked at my older brother, his eyes lingering on the urn resting behind him. My father released his hold on Royce and took a step back. His curious eyes found mine. I shook my head, indicating I'd had no warning or clue that Cassio was going to show up here today. I'd told him when Kallie passed and let him know Royce was having a very hard time, but he hadn't said much in response. He must've asked Zowen to fill in the blanks for him since he'd not only shown up for the wake, but had also come equipped with a bag that looked like he was ready to travel.

"What are you doing here, Cassio?" Royce's voice sounded like he'd been eating razor blades for breakfast, lunch, and dinner.

"What's it look like, *mi amore*? You're off to see places unknown. I'm going with you."

Royce scowled and his hands clenched. "How do you know that?"

My brother turned to glare at me. I shook my head again. I really had no idea what was happening.

"How I know doesn't matter. It's *what* I know that is important. You have a big, scary task in front of you. You shouldn't go alone." Cassio's slightly accented voice dropped to a low tone only my brother was close enough to hear. "Even if you don't let me tag along, I'm going to be wherever you are. I'm going to make sure you do what needs to be done while not losing yourself in the process. We can tackle this as friends or fight our way through as enemies. Either way, I'm going with you."

The two men faced each other in a silent standoff while Daire dragged me away, saying they didn't need an audience to figure things out. I let her lead me away, mostly because there was finally an expression on my brother's face other than sadness. Cassio had always managed to get a rise out of him, and it seemed that remained true, even under the umbrella of grief.

I followed Daire to where Zowen and Campbell were waiting with the baby. Zephyr was asleep in Zowen's arms, and the two men were quietly having a conversation. My eyes met Zowen's, and I lifted an eyebrow questioningly.

"Are you responsible for Cassio being here?"

He shrugged the shoulder the baby wasn't resting against. "No. Your brother is responsible for him being here. He just doesn't know it."

It was a cagey answer that made me roll my eyes and had Daire snickering.

My best friend reached out to give me one last hug before she dragged her fiancé off. I took the baby from Zowen and rubbed a knuckle across one of his feather-soft cheeks. He puckered his tiny mouth in response. His eyes stayed closed as he snuggled closer to me. Zowen watched the scene with love and satisfaction clear on every feature of his handsome face.

It was wild that this man had gone from calling himself a murderer to referring to himself as Dada in a high-pitched voice in such a short amount of time. The change was remarkable and one of my favorite things to witness as Zowen had evolved into a very invested and hands-on father.

"Let's go. We can check in on everyone after Zee eats and you both get some rest." Zowen put a hand on my lower back and led me away from the reception hall.

Before the baby had been born, his parents had gifted us a condo on the outskirts of Denver. Since we were staying in LA, they wanted us to have a place of our own when we visited Denver. Zowen's mom admitted she selfishly wanted it to be as easy as possible for us to bring the baby to Colorado for a long visit. Initially, Zowen turned the gift down. It was too much and felt too imposing. However, when his dad had convinced him that we could use the property as a vacation rental during the times we weren't there, he had relented. It was a simple way to make passive income that could go to paying off some of his still-outrageous legal fees.

After I fed the baby and took a shower and a quick nap, I got up in search of my wandering Archer. Zowen rarely sat still. He always seemed to find something to keep his hands busy. I couldn't complain because nine out of ten times, that something was me. Back home, he was building a custom bike. Here, he was cleaning the condo from top to bottom, like the property manager didn't have a cleaning service come in after every rental. He'd said he had a lot of pent-up energy from not being able to do anything without permission for all the years he had been incarcerated.

Once he hopped down from cleaning the ceiling fan, he caught sight of me and asked what I wanted to eat for dinner.

I surprised him by asking a completely different question. "Zowen, do you ever want to get married?"

He paused and cocked his head to give me a puzzled look. "I *only* want to marry you. If you want to get married, then so do I." It was similar to his assertion that he would *only* ever love me.

He smiled at me, and it tugged at every heartstring I had. It was still a rare occasion when his whole face lit up from within like that. Usually, it was when he was looking at me or his son.

"Are you proposing to me?"

I laughed and leaned a shoulder against the wall. "Maybe. It's been on my mind a bit since we had Zee. I'm not ready for it today. But I might be in the near future. I won't give you a weak proposal. I'll make it worth your while. You can wait for me, right?"

With zero hesitation, he replied, "*Always*."

The End

AFTERWORD

And we've come full circle. As I wrap up Zowen and Aston's story, I realize I should've called this the Archers' spin-off rather than a second-generation spin-off. Those Archers—they just have a habit of ending up at the center of everything.

I hope you enjoyed the trip to the theoretical future and all the memories from the past. I never intended to write a series for the kids from the Marked Men and the Saints of Denver. However, once the pandemic started, I kept hearing from so many readers that they were rereading both series as a comfort read during a really stressful time. It touched me. And it inspired me to give something back to those who had followed my career from the start. This second-generation series was super fun to write, so it was a gift for me as well as you. I enjoyed my time back in Denver and with the beloved characters immensely. I hope anyone reading this did as well.

When I made the decision to dive into the kids, I told myself that I was going to write books that really tackled issues adult children faced. And I was determined to show the parents from previous books as people with real lives and real generational trauma that would affect how they parented. Even though the first generation is beloved, they are so because of their very human flaws. I thought about the issues I'd faced as an adult child. Things like distance, disappointment, serious illness, the loss of a parent, conflict with ideologies, disapproval … I wanted to touch on all those very authentic hurdles we face as we grow into our own lives and stop being an extension of our parents. The one thing I left out was divorce. I mean, that's the one thing I know better than all the rest—LOL—but this is still romance and very much a collection of stories about love and happily ever after. Even though I was very tempted to push that boundary, I reminded myself this was a series I was writing as a thank-you note to my ride-or-die readers. Breaking up one of the OG couples would've totally defeated the purpose I'd started out with. Occasionally, my common sense and compassion do win out over my critical and creative impulses.

It also made sense for me to have the kids' books out there after it was announced *Rule*, the book that had started it all, was becoming a movie. It'll be released in 2024—beyond that, I have no new information to share.

I know there are a handful of readers who are going to be agonizing as to whether I will write a book for Cassio and Royce. I've said that I'm done with the kids' books, and I mean it. They simply are nowhere near as profitable as I need them to be to justify writing more of them. And while writing romance novels is a passion and true love of mine, I also need it to pay the bills. That's just the harsh reality of the matter. But don't fret. I'm sure I can figure out a way to give the boys a story down the road. Be it bonus content, or a preorder incentive, or maybe a one-off novella … there is still hope if you find yourself wanting more the boys. The truth is, I would've extended the series to six books if they'd performed better, but it is what it is. That's a hard lesson I've learned over the past decade of writing series.

Regardless, there will be more books coming because I always have something lingering in my mind, looking for a chance to shine.

Thank you so much for reading. Thanks for being here—especially after my unplanned, extended hiatus. Thank you for engaging with me, coming to see me at events, and just in general being the best readers a grumpy gal like me could ask for.

If you've made it this far, please consider leaving a review on whichever site you purchased *Wayward Son*. I'm aware you've probably seen authors ask all the time, but we really, really do need reviews to help boost a new release's visibility. I know it seems like going above and beyond, but your effort is endlessly appreciated.

The full Forever Marked series is now available.
https://www.jaycrownover.com/forever-marked
Fortunate Son: Ry and Bowe's story
Prodigal Son: Hyde and Remy's story
Son of a Gun: Campbell and Daire's story
Wayward Son: Zowen and Aston's story

ACKNOWLEDGEMENTS

We wouldn't have this second-generation series if it hadn't been for the readers who reached out during a difficult time and let me know how much my books and words mattered to them. If you're ever wondering if you should contact an author when their work moves you in some type of way, this series is proof that you absolutely should. At the end of the day, my heartfelt gratitude goes out to all my readers. Be they new to my work or here from the start, casual or die-hard, local or international, any and all forms of reader are the biggest reasons I've managed to live my dreams and beyond for the past decade. So, thank you to each and every single one of you.

Along with my readers, of course, I greatly appreciate all the reviewers and bookish influencers who have given my books a chance over the years. I'm sure it can feel like a thankless endeavor, but know you are deeply revered by the folks writing the words.

Huge shout-out to my beta team. I've struggled with life and time management skills for the last couple of years. I've been behind on everything, which makes getting books ready for publishing twice as hard as it typically has to be. It's one thing to push myself to scramble under an unrealistic deadline. It's an entirely different thing to ask very kind people who are offering their time and talent for free to work under the same ridiculous conditions. The team I have working on my extremely messy and ugly rough drafts never fails to come through at the zero hour. I'm always amazed and honored to have a dedicated group working on my words under any circumstances. I will forever say that the books that end up in my readers' hands are a thousand percent better because Teri, Pam, Sarah, Alexandra, Cheron, Kelly, and Mel go over them with a fine-tooth comb before I send anything off to editing. They are truly one of my greatest assets as an author.

Mel wears more than one hat in my author world, and there really aren't enough ways to thank her for all she does. Putting her in each and every acknowledgment doesn't seem like enough, but I'll never forget to thank her for just being all-around awesome and super helpful. It's unlikely you would be holding the book in your hand if it wasn't for her keeping track of my squirrel-like brain behind the scenes.

As always, I'm grateful for the professional team I work with. There have been some new faces added to the mix as of late because, once again, I suck and cannot keep myself on a reasonable timeline. Big thanks to Autumn from Wordsmith Publicity (https://wordsmithpublicity. com/) for not only helping make my release days and promo a piece of cake, but also for coming in hot with an editor when I was down to the wire and in dire need. (I owe Alison Rhymes (https://alisonrhymes.com/) more than one cocktail for recommending Autumn and all her amazingness. Be sure to check out her books if you like BIG angst and some seriously taboo relationship dynamics.) Speaking of the brave editor willing to tackle a project at the last minute and under a unfriendly, over-the-holidays deadline, I have to thank Jovana Shirley from Unforeseen Editing (https://www.unforeseenediting.com/)for agreeing to take on the task. I'm not sure what I would've done if she hadn't agreed to squeeze me into her very busy schedule.

Along with my new collaborators, of course, my longtime favorites still deserve endless praise. At this point in my independent publishing career, I don't know that I could put a book out without Elaine (https://allusionpublishing.com/) and Hang (https://www.facebook.com/designsbyhangle/). I feel like they are as much a part of my books as I am anymore. If you're ever in need of someone to make sure your work is as beautiful inside as it is out, I can't recommend these ladies enough.

Everyone I mentioned is linked at the beginning of the book. Go give them all your pennies.

other books by JAY CROWNOVER

Marked Men Series:
https://www.jaycrownover.com/markedmenseries

Saints of Denver Series:
https://www.jaycrownover.com/saintsofdenver

Forever Marked Series:
https://www.jaycrownover.com/forever-marked

Welcome to the Point Series:
https://www.jaycrownover.com/welcometothepoint

Breaking Point Series:
https://www.jaycrownover.com/thebreakinpoint

Getaway Series:
https://www.jaycrownover.com/thegetawayseries

Loveless Series:
https://www.jaycrownover.com/lovelesstexas

Standalone Books:
https://www.jaycrownover.com/standalones

about the AUTHOR

Jay Crownover is the international and multiple *New York Times* and *USA Today* best-selling author of the Marked Men series, the Saints of Denver series, the Forever Marked series, the Point series, the Breaking Point series, the Getaway series, and the Loveless, Texas series. Her books have been translated into many different languages around the world. She is a tattooed gal with very colorful hair who happily calls Colorado home. She lives at the base of the Rockies with her awesome dogs. She can frequently be found enjoying a cold beer and taco Tuesdays.

And if you haven't heard the news, Jay's first book, *Rule*, is being adapted into a movie by Voltage Pictures. It'll be out in 2024!

The following is a list of all the places you can find her:
Reader Group: facebook.com/groups/crownoverscrowd
Bookbub: bookbub.com/authors/jay-crownover
Website: jaycrownover.com
Merch: shop.spreadshirt.com/100036557
Facebook: facebook.com/AuthorJayCrownover

Twitter: twitter.com/jaycrownover
TikTok: tiktok.com/@jaycrownover
Instagram: instagram.com/jay.crownover
Pinterest: pinterest.com/jaycrownover
Spotify and Snapchat: Jay Crownover
Email: JayCrownover@gmail.com

For the *Rule* movie:
#markedmenmovie
Facebook: @MarkedMenMovie (https://www.facebook.com/markedmenmovie/)
Twitter: @MarkedMenMovie (https://twitter.com/markedmenmovie/)
TikTok: @MarkedMenMovie (https://www.tiktok.com/@markedmenmovie)
Instagram: @MarkedMenMovie (https://www.instagram.com/markedmenmovie/)